Claire Cullen Mack

Imitation of Life:
the Next Millennium

CLAIRE CULLEN MACK

iUniverse, Inc.
New York   Bloomington

Imitation of Life: the Next Millennium

Copyright © 2009 Claire Cullen Mack

This is a work of fiction. All of the characters, names, incidents, organizations, and dialogue in this novel are either the products of the author's imagination or are used fictitiously.

iUniverse books may be ordered through booksellers or by contacting:

iUniverse
1663 Liberty Drive
Bloomington, IN 47403
www.iuniverse.com
1-800-Authors (1-800-288-4677)

ISBN: 978-0-595-53181-3 (pbk)
ISBN: 978-0-595-51946-0 (cloth)
ISBN: 978-0-595-63240-4 (ebk)

Printed in the United States of America

iUniverse rev. date: 7/30/2009

Contents

Characters vii

Prologue xi

Chapter 1   Kacy 1

Chapter 2   Coyote Point 5

Chapter 3   Meeting Eva 12

Chapter 4   Michael 17

Chapter 5   After Graduation 20

Chapter 6   The Trial 22

Chapter 7   Eva 25

Chapter 8   The Bakery 32

Chapter 9   Monday at the Bakery 38

Chapter 10   School 41

Chapter 11   The Theory 44

Chapter 12   How'd You Do It? 48

Chapter 13   The TV Show 50

Chapter 14   Reverend Davidson 59

Chapter 15   The Proposal 62

Chapter 16   Church Sisters and Brothers 67

Chapter 17   No Better Than Mine 73

Chapter 18   Dr. Ozzie Hutchinson 79

Chapter 19   Lillian 85

Chapter 20   Tina 92

Chapter 21   Questions on Religion 94

Chapter 22   The Octopus 97

Chapter 23   Andrew, Lillian and Tina 106

Chapter 24   Jump the Broom Time 113

Chapter 25   The Wedding 116

Chapter 26   Confession 127

Chapter 27   Word Worm 132

Chapter 28   Bakery Love 137

Chapter 29   Preparation 144

Chapter 30   Ozzie Wakes Up 146

Chapter 31   Bless Us 149

Chapter 32   We're With You Vignettes.............................. 151
Chapter 33   Junebug and Skeet 156
Chapter 34   Trash 162
Chapter 35   The Funeral.. 168
Chapter 36   Sharing Information................................... 177
Chapter 37   Cheyenne.. 188
Chapter 38   Ray & Stevie 200
Chapter 39   The Meeting.. 204
Chapter 40   McNairy's 209
Chapter 41   The Trestle 221
Chapter 42   A Pharmacy 229
Chapter 43   The White Suit 238

Add "Eva"

Characters

1.	Kacy Murphy	Eva's white partner
2.	Moving Man	
3.	Dovie Hudson	Mississippi Activist
4.	Tina Murphy	Kacy's Daughter
5.	Dorothy Easter	Friend
6.	The Martin Twins	Ex Bakery Employees
7.	Lillian Garrett	Eva's Daughter
8.	Teacher	
9.	Marcus Cullen	Eva's first husband - Black
10.	Marcus Cullen, Jr.	Eva's son
11.	Tom Garrett	Eva's second husband
12.	Rev. Clifford Michael Davidson	Eva's third husband
13.	Rev. Hubert Ellwood	Head Minister, Prophet Church
14.	Mrs. Ellwood	First Lady, Prophet Church
15.	Mr. Chancellor	President, Usher Board
16.	Jack Vason	Kacy's Father
17.	Mrs. Vason	Kacy's Mother
18.	Michael Murphy	Kacy's Husband
19.	Grace Canon	Food Network Producer
20.	Gayle Teal	Food Network Producer

21. Mr. Hemins	Food Network Exec
22. Deacon Older Than Dirt	Old Fool
23. Andrew Garrett	Eva's Son
24. Robert	Andrew's School Friend
25. Reacie Florence	Andrew's Posse
26. The Octopus	An Ass
27. Eddie	Andrew's Posse
28. Alan	Andrew's Posse
29. Mr. Swann	School Counselor
30. Mrs. Rumsfeld	Asses Mother
31. Steve Kinney	Lillian's Mentor
32. Mrs. Samms	Church Biddy
33. Mrs. Johnson	Church Biddy
34. Larry Corley	Minister of Music
35. Kenneth Hackett	Minister of Music
36. Betty Calvin	Breast Center Director
37. Marion York	Nurse Practitioner
38. Dr. Ozzie Hutchinson	Kacy's Boyfriend
39. Dr. Turner	Oncologist
40. Phelicia Jones	Andrew's Girlfriend
41. Dr. Sells	OBGYN
42. Mary Anne	Kacy's
43. Mr. Gonzales	Junebug's Daddy
44. Mrs. Gonzales	Junebug's Mama
45. Junebug	Dumb
46. Skeet	Dumber
47. Police	
48. Judge	
49. Officer Cannon	SMPD
50. Chief Man	Chief of Police
51. Officer Petrie	SMPD
52. Bucky	San Mateo Local
53. Lacy	Skeet's Girlfriend
54. Mr. Wainwright	Skeet's Daddy
55. Mrs. Dottie Wainwright	Skeet's Mama
56. Snake	San Mateo Local
57. Dean Courtney	Cornell University

58. Officer Passinissi   SMPD
59. Tremaine Hawkins   Gospel Singer
60. Funeral Director
61. Girl at Church
62. Girl at Church II
63. Second Funeral Director
64. Detective Ed McGinnes   SMPD
65. Cheyenne Norman   Private Detective
66. Professor Arnold Webb   Forensics Professor
67. Ms. Thang   McNairy's Waitress
68. Bartender

Prologue

"What will I watch on TV tonight?" I flick to channel 11, the TV Guide on my set. The title of a movie catches my eye. *Imitation of Life*, the 1934 version with Louise Beavers as Delilah, Fredi Washington as Peola, Delilah's daughter, Claudette Colbert as Bea and Rochelle Hudson as Jesse, Bea's daughter. I haven't seen that version since I was a child. It'll be on in a few minutes, so I'll go to the kitchen, get a drink and settle in.

I really wanted to see this film because this was the first and last time that Hollywood allowed a light-skinned Black woman to play a light-skinned Black woman. In subsequent films, studios used white actresses wearing Negro #2, a makeup made by Max Factor to help Caucasian actresses blacken up. Actresses such as Helen Morgan in the 1936 version of *Imitation of Life* and Ava Gardner in the 1951 version of *Show Boat*, Jeanne Crain in *Pinky*, a 1949 film and Susan Kohner in the 1959 and second *Imitation of Life*, were users of Negro #2.

Fredi Washington was a Black beauty who could pass for white and declined to do so, although her career, according to studio heads, would have soared. Knowing Fredi's history made me really want to watch the 1934 version of *Imitation of Life*. An hour and fifty minutes later, I was fuming. That movie made me so angry, I was hopping mad. I couldn't even speak coherently.

The next day, I started polling friends. "How do you like the movie *Imitation of Life*?" I'd ask. I made this inquiry of over twenty-five friends, mostly Blacks. All of them told me how they loved the film, especially the 1959 version with Juanita Moore as Delilah, Lana Turner as Bea, and Susan Kohner as Sarah Jane. Everyone gushed over how they loved the funeral scene with Mahalia Jackson singing and the horse-drawn hearse.

I wanted to puke and didn't hesitate to set my friends straight, according to me. All of the people I spoke to had missed an important part of the film, although the 1959 movie version of *Imitation of Life* was not as true to Ms. Hurst's novel as the 1934 movie had been.

In Hurst's novel, two widows happen on one another; both are in need of childcare. They help each other: Delilah trades childcare and domestic services in exchange for a roof over her and her daughter Peola's head.

Delilah has a special recipe for pancakes and waffles. Bea, whose husband had been in sales, opens a restaurant and the two women are in business. The business doesn't go well, but Bea finds a way to franchise the restaurant with Delilah's recipe as the lynchpin. Bea tells Delilah that she, Bea, will take sixty percent of the profits and Delilah can have forty percent. Delilah demurs and tells Bea that she doesn't want money. "I only wants a big funeral when I dies."

Once again, I came very close to vomiting. Fannie Hurst wrote *Imitation of Life* after taking a road trip with her good friend and folklorist, writer Zora Neal Hurston, the author of *Their Eyes Were Watching God*, *Mules and Men* and several other novels. Hurst was going to call the story *Sugar House* but changed it to *Imitation of Life* just before publication.

I don't care what Fannie Hurst titled her story; the racism in the story makes me bilious no matter what the novel is called. I was so furious after watching that damned 1934 version of the movie that I dashed to my computer and started pounding the keys, attempting to right some of the wrongs in a work that was written so many years ago. I'm calling my version *Imitation of Life: the Next Millennium.*

I'm pleased to say that I'm not the only person in the world who has become irate about *Imitation of Life* as written by Fannie Hurst. Langston Hughes, the great poet and writer, was so offended by the original work that he wrote a play called *Limitation of Life,* which was staged in New York, premiering in 1938. Fannie Hurst not only outraged Black folks. Whites, too, were enraged by the film, as they didn't feel a Caucasian woman would go into business with her maid. Delilah was not Bea's maid!

I believe that Hurst's heart was in the right place. She was an activist and wrote the best she knew how about changing racial injustices in 1930s America. But Fannie Hurst, as a young Jewish woman whose best friend was the famous anthropologist and writer Zora Neal Hurston, should have known more about Americans of African descent. Fannie Hurst wrote her melodramatic *Imitation of Life* to help right some American wrongs. She wrote with the same motivation as Mark Twain, who tried to show the humanity of Jim, the Black character in *Huckleberry Finn,* did. But, Ms. Hurst's lack of knowledge of how Black woman lived and how they thought and felt fell woefully short of her goal, even for the 1930s.

In the 1934 and the 1959 film version of Hurst's novel, there are heart-wrenching funerals, which rivet audiences. We all love tearjerkers and Delilah's request for that magnificent funeral is fulfilled. But the Black character, through Ms. Hurst's friendship with Ms. Hurston, should have had some knowledge of Sarah Breedlove, AKA, Madame C. J. Walker. Madame Walker is the first woman on record in the history of the United States to have earned what was the equivalent of $1,000,000. Every other American woman up to that time who was a millionaire, inherited her money from her husband or her family. I wish Zora had told Fannie about Madame Walker and had incorporated some of Walker's knowledge of accruing financial stability. Yet, Fannie Hurst wrote about what she knew and what she felt.

Although I am disappointed with the original version of *Imitation of Life,* and deeply disappointed with Hollywood's film versions, I am not disappointed with Fannie Hurst. She at least tried to help improve race relations with her writing. And her friendship with Zora Neal Hurston stands for something. But because Hollywood's two films are still being shown on television in the twenty-first century, I wanted to speak my piece.

I don't want you to read my book and think that it is a Black version of Ms. Hurst's book. It is not. I certainly started out with that in mind but, like *The Wiz* as a version of *The Wizard of Oz*, my novel takes many turns and ends up with just a bit of the original story. *Imitation of Life: the Next Millennium* veers off, introducing chaste Black folks, bright, intelligent Black children, a little mischief, a little church, some mayhem and a few murders.

I hope you will enjoy *Imitation of Life: the Next Millennium*.

Chapter I
Kacy

"You could have given me a few more days. I could have come up with the money!"

Kacy was an attractive young blonde woman, age twenty-four years old with a great figure, long legs, and big blue eyes with long dark lashes. Her hair was pulled back in a rubber band and wisps were flying all over her head. At Kacy's knee stood young frightened Tina, her beautiful daughter and the only good thing to come from her failed marriage to a loser.

Kacy and Tina stood on the sidewalk, looking at their meager collection of furniture that had just been dumped on the pavement.

Kacy was the victim of a down turn in the economy and she and Tina were on the street. No money and no place to go.

"What are we going to do?" Kacy wondered aloud.

"Woulda, shoulda, coulda . . . Lady, just get out of my way," the burly man with prison tats on his biceps barked. "I'm doing what your landlord, Mr. Brown, paid me to do! Move, dammit!"

Startled and scampering out of the bully's way, seven-year-old Tina, a miniature of her mother with pale blonde, cornrowed braids that fell on her shoulders, almost tripped retreating from the intimidator's verbal abuse.

"How can people be so damned unkind? So mean!" Kacy blurted. The only blessing was that today was Saturday and there weren't as many people on the street to see them being thrown out. She kept that thought to herself though, not wanting to anger the tattooed jackass any further.

Kacy and Tina backed away from the tattered floral print couch, broken-down chrome kitchen set with three lopsided chairs that didn't match, a 17-inch black and white TV, an army cot, some blankets and a few clothes.

The two of them were dressed casually - Saturday clothes: shin-length jeans, tee shirts, and sweaters - clothes for a day that was starting in a nightmarish fashion.

"How am I going to find a place to live on a Saturday?"

Are there shelters open today? She remembered that the only shelter in town had been moved because the neighbors were fed up and demanded the County Board of Supervisors get the thirteen-year-old "temporary" shelter out of their neighborhood.

We can sleep in the car tonight, but where will we park? I know, we can drive up to 280 and park at the Father Serra statue, but do I have enough gas to get up there? There's the frontage road over near Econ Market. We can cover ourselves with blankets there. But would that be safe? Maybe we can park in the Samaritan House parking lot. Heck, too many cars filled with indigent people are sleeping there already.

Kacy stepped to the curb holding Tina's hand. They both sat down. Kacy rested her head on her folded arms and was about to tear up when she felt a tap on her shoulder. She looked up and there was her neighbor, Mr. Collins. He jammed a wad of bills into her hand and walked back across the street to his house.

Mr. and Mrs. Collins, a handsome couple in their early seventies, were the hard working mother and father of a son and daughter who visited their folks weekly. Mr. Collins had been a cement-finisher in construction. A handsome brown-skinned man, he was six feet tall with movie star good looks. Mrs. Collins was an extremely light-skinned woman who could pass for white; she had been born and raised in Mississippi. Her cousins were famous for their civil rights work and much of their feistiness was evident in Mrs. Collins.

Mrs. Lomie Collins had worked as a domestic, but that was only because of the times. Had northern California not been so expensive to live in, Mrs. Collins would have been an activist like her cousins, Winson and Dovie Hudson. But living in an expensive community like San Mateo, California made it more important to have a job that paid steady money.

Winson and Dovie Hudson were committed community activists in rural Mississippi for decades. They, on behalf of their children, were the first Black plaintiffs to file a school desegregation suit against the state. The sisters were also instrumental in democratizing voter registration, establishing preschool centers, and implementing nutrition programs.

On voter registration and being discouraged by the Ku Klux Klan: "A lawyer from the Justice Department came here (Carthage, Mississippi) and investigated (why we couldn't register to vote). When we went back to register, the registrar gave me a thing to fill out again and instead of filling it out, I wrote down there, 'It said what it meant, and it meant what it said.' He say, "Well, you pass." Dovie Hudson from the book, I Dream A world, by Brian Lanker.

The money placed in Kacy's hand by Mr. Collins was like a gift from heaven. Kacy didn't really know Mr. and Mrs. Collins. They were neighbors she waved to when she was coming or going. Now, the Collins proved to be more than friends or neighbors. As far as Kacy was concerned, they had just earned the rank of angels.

"Where are we going to go?" Kacy said aloud, as she watched Mr. Collins disappear through his front door.

She opened her hand and counted the clump of bills that came to one hundred dollars.

"We're not going to worry about anything right now, Tina. Let's have a picnic and eat something other than cold cereal. We'll go to Safeway, buy some sandwiches, soda, potato chips and cookies.

Then we're going to enjoy nature and have a great time at good old Coyote Point."

Kacy turned back for a final look at her tattered belongings. She grabbed the TV and the blankets, carried them to her beat-up white 1968 Toyota and put the items on the passenger side of the front seat. She went back and retrieved Tina from the curb. Then, between the two of them, they picked up as many clothes as they could handle. Tina climbed into the back seat and bundled into a blanket. ~~California mornings can be chilly.~~ Kacy put the rest of their stuff in the trunk, walked slowly to the front of the car, sat heavily in the front seat, put the car in gear, and off they went to the grocery store.

to offset the chilly
California morning.

Chapter 2
Coyote Point

"Thank goodness we made it here before the guards come on duty. If they were here, we'd have to pay to get in. The parking lot's empty, Tina. Which space should we take?"

"Eeny, meeny . . . Mom, how about that one?" Tina pointed.

"Good choice, my dear. That's the one we'll take. I'll be able to see you at the water's edge from here."

Kacy pulled into a space and they both exited the car. Tina was still wrapped in their old blanket and Kacy held two bags of picnic goodies.

She was glad to see that Tina had perked up a little bit. Dropping the blanket on the sand, Tina took off at breakneck speed to the murky water of San Mateo Bay, anxious to wet her bare feet. It was then that Kacy let go of a flood of tears; they blurred her big blue eyes and sent black mascara lines down her cheeks. Kacy was thankful she'd been able to hold back the tears for so long. She didn't want Tina to know how bad she was feeling.

"How'd I let us get in this mess?" Kacy muttered, gazing through teary blue eyes.

Through her tears, she looked skyward. Three huge jet airplanes were floating toward their destination, unfolding their wheels as they approached San Francisco International Airport, just two miles from where Kacy was seated on the sand.

She watched Tina play at the edge of the brownish, green-gray water of the Bay.

About half an hour passed and more people were beginning to stream into the park. To the right and in back of Kacy's blanket was a Black family setting up for what looked to be a huge birthday party. They were decorating with balloons, crepe paper, card tables, fancy birthday tablecloths with napkins and plastic utensils to match.

"I wonder if I will ever be able to have birthday parties like that one for Tina ever again?" Kacy asked no one.

As Kacy was lost in thought, a little cutie of about eighteen months came waddling toward her. The little girl had skin the color of melting See's milk chocolate. There were pompoms in her thick curly black hair and liquid dribbling from her snotty, unwiped nose. The little girl's behind was pooching out because of a Pamper that made her rear move as though it didn't belong to her body.

"Claudia, come back here," yelled one of the adults. But Little Claudia just kept going the way she was going. She was wearing tiny sandals and a checkered playsuit that made her look like a model for a Tiny Tot ad.

Claudia saw someone she hadn't seen before and also spied the goodies on the blanket. Kacy put her arms out and Claudia toddled right into them.

Kacy yelled back, "She's okay. My daughter is just over on the beach and Claudia won't be any trouble."

"Okay," smiled the woman. "If she bothers you, just bring her back."

Kacy "kitchy cooed" with Claudia, wiped her nose and cuddled and kissed the cute little girl.

Tina came back from the beach, wiping sand from her feet and legs. She'd forgotten some of the woes of the morning and was happy to see her mother with this darling little Black girl. Tina held her arms out and Claudia left Kacy for Tina.

"Mommy, look! She likes me, too," squealed Tina.

Claudia's family were hauling coolers of drinks, salads,

sandwiches, barbecue, loaves of bread, a huge grill, and all the fixings for a party. This was going to be a big one.

Although Kacy was enjoying the little one, she began to feel self-conscious and decided to move farther down the beach. But the lady who had been yelling at little Claudia started walking toward Kacy and Tina, coming to retrieve the child.

"Hi! I'm Dorothy Easter. Thank you for looking after Claudia. She's a handful."

"Not at all. She's a love. I didn't mind her being here at all. I think I've kissed most of her skin off," Kacy said to the baby's mother.

Dorothy noticed the few food items that were on the blanket and an idea came to her.

"Hey, why don't you and your daughter join us? We have enough food for an army and Claudia has already adopted you. We'd love to have you come on over. My name again is Dorothy Easter. This little one is my daughter Claudia. And since she has embraced you, you're practically members of the family. What's your name?"

Dorothy was a beautiful Black woman with a short natural, a beautiful smile, and dimples that looked as if they touched each other. She was a chunky woman with a good figure. She dressed in khaki slacks, sandals, and a cotton red plaid shirt tucked in at the waist.

Kacy stuck out her hand and said, "My name is Kacy Murphy and this is my daughter, Tina Murphy."

Kacy hesitated for a second, then Tina said. "Mommy, can we, please? Look at the food!" Ahhed Tina.

It had been a long time since Kacy and Tina had had anything other then cold cereal for breakfast and dinner. The aromas coming from where Dorothy Easter came from were becoming overwhelming.

"Yes, we'd love to join you. Claudia has become my best friend in just minutes. She's so cute I could just smooch her to pieces!" Kacy said, having already started that process.

Dorothy bent over and started helping Kacy pick up her belongings. Kacy waved Dorothy off. "No, you don't have to do that, I'll take care of this later."

"Good. I'm glad you're going to join us, Kacy and Tina. I know why Claudia became fascinated with you. You both have the bluest eyes I've ever seen."

More people arrived and soon there were about ninety partygoers. The last thing to arrive at the big gathering was a catering van with a hand-painted sign noting "Eva's Cakery."

When Eva left the driver's seat, she walked to the side of the van and slid open the door, revealing the most unusual birthday cake Kacy had ever seen.

First of all, the cake was huge. It was placed on a board that was at least six feet by four feet. It looked like a bas-relief from a building. The saxophone on the cake looked as though it was made of real metal, but it was cake.

On each corner of the cake was a round cake on short pillars. One round featured a piano, the second a set of drums, the third had violins, and the fourth had a big bass with musical notes and "Happy Birthday" jutting into the air.

With Claudia on her hip, Dorothy eased Kacy and Tina away from the van and started introducing them all around the crowd as new family members adopted by Claudia. Kacy fell into conversations with different groups and almost everyone at the gathering wanted to know about the Easters' new-found "family members." Kacy was careful not to give too much information about herself, but she enjoyed tidbits with this uncle, these aunts, and those cousins. When there was a lull, Kacy sidled over to her abandoned blanket and food she'd bought earlier. She quietly folded the blanket, packed the other items back into the paper bags and slipped all of it into her car.

◊

The Martin twins, Polly and Peter, were there. Polly and Peter used to work for Eva at the bakery when they were in high school. They used to clean the bakery and had learned the basics of cake filling and decorating.

"Hi, Mrs. Garret," Polly Martin greeted. "Do you still have the hottest bakery in San Mateo?"

"Yes, I do, Polly, and one of these days I'm going to become the millionaire I should be. Where's Peter?"

Eva was tall and tan and young and lovely, not from Ipanema but born in San Mateo. She had a slim model's figure, small breasts, a narrow waistline, a Black woman's behind, and a cap of black shiny curls. Her teeth were beautiful and white and framed by full lips and demure dimples. Many of the people at the party agreed that she should have made that million. Some said that if Eva weren't Black, she'd have been the Julia Child of the cake world a long time ago. Eva took it all in, nodding affirmatively with her left fist on her hip!

Dorothy surveyed the picnic scene and decided that everything was in place, so she waved at Aunt Irene, the oldest family member in attendance. After asking everyone to quiet down, Aunt Irene blessed the meal. When amen was said, everyone lined up on both sides of the card tables and started heaping their plates.

There was corn on the cob and numerous salads including cucumber, three bean, potato, macaroni, green, celery root, and carrot and raisin. There were Jell-O salads, ambrosia, garlic and cheese breads, fresh rolls, and crispy French baguettes placed on the tables. There were enough bean dishes to fuel a gas station, baked beans, pork and beans, pinto beans, and red beans with rice. Meats included hamburger patties, sausages, hot links, cold cuts, steaks, and chops. Fattening, gooey desserts abounded, with several banana puddings, apple pie, peach cobbler, and the birthday cake. Someone had even brought custard for ice cream that would be hand churned later in the day. Kacy and Tina ate until their stomachs hurt.

The birthday boy was John Dandy, a famous jazz saxophonist. Many of his musician friends such as Vernon and Eddie Alley, Jules Broussard, Dick Conte, Jym Marks, and Fred Berry came to join in the festivities. As the eating part of the party wound down, the musicians went to their cars and brought out their trumpets, saxes, drums, guitars, and an electric keyboard. Then they started jamming.

Kacy couldn't believe her good fortune. That morning she had been thrown out of her room and Mr. and Mrs. Collins had given her one hundred dollars. After she had had a private pity party, she and Tina had been invited to have a great and much needed meal. And to top it off, she was listening to some of the best music this side of heaven. There were even three fabulous vocalists in attendance: Stacy Carter, Pam Hawkins and Dr. Margie Baker were there to add words to the music.

When the vocals started, it was Eva's cue to bring the cake to center stage. She needed the help of Dorothy and the Martin twins, Peter and Polly, to put it on the table in front of the impromptu band.

"Darn, Eva. My arm is sore from cranking that ice cream. Almost everyone here took a few turns. What kind of cake is it?" Peter asked.

"It's chocolate on one side and white on the other and the rounds are carrot, spice, lemon and nut. We'll tell people what their choices are and allow them to choose what they want. Hand me the lighter will you, Peter? Gotta light the candles," Eva said.

The candles were lit. John acted embarrassed as everyone sang the jazziest Happy Birthday ever sung, with an even lustier version of the Stevie Wonder rendition. Everyone hurriedly lined up for desert.

Someone in the crowd, through a mouthful of cake, said, "Eva, if there was an ounce of justice in this world you'd be a multi-millionaire. This cake is awesome. It not only looks great, it tastes magnificent!" An amen corner affirmed in favor of Eva's cake.

Eva, with the help of Peter and Polly, cleaned up the mess left from the massive dessert, put her things together and left the park. Kacy and Tina stayed to help with the clean up, too, because they had no place to go.

People were putting things in their cars and saying good-byes and call me's. Then someone discovered Eva had left a box of her equipment. Eva's shop was located in the southern part of downtown San Mateo and everyone else was headed north to Burlingame, Daly City and San Francisco, or east across the bridge to Fremont, Hayward and Oakland.

"Darn!" Dorothy said. "I won't be able to get this stuff to her until next week. Is there anyone who can take these things to Eva?" No one responded, so Kacy said, "I'll be glad to take them.

"I know about where it is, but I'll need directions. Dorothy, thank you so much for inviting Tina and me. We had a wonderful time. Thank you so much. Hope to see you again sometime." Kacy waved goodbye and headed to her car with Tina in tow.

"Same here!" Dorothy said, not thinking their paths would ever cross again.

Chapter 3
Meeting Eva

Eva's box of pillars and separating plates were safely placed in the back of the car, ready to return to Eva.

Kacy and Tina piled in the old white Toyota and pulled out of the park. They had a hint of where Eva's shop was because her address had been on the side of the van, 618 South B Street, San Mateo and Dorothy Easter's directions would make it easier to find. But Kacy wanted to double check.

After crossing highway 101 on the overpass, she was on Poplar Street headed west. Pulling to the curb, near San Mateo High School, she told Tina, "I want to check these directions again, honey." Kacy looked at the piece of paper with the directions scribbled on it. Then she looked at the beautiful, two-story brick school building and slipped into reverie. "I went to this school, Tina. How many years ago? To think that Merv Griffin and Kris Kristofferson went to school here. My goodness! Even Barry Bostwick, who played in something on TV. I don't remember the name of the show. And Diane Varsi of Peyton Place fame went to school here. I wonder if anyone besides me remembers her."

"Mommy, I don't know who you're talking about. Can we go, please?"

"Okay, okay! Here we go," Kacy said, regaining her senses and putting the car back on the road.

After making a few wrong turns, Kacy was able to locate Eva's bakery. Tina, on her knees in the back seat of the car, exclaimed, "Look, Mommy, there's Eva unloading her truck."

"That's a van, Tina, and you're right, there's Eva. We made it to the right place."

"Mommy, Mommy, may we please go in?" Tina begged. "The door to the shop's open and there's Eva. People at the party were talking about her shop, and I want to go in."

"Just wait a minute, Honey. Let me see if it's all right with Eva."

Kacy got out of her car and walked toward the shop. "Hi, Eva," Kacy greeted. "Here are some things you left at the picnic."

"Girl, if I didn't have people like you, my shop would be all over creation. Thanks for bringing me those things," Eva said with a big dimpled smile. "Would you and your little girl like to come in and take a look around?"

"How did you know that's just what we wanted to do? Tina's dying to see the bakery," Kacy replied.

Eva gestured toward the car and called, "Come on, Tina. Come and take a look at the shop."

"Be sure to lock the car, Tina," Kacy yelled.

Tina locked the car and went bounding toward the bakery.

Eva was already in the shop, moving toward the sinks. She had to put the dirty pillars that had held up the smaller round cakes and other things in to be soaked.

"Wow!" Kacy and Tina said as they entered the bakery.

"What a great place! And it smells sooooo good!" exclaimed Tina. Kacy followed Eva's lead and placed items from the box into the sink, which was quickly filling with hot water.

There were three main parts of the bakery. The main workroom was a huge room and had three waist-high, long tables. The tables were where the splitting, filling, and decorating was done. There were more refrigerators and freezers lining the walls than Tina had ever seen. The next room had huge ovens, mixing bowls, and every size and shape of cake pan known to man. There were bins for the dried ingredients and cake mixes.

Next to that room was the front of the store with a display case and hundreds of picture albums. Photos hung on the walls of the famous people Eva had made cakes for: Liberace, Willie Nelson, Clint Eastwood, Jim McKay, George Schultz, Madonna, Frank Sinatra, Jesse Jackson, Joe Montana, Jerry Rice, Hugh Grant, Garth Brooks, Carol Channing, Andy Gibb, Jerry Seinfeld, Bob Hope, John Lee Hooker, Julio Iglesias, Neil Young, Glenn Campbell, Willie Brown, Willie Mays, Willie McCovey and hundreds of localites. It was the most unbelievable space Tina and Kacy had ever been in.

"Tina, look in this book. It's full of children's birthday parties." "There are five full albums of just children's birthday cakes. Have a ball," Eva said.

As Tina was looking in the books, Kacy asked, "Eva, where's the bathroom?" Reality for Kacy was beginning to set in.

Walking into the tiny room with a toilet, washbowl and mirror and closing the door, Kacy looked at her reflection and asked, "Where are we going to sleep tonight?" The image in the mirror didn't have an answer. Her sad blue eyes peered back, filling with tears.

Once again, Kacy thought about homeless shelters, rest stops, the inside of the car, the parking lot of a local charity. She had choices and none of them were palatable.

As Kacy exited the restroom, she could see that Eva was decorating something. Kacy walked over to see how it was done.

Eva had a pastry bag of frosting in one hand and something Kacy couldn't figure out in the other.

"Come closer, Kacy. I'm decorating cupcakes for you and Tina. I'm just finishing the one with Tina's name on it. Yours is on the table," Eva said gaily.

"What I did was add mint to your frosting. I buy mint wafers by the pound and grind them in the blender to powder them. I add the powder to the frosting for an extra-added mint wow to the flavor. It's quite an exciting taste. Everyone wants to know how I do it, but it's a trade secret. For your cupcakes, I just mashed a couple of the wafers into powder with the back of a spoon and mixed it into the frosting. If it is done correctly, a person will never know there is a powdery substance in the goop. They just know it tastes good."

"I can't wait to taste it but, Eva, this has been a very interesting day for Tina and me," Kacy said, tears spilling. "We were kicked out of our rented room this morning and, as luck would have it, we happened to sit on the beach for a picnic near your wonderful friends. Dorothy and Claudia and everyone made us feel so welcome. We had the best meal we've had in weeks. But I don't know where we're going to sleep tonight." Kacy's sparkling eyes became sadder and, again with her hand, she wiped away tears. Her nose and cheeks were turning bright red.

Eva put down the cupcake, grabbed some tissue from a box, and put her arm around Kacy. "Just calm down. Things are tough, but let's see what we can do about it. You're not the only folks with problems," Eva said, dabbing her own nose with a tissue.

"My not-too-bright Ex moved out, and I have a big house. Just me, my kids and two dogs. You can stay at my house tonight, and we'll figure out what you can do tomorrow. You need a good night's rest and so do I. Where's Tina? Come on, Kacy. Let's shake this joint. Both of us have problems. We seem to be two intelligent, good-looking women. Between the two of us, we can get back on our feet. Come on!"

Eva put the cupcakes in a box and she and Kacy walked to the front of the store to find an exhausted Tina asleep with her head on the pages of the picture album.

Kacy bundled Tina up and asked Eva, "Are you sure?"

Eva said "Girl, come on. If we have something to give, we're supposed to give it. Put Tina on the back seat and we're off to my house. Lillian and Andrew are at friends' houses, having a weekend over, so we have the place to ourselves."

In a two-car caravan, they traveled through San Mateo's beautiful suburban streets. It took about five minutes to reach Eva's house. They pulled into a driveway that had room for three cars. The little white beat-up Toyota looked out of place, but beyond the driveway was a place for Kacy and Tina to sleep for the night.

When they stepped inside the house, Tina sleeping on Kacy's shoulder, Kacy said, "Eva, at least you have a house to invite us to stay in. I have it a little tougher. I have absolutely nothing except the few scraps in my car."

"Shush. You're going to wake Tina and you're going to start crying again. Knock it off! Stop it! Pillows and blankets are in the hall closet. Get what you need, and I'll see you in the morning. That room over there is the guest bedroom, The room where our foster children used to stay. Get settled in. Goodnight! I'll see you in the morning. I'll show you the kitchen and the rest of the house tomorrow. I'm beat, goodnight!" Eva flew up the stairs.

God must have been looking over Kacy because her life, as terrible as it seemed, wasn't so terrible after all. Every time things looked bleakest, something good popped up.

Chapter 4
Michael

Kacy's life wouldn't have been quite this bad had she only fallen in love instead of in lust. She hadn't listened to anybody.

"Kacy, that boy is a jackass and a loser," Jack Vason had told his daughter.

"Daddy, you're just being hard-hearted and mean because Michael's family lives in a trailer. According to what you've said about your family, Daddy, you weren't born with a silver spoon in your mouth. Michael just needs someone to be nice to him."

"Kacy, you're an A student and selected to be one of the valedictorians of the class. That's a 4.0 grade point average. You are a California Scholastic Life Member and a National Honor student. I don't understand why you are being so dense about this juvenile delinquent. You think your father doesn't know, but I know guys like Michael, and I don't want his type around my daughter. Regardless of what you think I think about his humble background, he's just going to bring you down, honey."

"But Daddy, he's so cute and helpless. He needs me."

"Kacy, your Dad's right, but since you're going to be as hardheaded as he is, I want you to promise us a few things," Lois Vason interjected.

"What, Mother?" Kacy said in a snotty tone.

"Now, don't get snippy with me, young lady."

"Yes, Mother, I'm listening," Kacy pouted.

"I want you to promise us you'll finish college. And since you insist on dealing with this horrible young man, yes, I feel about him as your father does, I want you to get over to Planned Parenthood Monday and get condoms, a diaphragm, and as much spermicidal cream, jelly, or ointment. . . whatever that stuff is. And I want you to use them! All of them at once if you have to. Do you want me to take you over there, or can you get there on your own?"

"You two are so mean. I hate you! I can get there on my own," Kacy cried rebelliously.

In high school, she had majored in English Literature, immersed herself in the classics and creative writing, and breezed through tough courses during three years of college.

BQ. Characteristics of English Literature
    1. Language and Form
    2. The English Author and Society
B. The Beginnings (500–1500)
    1. The Anglo-Saxon Period
    2. The Anglo-Norman Period
    3. The Age of Chaucer
    4. From 1440 to the 1550's
C. The Flowering (1550–1660)
    1. Elizabethan Poetry and Prose
    2. Elizabethan Drama
    3. Cavaliers and Puritans
D. The Classical Age (1660–1798)
    1. Restoration Poetry and Prose
    2. Restoration Drama
    3. The Age of Swift and Pope
    4. The Rise of the Novel
    5. The Age of Johnson
E. The Romantic Age (1798–1832)
    1. The Pre-Romantic
    2. Romantic Poets
    3. Romantic Prose Writers

F. The Victorian Age (1832–1900)
   1. Poets and Essayists
   2. The Great Victorian Novelists
   3. The Irish Literary Revival
G. The 1900s
   1. The Novel
   2. Drama Reborn
   3. Poetry

Kacy sailed through the College of Notre Dame in Belmont and graduated early. There were no unplanned pregnancies and Michael was waiting to marry the intelligent, blue-eyed beauty the day after her graduation.

Chapter 5
After Graduation

ital.

"Mom, I've got a job. It's with the Independent in Burlingame. I'm a beat reporter, covering San Mateo."

"That's nice, Kacy, but that's a Podunk newspaper. You're going to need a better job than that. A roof over your head and food in your mouth and your baby are far more important than bedroom sessions with that loser you call a husband."

"Oh, Mother! How's Dad?"

"Still stubborn, just like you!"

"I love you, Mom. I'll talk to you later."

Michael was good in bed. But that was the only place he was good. He didn't look for a job, he didn't like to shower, and he was disrespectful to Kacy's parents. He only wanted to stand on the corner and sell dope when Kacy was at work.

Michael was a Sean Penn lookalike. A ferret-faced, six footer with brown hair, blue eyes like Kacy's, and a nice build. He was a trailer trash, wannabe gangsta.

One night, all hell broke loose and no one had to fight with Kacy about distancing herself from Michael Murphy after that.

"Michael, wake up! What's that noise at the door? Somebody's pounding on the door."

Michael jumped out of bed in his shorts and stumbled to the front of their tiny rented, two-bedroom bungalow.

"Who is it?" Michael barked.

"San Mateo Police! Open up!"

Michael bolted for the back of the house, grabbing a pair of pants on the way. He swung open the back door, ready to run across the grass to the fence and ran straight into the arms of two additional police officers.

"Fuck you, man. I'm innocent. Gitcha hands off me! I got rights!"

"Read him his rights, Smitty," Officer Brown said.

"Okay, Downtown," Smitty said.

"You have the right to remain silent, etc." Smitty repeated mechanically.

That was the night the light came on and Kacy heard her dad's words echoing in her ears. She realized what she knew down in her heart: her Dad was right. Michael had to go! A cute to her no-good guy was no longer good for her or Tina's future.

Chapter 6
The Trial

The case was assigned to Judge Cosby Shelton's court. He was one of the sternest judges in the entire county.

"Mr. Murphy, will you rise, please. You are being sentenced to Pelican Bay State Prison for twenty years, with parole not to be considered sooner than ten years. You are a scourge to our community. I have had many people come before me in my days on the bench, but your crime of selling drugs, poison to minors is reprehensible. And when it is considered that the Police Chief's son was among your customers/victims, I'm sorry that the law only allows a maximum of twenty years.

"Usually people are sent to San Quentin until it is decided where they should be placed. But I am recommending that you be sent immediately to Pelican Bay State Prison. Case closed!"

The district attorney, a young Black man who graduated from Howard University School of Law, told Kacy, "There are big differences in the sentences white men and Black men receive after being convicted of selling crack as opposed to powdered cocaine. Powder is the cocaine of choice for the white boys and crack, the cheaper less purified stuff, is the substance that is dumped in Black communities for Black boys," he confided to Kacy.

Kacy said, "Thank you sir, but at this point, I don't care."

"At least Michael has bed and board. 'Three hots and a cot, as those who love going to jail call it. He has a roof over his head," Jack Vason said, when he heard about his loser son-in-law's sentencing.

His daughter Kacy was out in the cold. But hardheaded Jack Vason was intent on giving Kacy a large dose of "tough love." He was going to let her stay out in the cold until she learned she could take some of his advice.

The straw that had broken the camel's back for Kacy's Dad had come shortly after Kacy and Michael married. Lois and Jack Vason invited Kacy and Michael to dinner at Viognier on the top floor of Draeger's Supermarket, in downtown San Mateo. Before they ordered dinner, Jack Vason went to the restroom and Michael excused himself and went, too. In the restroom, as Jack Vason finished using the urinal, he stepped over to the wash basin and washed his hands. Michael didn't. Michael just zipped his pants, brushed his bed-head hair-do with his hands and headed toward the door.

"Michael, aren't you going to wash your hands?"

"Jack, when I'm out in the woods hunting, I never wash my hands after I take a piss. I don't see why I need to do it here!"

The two men returned to the table. Jack said to Kacy and her mother Lois, "I don't feel well. Lois, come on. Will you drive? I'll pay for your dinners on the way out."

"Okay, Jack," Lois said, puzzled, as she picked up her purse and took out her keys.

"Okay, Mom," Kacy said, looking even more puzzled than her mother.

"Michael, what happened in there? Did Daddy look ill?"

"I didn't look at your dad. I don't know what his problem is. He'll be okay. At least he paid for the dinner."

Kacy glared at Michael, then turned and looked sadly as her parents walked away. Kacy's Mom and Dad left the restaurant. Kacy didn't see her parents again after that night.

Unfortunately, Kacy's newspaper job couldn't sustain her. Yet, her passion and experience in writing helped her get a good job at See Frank, a worldwide financial institution that had its headquarters in San Mateo. But when Black Thursday hit, Kacy was out on her butt again.

Chapter 7
Eva

Eva had been born and raised in San Mateo, California, to working-class parents. She married right out of high school to Marcus Cullen.

"When I walked out of San Mateo High, I said 'I do' and I did. Andrew was born nine months after Marcus and I married. And Andrew was the greatest contribution that Marcus made to our marriage. I divorced Marcus when Andrew was two. Stupid is a word that didn't need to be defined when spoken in reference to Marcus."

Eva said all of that to Kacy with her fist on her hip, standing in front of her work station at the bakery, while Kacy sat on a stool on the opposite side of the table.

"Marcus was tall, dark, extremely dark and handsome, at least to me," Eva continued. "He thought he was a mechanic, among other things. He once wanted to see how much gasoline was in the tank of an old car he was working on. When he looked into the tank, he used a match instead of a flashlight. Marcus was a sight with singed eyebrows and moustache," Eva laughed.

"His next adventure was cleaning some car parts with gasoline in the closed garage. That time, we only lost the entire garage to fire because the pilot light from the water heater set the fumes alight," Eva said, shaking her head.

When he lit the kitchen curtains on fire after twisting a piece of paper around his finger and lighting it, Eva said good-bye to pyromaniac Marcus. The only way the kitchen was saved was by Eva rushing in, grabbing the sink hose and dousing the curtains and Marcus.

After Marcus became history, a wonderful Irish dude named Tom Garrett swept Eva off her feet. Tom was Irish and Eva American of African descent. And that was the least of their problems. Together, Tom and Eva had a lighter than light-skinned baby girl named Lillian. Lillian and Mrs. Lomie Collins (the woman who helped Kacy out) were complexion look-alikes.

Eva, too, had Irish ancestry, which she had inherited from her father's side. Eva's great grandfather had been the son of the plantation owner and Lillian's dad, Tom, was from County Cork, Ireland, and a first generation, naturalized American. Tom, though, was related to Marcus Cullen, Eva's first husband, when it came to gray matter.

Tom, another dreamboat, had dark brown hair, big blue eyes and a six-pack stomach. No pyromaniac but he was into get-rich-quick schemes. He wanted to sell their friends everything from time-shares to pots and pans and vacuum cleaners.

One evening with her left fist on her hip, Eva asked, "Tom, have you seen the Sears bill lately? We have to cut back on the gift giving. Neither of us has the money to pay the bill off each month and the interest is killing us. I let you use my Visa card to get your car repaired, not as a carte blanche ticket to QVC and the Home Shopping Network," Eva snarled angrily.

"Eva, don't be so stodgy and tight-fisted. In fact, you need to take that fist off your hip and open it up," Tom said in his thick Irish brogue. "Are you sure your ancestors are Irish and not Scots? It's not going to hurt to run the bills up a little bit. Everyone in America is in debt."

"Little bit my behind! If you disappear or drop dead tomorrow, I'm the one responsible for these bills.

"That's all right, darlin'," Eva said, doing a poor imitation of

Tom's Irish accent. "I know it's time for these credit cards to evaporate, and I think. . ., no, I know that you, dear Thomas, need to disappear, too!

"Plus, Tom, you're lucky that I keep my fist on my hip. I really should take this fist and put it in your eye."

Eva cut up the credit cards, invited Tom to vacate the premises, and decided she could live better and happier without a husband.

She would say to friends, "I have a neon sign on my forehead that says, 'Stupid men, apply here!'"

Andrew, by Marcus, Eva's first husband, was a beautiful, very dark-complexioned young man who reminded everyone of the golden mask of Egypt's King Tutankhamun. Lillian, her daughter by Tom, was a paler version of Halle Berry and had the complexion of Mrs. Collins, the across-the-street neighbor who had been so kind to Kacy. Most people didn't know Lillian had any Black relatives at all. Yet, Eva raised both of her children with such pride in their rich Black heritage that these two children exuded self-assuredness from the bottom of their feet to the top of their heads. Good sense and good manners oozed from every pore, and they had no qualms about being Americans of African descent.

Eva worked on her children in-vitro – in the womb. "Dr. Sells, what I do is, when I'm listening to a book on tape or reading a book, I put another tape of ABC's, Dr. Seuss, Shakespeare, Lerone Bennett or Toni Morrison in another recorder. I put the earphones on my belly and let my unborn listen to what I consider good literature."

"Eva, you are driven," Dr. Sells said, shaking his head.

In that same fashion, more so after birth, she repeated over and over how beautiful Andrew and Lillian were and how much pride they were to have in their heritage. She told them how wonderful it was to be who and what they were, of African heritage and Irish heritage, something both children shared. This combination was the highest and best combination in the world, according to Eva's indoctrination.

Andrew and Lillian's library included every Ebony magazine from the company's inception. Books of poetry by Countee Cullen, Langston Hughes and Paul Laurence Dunbar were Andrews's favorites. And Andrew, Lillian and Eva enjoyed the records of The Last Poets of the 1950s and Amiri Baraka. Books by W.E.B. Du Bois and Booker T. Washington, biographies of Harriett Tubman, Sojourner Truth, Frederick Douglas and other early Black American heroes crowded bookshelves that reached the ceiling. Andrew and Lillian knew about themselves and a slice of American history that wasn't written in their school textbooks. Eva embraced and taught her children about Irish authors, too. Among the family's favorites were W.B. Yeats, George Bernard Shaw, Samuel Beckett, Seamus Heaney, James Joyce, Flynn O'Brien, Oscar Wilde, and Jonathan Swift.

Lillian and Andrew were Eva's pride and joy. They had seemingly both received all of their brains from their mother, but their looks were a combination. Eva was adept at finding good-looking, empty-headed-men.

At the bakery one day, Jason, one of the bakers, asked, "Eva, why do you keep calling your ex-husbands the Pid Brothers? You always call them that."

"That's because they act like their first names were Stuart, Stu for short," Eva explained.

Jason walked away shaking his head; he didn't understand. All of a sudden, a huge roar came from the back table where Jason was working. It seemed as though the little cartoon balloon had appeared above Jason's head. He started laughing.

"Stu – pid, ha, ha, ha, ha, ha! Oh my goodness, stupid! Eva, you should be ashamed of yourself. Stupid! The Pid Brothers, Marcus and Tom. Shame, Eva!" Jason laughed uncontrollably.

Eva was hard on both of her exes because neither of them had the intellect she was looking for. However, they were good fathers to their children. Child support was no problem, and they both helped to make two beautiful children.

When people saw Eva, Andrew, and Lillian together, they often thought Lillian was a friend of the family instead of the youngest daughter and Andrew's sister, even though Lillian looked a lot like her mother.

Most people who made the mistake of thinking Lillian was a little white girl rued the day. From when Lillian was five years old and older, many whites would say things they shouldn't have said about Eva or Andrew when they thought they couldn't be heard. Or they would make remarks about Black people when they thought they were standing near another white person. Lillian would light into them and make their faces turn red, making them sorry they made disparaging remarks about anything black. They would scurry off embarrassed because they had been caught with their "sheets" showing. Ku Klux Klan sheets!

Eva would always know when Lillian had overheard a nasty remark about her brother or herself. The doting, ever watchful mom would rush to Lillian's side when Lillian blurted out whatever was on her mind, giving a rejoinder such as, "The blacker the berry, the sweeter the juice." Or, "Don't you dare talk about my mother!" Those outbursts meant that someone had referred to Eva or Andrew's color.

If just a snide remark had been made about Black people in general, the Tourette's Syndrome-like comment would sound something like this, "You stringy haired haint!"

Eva inherited her Irish lineage from her father's side. Eva's great grandfather had been the son of the plantation owner and Lillian's Dad was from County Cork and a naturalized American. The family found as much joy in celebrating St. Patrick's Day as they did in celebrating Kwanza and Christmas.

Because of Eva's business, every holiday was important. Holidays sold cakes. Eva had loved to cook since childhood. She made the culinary business her priority for higher education and was a graduate of the local Culinary Institute. Upon leaving the Culinary, she became a pastry chef. But she loved baking and making cakes better than crepes, tarts and cream puffs. She found that cake baking and decorating opened her artistic mind. She could sculpt and design with cake. Cakes and cake decorating could be the clay of the potter, the steel of the forger, the palette of the painter, or the marble of the sculptor. She could make a cake statue of David or cake cartoon characters like Porky Pig or Mickey Mouse. Cake baking and decorating made Eva's artistic juices flow.

Yet, even with the business being about 5 years old and even with the acclaim she received from being on local TV shows and

five

doing cakes for stars, Eva wasn't making money. She was getting by. Now, without the two stumblebums she had been hooked up with, she knew she could do more. She didn't want to be just the other bakery in town. She wanted to be THE bakery in town.

Eva's business acumen was lacking. She read trade books, manuals, and magazines, and attended classes and seminars, but turning a small business into a small moneymaking business was her goal. Eva wasn't greedy, but she wanted to make enough money so Andrew, Lillian, and she could live comfortably. Eva also had plans for both children to graduate from college.

She wanted to do more than just make the house payments. She wanted to own her own building and have the bakery in one part and rent out the rest. She wanted to capitalize on her investments and not have to work hard all her life. She wanted to work smart, not hard. There was a way to do it, but running the business and being the chief cook and bottle washer kept her on a treadmill. She was doing okay, but okay wasn't good enough.

Eva told Kacy about her short run in the corporate world. She stood tall, with her legs parted and her left hand on her hip. "I had a job for a few years with Benjamin Funds, the biggest firm in the area. Navy blue suit and white blouse were the uniform of the era."

Eva related, "I became tired of the times my white co-workers would see two or three of the Black employees talking and ask us, 'What was that meeting about?' Or when a white colleague would say to me, 'You know I really like you. When I'm with you, I don't see color. I don't think of you as Black.'"

"Kacy, I'm Black and I'm a knockout. I want them to say, 'Look at that beautiful Black chick!' But they say, 'Isn't she exotic?' Hell, I'm not exotic. I'm beautiful and a damn sight better looking than Gwenneth Paltrow or Nicole Kiddman. I know I'm smarter than Kiddman, too, she smokes. My Momma told me I was beautiful. My mother used to say, 'Even a buzzard thinks its baby's beautiful!' Screw exotic!"

"I was told I was decreasing my effectiveness with my aggressiveness. Those jerks always wanted to shorten my name and call me Eve instead of Eva. They wanted to know if I could tan in the summer. I'd look at my arm and say, 'Last time I looked this was still skin!' There were questions about my hair: Why did I change the style so often? I told them because I can! Natural today, straight tomorrow, curls the next week, and then braids. About my clothes: Why did I always dress up? 'Cause I didn't think jeans were appropriate for the office, et-cet-era, et-cet-era!" Eva drew each word out.

"After Marcus Cullen, Tom Garrett, and the corporate world, I decided to strike out on my own. It's not that I have completely avoided stupidity but, in my own business, I can handle it on a different level. If employees get too stupid in here, I can fire them! Or put ground glass or poison in their cake, maybe just in the icing," she said, laughing.

Eva raised her hand to get a high five from Kacy, but Kacy recoiled and flinched. Eva laughingly said, "Be cool girl, I was only trying to get a high five."

Kacy interjected, "Eva, I don't have that many Black friends, but if I say something stupid about race or color, please be gentle with me, puh – leeze?"

"Kacy, I'll be as gentle as I can be. But I have to warn you about my daughter, Lillian. She doesn't suffer fools and takes no prisoners. So I'm warning you in advance. I'll be as helpful as I can, but I won't always be around to save you."

Chapter 8
The Bakery

It was Sunday morning and both women had a new day to face. Eva rose early as she had cakes to finish. The bakery would open at ten o'clock for people who had to pick up cakes, candles, or balloons. On Sunday, she closed the doors at one o'clock.

Eva popped her head into the room where Tina and Kacy were sleeping.

Kacy was lying awake in bed, eyes open, ruminating on the bleakness of the last two days when she heard the doorknob twist. "Good morning, Eva, and thank you," she blurted out the instant the door opened.

"I'm on my way to work. There's plenty of food in the fridge. You and Tina can come down to the bakery when you get yourselves together, if you want to. If not, just hang around here. I'll be back home around two."

"Thanks, Eva," Kacy said again. "As soon as Tina wakes up and I get her fed, we'll come down to the bakery and give you a hand."

"That will be wonderful, Kacy. I can always use extra hands down at the bakery. And if you say 'thank you' one more time, I'm going to strangle you."

Eva was out the door, into her van, and on her way to work.

Kacy removed herself from the bed, showered, shampooed,

and made herself presentable. Tina woke up whimpering. She was disoriented and couldn't remember where she was.

"Shhh, baby, you're okay. We're at Eva's house. We're fine. I'll help you get yourself showered and dressed, and we'll go to the kitchen. We're going to have a real breakfast today. What do you want? Pancakes?"

"Bacon and eggs, Mommy. Bacon and eggs."

"Okay, Tina. Today you won't have to eat cold cereal."

Kacy cooked eggs, bacon and toast for both of them. Tina drank a big glass of orange juice while Kacy had orange juice and hot coffee. After the nice breakfast, she washed the frying pan and put the dishes in the dishwasher. Kacy brushed Tina's hair, put it in a ponytail and off they went to the bakery.

When Tina and Kacy walked in, they saw a staff of people busy doing everything at once. Some were taking orders, some decorating cakes and others waiting on customers who came to pick up various items. It was a hustling, bustling place.

Kacy went to the sink and began to add strong detergent and more hot water to last night's cold, greasy gook. She rolled up her sleeves and started washing and scrubbing.

"Boy, these things are greasy!" she said to no one in particular.

Hot water and detergent, along with some elbow grease, did the job. Constant chatter and a small hubbub were the norm in this beehive, even on a Sunday!

Kacy, with Tina's help, washed everything in the sink. Tina had a great time trying to figure out where all the items went. Her job was putting the pans, utensils, pillars and decorating tips back in their proper places. This kept the youngster busy most of the morning.

Kacy wiped her hands on a paper towel and went to the table where Eva was tubing an elaborate peacock on a cake. Kacy brought Eva up-to-date on why she and Tina had no place to stay, no credit, and why the Murphy women were trying to live on minimum wage.

Eva chuckled, placing her hand on her hip and said, "Look, I need some help at the bakery. Is there anything else in your résumé beside divorcée and dishwasher?"

Kacy laughed, too. "For a roof over my head, I'll become anything you want me to be. Maybe working together, I can help you become that millionaire I heard you talking about at the picnic. In fact, I want to be a millionaire, too. So maybe we can find a way to do it together!"

"You're on, little sister! But that means we have to make two million!" Eva smiled warmly at her eager guest.

Kacy began to tell Eva more about her background. "Eva, I'm a writer. I'm Pulitzer material, but I've sorta lost my way. As a child, I wrote stories and plays, usually about the underdog and how I could nurture them and single-handedly uplift the human race. I have always wanted to write and have always wanted to take care of those I felt couldn't take care of themselves. In a way, I guess that's how I became mixed up with my ex, Michael.

"I was going to reform him, clean him up. He was going to be a model husband and father. And I guess today he has probably become a model something or other - a model prisoner."

The two women worked way beyond two o'clock. Tina was in the front of the bakery going through the albums. This activity had become her favorite pastime and on a warm Sunday afternoon, with the sun heating up the space, going through the albums always put Tina to sleep.

When Sunday's work was finally done, they ordered a pizza. With greasy fingers and between chews, Eva walked Kacy through the entire bakery. The two women peeked in at Tina, and there she was, head down on a display table, dead asleep. Eva continued to tell Kacy as much as she could about the ups and downs of the bakery business.

"Kacy, Monday is going to be a big day for you. You will begin to learn Baking 101, as taught by Eva Garrett.

"Because the bakery is open on Sundays, I miss morning church services. I have to have something for my soul, so I've started going to Sunday night services.

"Now, I have to go home, take a shower, and get to church, or I'm going to be late. I attend Prophet Baptist Church. The evening services aren't very long, not as long as most Baptist services, and I've got the hots for one of the ministers. There's a new hunk of a minister over there, and it makes the service even better. I think he's eyeing me too!" Eva laughed.

"Well, I'll meet you back at the house," Kacy said as she helped sleepy Tina into her jacket and started for the door. But she hesitated and asked, "Where is Prophet Baptist Church?"

Eva told her how to find the church, then asked, "Why do you want to know?"

"Eva, God has been so good to me, and I need to say thank you too. I'm Lutheran and not very religious, but today I need to give a lot of thanks."

"Okay," Eva answered. "Should I wait for you?"

"No," Kacy whispered. "I'm going to go and put Tina to sleep. I'll meet you at the church as soon as I can."

After Tina closed her eyes, Kacy took off her clothes, jumped in the shower, and put on fresh make-up and a cute dress. She quietly slipped out the front door. Finding the church, she parked her car and ran in. Arriving just as the minister was winding down the sermon and was preparing the congregation for the collection, Kacy took a ten-dollar bill out of her purse. She squeezed Alexander Hamilton hard, closed her eyes, and gave great thanks to the Lord who had seen her through two interesting days.

The ushers told the people in the last pew to come forward first. Each row was to follow in succession. They marched by a table and put their contributions into one of several baskets. Because the line was taking so long, Kacy reached in her purse and pulled out another ten and a five. When it was her turn to march past the baskets, she put in twenty-five dollars. A warm glow came over her.

Then the music became louder. There was a drummer, a guitarist, a bongo player, an organist, and two piano players. The choir director lifted his arms and the choir members opened their mouths. Kacy felt that she had just been transported and lifted to a rhythmic Nirvana. The song began, "The spirit of the Lord is here, I feel it in the atmosphere..." Moving their arms and feet to a definite beat, the congregation was almost military in their foot pounding. Kacy pumped her arms, stamped her feet, and swayed along with the rest of the congregation. Anyone who could remain motionless and in one spot was obviously deaf and blind. This was not the Lutheran Church!

After that rousing tune, a Mahalia Jackson lookalike started singing "Precious Lord Take My Hand." The tune was so beautiful, slow, and touching that tears streamed from Kacy's blue eyes. This time they were happy tears because Kacy felt as though she were levitating. She knew that God had truly touched her life this day. But was it luck or was it God? "Because I'm in church," she thought, "this is a no brainer: of course it is God!"

The service ended and the congregation started pouring out of the building. Eva passed by the pew where Kacy was. Kacy stepped out, grabbed Eva's arm, and they walked toward the big church doors together.

Several ministers were waiting in the foyer to shake hands with the exiting congregants: Rev. Brewer, Rev. Walker and Rev. Clifford Davidson. That minister is really good-looking, Kacy thought. And with that thought, Eva squeezed Kacy's arm and Kacy knew exactly who Eva had been talking about and now squeezed about.

The two women stopped in front of the hunk. "Rev. Davidson, I hope you remember me. I'm Eva Garrett and this is my friend Kacy Murphy. I think Kacy might be interested in joining Prophet."

"Is that so, Ms. Murphy? There is always room at Prophet for someone who is looking for a church home. I hope Prophet Baptist Church can and will fit your needs."

"Rev. Davidson, I enjoyed the service and the music was beyond belief. I'll be back," Kacy mumbled.

"Mrs. Garrett, of course I remember you. I recall you were looking for a person to fix some shelves. I think I might be able to help you with that problem. Please give me a call."

"I certainly will, Rev. Davidson. You'll hear from me tomorrow. Should I just call the number here at the church?"

"Yes, Mrs. Garrett. I pick up messages all day from that number."

"I'll leave a message early tomorrow morning," Eva replied.

The two women hurried down the church steps. When they

reached the bottom, Kacy said, "Eva, why did you tell him I was going to join church?"

"Kacy, I couldn't think of anything else to say to him, but did you hear him? He's going to help fix the shelves at the bakery. I can't wait to call him."

Kacy and Eva were both parked at King Center parking lot, half a block from the church. The two women skipped all the way to the lot, giggling like two schoolgirls.

Chapter 9
Monday at the Bakery

"Kacy, I know there are ways to save. I just don't have the time or the inclination to look for them."

"Let me look at this stuff for about an hour, Eva. I'm going to the desk in the back."

"Great! I'm sure looking at the paperwork for this bakery is going to be better reading than a sexy novel."

"Don't bother me for about forty-five minutes, Okay?" Kacy said.

An hour and a half passed. Kacy was back with a tablet completely filled with proposed changes.

"What we need is a computer. All the orders, equipment, ingredients, everything should be computerized."

"Kacy, I can't afford a computer right now, and I don't have time to do that paperwork."

"Don't worry about it, Eva. Kacy to the rescue! I'll get done what we need to get done. Paper and pencil are still fashionable. We can register everything we need to keep track of in ledger books for the time being, but we are going to bring this operation into the twenty-first century. I know many recreation centers and churches have an excess of older computers. People are always donating their out-of-date machines. I'm going to call around and see if the YMCA,

Prophet Baptist Church or St. James has a couple of computers in their basements that they'll sell or give to us for a nominal fee."

"Kacy, before I can get a computer, I have to do something about that van."

"You're right, Eva. We're going to buy a new van and have a professional sign painted on it. But we're not going to go into debt to do it. We're just going to tighten our belts."

"Sounds good to me. Do whatever you have to do," Eva agreed.

Kacy washed dishes, cracked eggs, learned to bake, arranged shelves, counted inventory, learned to make decorative edges, split and filled cakes and on and on. Every bit of the baking business was being crammed between Kacy's ears as fast and as comprehensively as Eva could do it.

Kacy was an excellent student. Her extra work and effort, with a tiny salary and bagged lunches, was helping to cut corners as predicted.

Kacy began going out on deliveries, as well as taking orders and making sales. In the past, most of the people in the bakery, including Eva, were content to let the business come to them. Eva ran ads in the local newspapers every now and then, but she did not have a consistent or comprehensive sales campaign.

Kacy proved to be an excellent salesperson. She gathered the staff together and sold them. "When a Mom comes in for that birthday cake, we have to be the ones to encourage her to buy her balloons from us. We want to sell her the candles. We don't want to sell her too much cake, but we are here to make money. We have to pay rent and your salaries. We need to sell the biggest cake we can get away with, but don't be pushy. You have to tell the mom how well cake freezes and that she can not only send a picture of the cake over the web to the grandparents, but frozen cake travels well and will be just fine sent by one day express. That way we can sell either a larger cake or an extra small one, so that grandparents, in-laws, aunts, uncles and cousins can also have cake."

"We need to tell the customers about placing an order for next year's event, too. We will put their name and information in the computer, so we can know when the next birthday, anniversary, or just a plain great day for a cake is approaching. Our new motto must be, 'Bring in New Business!'" Kacy added.

They don't have one yet.

Chapter 10
School

Tina was enrolled in Meadow Heights Elementary School near Eva's house, where she successfully sidestepped the new-kid morass.

It was the same school that Lillian and Marcus attended. The two Garrett children were in fifth and sixth grades and had sworn to keep an eye out for Tina.

One Monday, Lillian left her lunch at home. Eva brought the lunch to her school on the way to the bakery.

As Eva entered the schoolroom, the teacher looked up and greeted, "Hi, Mrs. Garrett."

Eva waved at the teacher, saying, "Here's Lillian's bag."

The teacher motioned to Lillian to stop her work and go to her mother to retrieve her sandwiches. Lillian took the lunch from her mother and Eva leaned down. They kissed and hugged each other.

During recess, several of the white kids came over to Lillian and asked in awe, "Was that your mother, Lillian?"

"I didn't know your mother was colored!" said one girl.

One of the boys started chanting. "Lillian's mother is Blaaaaack," in a sing-songy chant.

Lillian walked over to the boy with her hand in a fist and knocked the kid seven ways from Sunday. The boy grabbed his nose, which was starting to bleed and ran toward the restrooms. The other children made a wide circle around Lillian.

"Yeah, my mother is American of African descent, and she's proud of it and so am I. She's beautiful and smart and so am I. If anyone else wants a bloody nose, just say so and I'll be glad to give you one," bellowed Lillian.

Mrs. Croce came up to the crowd of children and grabbed Lillian by the arm. "What's going on here?" the teacher asked, raising her voice.

It seemed as though a thousand elementary school voices were trying to speak at once. But the teacher figured she knew what the issue was. Lillian didn't tolerate anyone talking about her mother or her brother. This wasn't the first time it had happened and probably wouldn't be the last. One day, Mrs. Croce thought, the kids in general and the white kids in particular, will get the message. Lillian wasn't a white girl and didn't want to be. She was proud of her heritage because her mother had instilled that in her. And please don't talk about her brother Andrew.

Mrs. Croce herded Lillian into the classroom.

"Lillian, you can't go through life hitting people. You have to control your temper. Here is some paper and a pencil. I want you to write, 'I will not hit.' one hundred times."

"Yes, Ms. Croce," Lillian said with no emotion at all.

When the class returned from recess, the teacher gave a long lecture on being kind to one another, on race relations, and how nature made many varieties and colors. Time-outs and non-violence were the theme of all Mrs. Croce's classes. You were going to have to take time out if you punched a fellow student. Punching was an act of violence. As students in Mrs. Croce's class, you had to practice non-violence.

"Class, do you remember our lessons on Dr. Martin Luther King and Mahatma Ghandi? They lived and breathed non-violence." Ms. Croce plodded on.

Lillian, from her desk, listened harder than anyone in the classroom. Her brow was knit in concentration, and she vowed to herself that she would hit the next kid who had something to say about her mother or brother even harder. I meant what I said, and I said what I meant.

Chapter 11
The Theory

"Kacy, I thank you so much for that great shot in the arm you gave the staff today. That was some pep talk. I really appreciate it," Eva smiled.

You sounded like me when I give the kids lectures. Not that you were lecturing, but when I talk to Andrew and Lillian about who they are and why they're supposed to be proud, Kacy, I'm as ethnocentric as they come."

"Eva, what does ethnocentric mean?" Kacy inquired, looking puzzled.

Placing her hand on her hip, Eva said, "I'll give you a definition later. And look at the hand I was dealt. Two children who couldn't be more opposite in this world. One white, one Black, and both mine. You can believe there have been some challenges!

"I want them to know they can be anything they want to be. I want them to use their minds and stretch them. I want them to be overachievers and not let anyone stand in their way because they are Black or American of African descent," Eva emphasized.

"Eva, I've never heard that term before. I've heard you referred to as Colored, Black, African-American but American of African descent? Where have I been?"

"People want to know why I use that term. Kacy, it's because we're Americans first. If a person is Japanese and from Japan, he or she is Japanese. Japanese! If he or she is Japanese and born in the U.S., that person is American- Japanese. Get what I'm saying? I want the American to come first.

"So, you're not German-American or Italian-American. The wording should be the other way around. A person should, in my opinion, be American-Nigerian or American- Irish. I'm an American. My kids are Americans. You and Tina are Americans. It's not rocket science for me. That's my pep talk for the kids and for the rest of the world – if the rest of the world would only listen. It's just me and Whoopee Goldberg with this theory. She's the only other person I've heard with the same philosophy. And ethnocentric means the belief in the superiority of one's ethnic or racial group! I don't believe in the superiority of anything, but I feel strongly about equality for my racial group and about not being stepped on. I'm just into my ethnicity and my people."

"I'm listening, Eva. It's an interesting theory. I don't know what I'd call myself, I'm a variety, I guess."

"Then you're just an American," Eva said. "That's okay too! My dad had a lot of difficulties about color issues. He would get a kick out of seeing my Andrew and Lillian. About Lillian he would have said:

'One drop of Jesus' blood will make you pure.

But one drop of a niggah's blood will make you a niggah sure.'"

"Eva, that's not a nice word. My ex Michael always used the 'N' word. My mother and father didn't raise me that way. I hate that word!"

"Don't panic. I don't like that word either, and it's not a word I like using. That's some old bugaboo theory and saying my dad grew up with where he was born in Texas, back in the 1890s. My dad was an old man when I was born. That's the way the so-called laws were back when my dad was a young man.

"Supposedly, no matter how light you were, if you had one drop of Black or African blood, you were considered Black. That has always puzzled me because history shows that many, many American Caucasians have Black or African blood in them, but they never talk about it. Millions of American Caucasians will tell you about their American Native ancestry, but you never, or rarely, do you hear them talk about their African side. You know, with all the sleeping around folks do and did, and with all the people who passed and are passing, there have to be more Americans of African ancestry than have fessed up!" Eva laughed.

"One of these days people are going to have to take DNA tests and some folks are going to be very surprised to realize that they are my relatives. I have to talk about this stuff to Lillian all the time. Her color does cause some issues.

"Can't you just see us in a futuristic setting? People are getting on the shuttle to go to the moon and they have to have a DNA test before taking the trip. There's a buzzer that goes off to let you know what the racial types are because science has learned that if you have Black blood, you can't go to Mars. If you have white blood, you can't go to Venus. If you have Asian blood, you can't go to Neptune."

"Yeah, Eva, I can see it," Kacy laughed. "I can see Mrs. Jefferson standing in line with her husband, who was born in the South and still flies the Confederate Flag in 2050. They have tickets for Mars.

"Yep and when the buzzer goes off after Mrs. Jefferson takes her test, poor Mr. Jefferson faints and Mrs. Jefferson is flabbergasted; she's removed in a straitjacket because she can't believe she has Black blood. 'Damn the DNA!' she yells as she is put into an ambulance." Eva and Kacy both laugh.

"Kacy," Eva continued, "You would have loved my Dad. If you think I'm a character, it would comfort you to know I didn't fall far from the tree."

"Eva, I think you would have liked my dad, too. He didn't like Michael. Michael was crude, rude, and abusive. Daddy knew it, and I just couldn't see it. My dad was even for school integration. He used to go to the school board meetings. He said he really liked that Ruth Nagler, she was the chairperson, and there was a guy named Bill Gillespie that my dad liked, too.

"Daddy would say, 'Those colored children need a chance and the best way to get it is through a good education. They could go to school in our neighborhood.' Yeah, Eva, you'd have like my dad.

"Can you believe it, Eva? My dad even joined The Council on Racial Equality? It was church people who came together to say that everyone in San Mateo should have a job and a good education. I think they did a good job.

"Eva, I can remember when they did the school bussing thing. There was a Black girl in our room named Kelsey Lax. She was shorter than everyone else. Michael began bullying her and spit in the little girl's face on the second day of school. Michael didn't know that Kelsey had a friend named Deborah Hayes. Deborah was tall, much taller than Kelsey, even taller than Michael, but she was in our class, too.

"Deborah was standing nearby when Michael spit on Kelsey. Deborah ran over to Michael, grabbed his arm and beat the crap out of him.

"When we got back in the classroom the teacher saw that Michael had been into something. His face was red and he had a big welt under his eye. But Michael lied and told the teacher he and some other boys had been fooling around at recess. Can you believe it, Eva? None of the kids told! But that stopped Michael from messing with any more of the Black kids. He might have done something I didn't hear about, but he left Kelsey alone after that.

"The other kids didn't like Michael that much. He was bussed to school, too. He lived in the trailer park that was across the highway," Kacy confided.

"You're right, Kacy. The school bussing in San Mateo did work pretty well. There were a lot of citizens who made sure it worked. That's why I like this city," Eva added.

Chapter 12
How'd You Do It?

"How did you get into this business, Eva?" Kacy asked.

Eva set her decorating bag on the table and placed her left hand on her hip. "I always knew I wanted to do something in the food business. I started cooking when I was seven years old. My mother had such bad morning sickness that she couldn't go near the kitchen. Every odor in the kitchen sent her to the bathroom to throw up.

"I had always shown interest in things that had to do with the kitchen. From the shopping to the last belch, I wanted to be involved. In high school, I took every cooking class the school had to offer. I went to the local community college to take what wasn't offered at the high school. I went to the Culinary Institute and ended up loving all aspects of cooking."

"The same thing happened to me only my passion was English and writing. What a coincidence!" Kacy interrupted.

"Cakes just seemed to turn me on. I found you could make anything out of cake. It's like having clay in your hands. I guess I'm just a frustrated sculptor and found out that I could do a Leonardo da Vinci, a Picasso, or a Whistler out of cake. I can be Romeare Bearden Andy Warhol or Varnett Honeywood. If it could be done

48

with acrylics, oils, clay, or marble, I could do it with frosting, filling, and cake.

"I also became involved in cake baking because, when Marcus and I were first married, we took in foster children. It was touching to see their faces on their birthdays. Those youngsters hadn't had the joy of having birthday parties, and anything we could do to make their lives brighter during the short time they were with us was a pleasure on our part. It made me feel extra good to provide a small item like a cake for those children. Something as simple as a birthday celebration brought a special light to those children's eyes."

Eva wrapped her arms around herself and danced across the room. She sang a few lines from the Stevie Wonder version of "Happy Birthday to yah . . ."

I've hired several artists who work with palette and oils. They've been amazed at what they could accomplish with frosting. Some bakeries use sprayers to apply the colors on white butter cream. I prefer mixing my own colors and drawing free hand. We turn out masterpieces every day. Only when the party's over, there's no trace left of our mastery. As you see, Kacy, we take pictures of each cake, particularly the unusual ones. And customers take pictures and send them to us, too. We've even had to hide some of the books and bring them out on request. We started missing photos and realized that rival bakeries were coming in here and taking the photos out of the albums."

Chapter 13
The TV Show

All the while, Kacy was watching Eva like a hawk. She studied Eva and she studied the bakery. After six months of being with Eva, Kacy surprised her one day by handing Eva a slim black briefcase. Inside, Kacy had placed a thirteen-week treatment for the television cake-show series, Eva's resumé, and newspaper articles about the bakery.

There were articles about the many cakes that were made for the San Francisco 49er parties in preparation for Super Bowl activities. Other articles were about Eva's demonstrations at the County Fair. There were more articles about the over five hundred Scout Troops that had earned their badges at the bakery by learning to decorate small loaf cakes or cupcakes.

Kacy also had been in conversation with the executives at the Food Channel and had set up an appointment for the two of them at the end of the month.

Eva and Kacy were once again acting like two schoolgirls getting ready for the big day.

Kacy was able to buy an expensive and great-looking navy blue suit from Nordstrom Rack. It had even been marked down at that store. Eva was paying Kacy a meager salary, but Kacy was becoming a master at pinching pennies. She was even becoming successful at teaching her spendthrift housemate, Eva, to do the same thing.

Both women were on a budget not just at the bakery but at home, too. That meant they had to eliminate the housekeeper and distribute household chores between themselves and the children. Everyone made their own beds before school. Everyone helped load and empty the dishwasher, make lunches, fold clothes, and clean the house. No one was exempt.

The navy blue suit, worn with a lighter blue turtleneck sweater, brought out the blue of Kacy's eyes. Low, chic, navy leather pumps and navy leather bag had Kacy looking spectacular.

Eva looked at Kacy and said, "Girl, you're looking very corporate there. Soon as we make some real money, we're going to shop at Nordstrom when there isn't a sale."

Kacy looked at Eva and laughed, saying, "We're going to make the Food Channel execs think we don't need their old TV series. We're going to step in the door and let them know we know what we're talking about, and that we don't need them. They need us! If this look is corporate, then let's look corporate!"

On the morning of their appointment, Eva wore a charcoal-gray, pin-stripped pants suit, Black low-heeled shoes, red scarf, and ruby earrings and bracelet. The jewelry was an expensive present from one of the Pid Brothers; Eva couldn't remember which one. She also carried a black leather shoulder bag and looked as though she had just stepped off the cover of Black Enterprise or Essence Magazine. Kacy could have captured the covers of Vogue or Elle.

"Eva, I've eaten a lot of birthday cake in my day, but I swear I haven't seen any cakes like yours anywhere," Kacy said.

When they reached the 15th floor of the Transamerica Building, all heads turned to watch the two beautiful and completely opposite women stroll down the hall. Kacy and Eva knew they were turning heads, and they loved every minute of it.

On the glass double doors, the sign stated FOOD CHANNEL. Eva and Kacy were in the right place. Their reflections were prominent in the glass of the doors. Make-up straight, hair neat, no slips showing. Of course not; they were wearing pants suits!

→ *mention Mr. Hemins here,*

Resumé and manuscript in the briefcase. Each woman knew her role.

As strong and confident as Kacy and Eva were, two executive producers at the Food Channel had doubts. Although they had not yet met Eva Garrett and her partner, cake decorating shows to Grace Canon and her assistant, Gayle Teal, were ho-hum viewing. After all, the Food Channel aired Emeril Lagasse and other high-powered chefs and Gayle and Grace had already turned down numerous cake-baking shows. — 2

"I've read the treatment, Mr. Hemins. It's not that different from several others we've received," Grace Canon, senior show producer, sighed.

"Me too, Hemins. I don't see what's going to make this show different from any other," agreed assistant Gayle Teal.

"See, that's where we differ, Ms. Canon, Ms. Teal. I went to the bakery as just a casual shopper. I looked around the place. Asked to use the bathroom while I was there. I saw the work being done. I saw the cakes. Although pictures were submitted with the packet, you really need to see the cakes in the display case and the people coming in and out of the store. I gained a feeling for the place by listening to customers' comments. You have to see the pictures on the walls of all the celebrities. You have to see the pictures of beautiful weddings. I saw everything first hand. You two need to do that.

"I have a gut feeling about this show. One of the other components that has convinced me is the fact that Garrett works with young people. I'm a sucker for young people. I want to see this thing work. Canon, you make it work."

"Yes, Mr. Hemins. I'll make it work," Ms. Canon said mildly, accepting the strong message from her boss.

However, Grace and Gayle just didn't feel it. From the treatment they'd read — cake mixes, use of pans, how to make drop flowers? What the hell was a drop flower? thought Grace.

Mr. Hemins left the office and the job was up to Ms. Grace Jones and her assistant.

Ms. Canon was a plain-looking woman, casually dressed in jeans and an open-necked, man's stripped shirt. Her assistant

?

Gayle was dressed in faded gray jogging sweats. They still were not convinced about the show, but they had their marching orders.

"Grace, who in hell makes cakes anymore? That's why we have Costco and Safeway. If you want a cake, go to one of those stores and buy one."

"Yeah, Gayle. We've already turned down at least twenty similar shows. But Hemins sees something we don't see. I bet this Garrett and her friend Murphy look like two sacks of flour. Who bakes, let alone decorates, a cake these days?"

The receptionist escorted Kacy and Eva into a long narrow conference room. A large mahogany table took up the center and comfy over-stuffed chairs made the room look crowded. After Kacy and Eva sat waiting for about five minutes, Ms. Canon and her assistant entered the room.

Both women's eyebrows raised when they saw Eva and Kacy, and they smiled, "My name is Grace Canon and this is my assistant producer, Ms. Gayle Teal. Gayle is the person you talked to on the phone. If your project is approved, she'll be the point person. Would you like coffee? Water? Anything?"

"No, thank you," said Eva. "We're anxious to tell you about our series. I'm Eva Garrett and this is my partner Kacy Murphy. Ms. Murphy will be the spokesperson today."

They took their seats and Eva placed her left hand on her hip and sat in that fashion through the entire meeting.

Gayle Teal sorted through her papers and said, "Excuse us for a moment, will you? I left the packet for your show in my office. The one I have is the wrong one. I need Ms. Canon to help me find it and now I'm the one who's thirsty. We're going to get some cold bottles of water. Sure you don't want some?" Gayle questioned. She stood up and headed for the door. Grace followed her from the room.

When they knew they were out of earshot and couldn't be heard by Eva and Kacy, Gayle said, "Did you see those two babes, Canon? I never dreamed that they would be so young and attractive. The Black one's making me drool!"

"Gayle, you'd better shut up! You know Molly would knock you in your head if she thought you were looking goo-goo eyed at anybody. But I get your drift. They're both to die for. Too bad we're both spoken for. I'd take either one of them. But good looking or not, I still don't like cake-baking shows, and they're going to have to jump through my hoops. I don't care what Hemins says. These women have to prove they're worthy of being on the Food Channel. And Gayle, you know I'm a one-woman woman. I'm just lusting. Doesn't everyone now and then?"

Just then, a male voice harumped. It was Hemins clearing his throat. He was sitting in his office next to Grace's, sitting where Grace and Gayle couldn't see him and the door connecting their office was ajar.

"Grace and Gayle, I know you think you really run this operation, but I still control the checkbook that pays your salaries. And yep, they are two babes! The blue eyes on that blonde made my heart jump. I looked deeply into them when I visited their shop. My wife, Marion, would bop me up-side my head, too, if she knew I was making goo-goo eyes. So that puts all three of us in the same boat. Now, we're all going to behave and make this show work. Got it?"

Laughing and a little embarrassed, Grace and Gayle echoed, "Got it!"

They had their orders and they had to help Eva and Kacy make a successful series.

Reentering the conference room, Gayle and Grace rejoined Kacy and Eva. Still, they gave Kacy and Eva the grilling of their lives. They didn't leave a stone unturned, asking questions about drop flowers, convection ovens as opposed to regular ovens, and why a person would want to use a comb on a cake. They still thought Kacy and Eva were too dressed up and pretentious, even if Canon, Teal, and Hemins found the two bakers to be living dolls.

Finally, after a grueling hour, Canon and Teal told Kacy and Eva that the Food Channel would accept the first thirteen-week treatments of the cake-baking show.

At the big conference table Kacy and Eva dissected the individual shows with Canon, Teal, and Mr. Hemins, who had now joined them.

"The first show: we'll start by picking out a great mix. A great mix! Yeah, nobody has time to make a cake from scratch. When we get to episode twenty-four," stated Kacy, "We'll do a retro show and demonstrate what it takes to make a cake from scratch. But not in the beginning!"

The script mentioned adding wine to achieve a particular flavor, Jell-O pudding for moistness and various types of other ingredients to achieve different textures.

"All of the brands are good, but if we feel a particular brand can help a viewer achieve something special, we'll emphasize that one and explain why. We'll tell the baker what to expect when using Duncan Hines, Pillsbury, Betty Crocker, or a generic brand. Every step will be laid out," Kacy explained.

"We'll make up a few mixes and talk about what might be best in what type of pan. For instance, a pound cake is better in a loaf pan, Bundt cakes in Bundt pans, etc. We'll show which pan to use if you make the wine cake."

Kacy continued, "In show number two, we'll demonstrate pans and how to make the shape you want if you don't have a pan that's shaped like Mount Everest. How do you get the skirt of a doll if there is no pan shaped that way? Well, there is a pan shaped that way, but it's not a pan you would think of.

"In show number three, we'll offer more ideas on how to cut a cake into the shape you want out of any type of rectangle. We'll show when to use round pans of cake to go with the rectangular ones and how to make a star or an extra large heart when you don't have pans in those shapes or that large. And yes," Kacy chuckled, "we'll explain what a cake comb is and why we don't comb our cakes at Eva's."

After Kacy completed her description of the thirteen shows, Ms. Jones thanked her and announced, "There are at least three companies vying for sponsorship. We have been contacted by a major food conglomerate, a sugar manufacturer, and a pan company."

Eva tried to remain professional and calm, but she wanted to jump out of her chair and shout. Kacy was feeling the same way, too. It was fantastic to hear that someone wanted their show idea and that the companies were in competition for a good show. Hopefully, their show. Damn, that felt good!

Another issue Ms. Canon and Ms. Teal hammered home was

that Eva and Kacy also needed to think about having young people incorporated into as many programs as they could manage.

"That will be no problem at all, Ms. Canon," Eva assured. "We can start with our own children and almost every scout troop in town has been to the bakery to earn a badge. So, I feel we'll have a cast of willing characters."

Before the meeting was over, Eva and Kacy had sold thirteen episodes and, the producers, now convinced, wanted to see more. Eva and Kacy were to return to the office in a week to sign the contract.

After they had shaken hands with Eva and Kacy and the bakers had headed for the elevator, Gayle looked at Grace and said, "They weren't as bad as we thought they would be."

"Yeah," Grace answered and we're going to have to give them all the help we can. And can you believe it? I never cared a whit about a cake comb, but now I know that Eva's bakery finds it more professional and esthetically pleasing to have a smooth-sided cake. Schlocky bakeries, according to our two experts, use comb-sided cakes to hide flaws. Who'd a thought it?"

The shows would be shot in the studios of the local community college so that Eva and Kacy would not have to make multiple trips to San Francisco.

The Food Channel producers scheduled a day to visit the bakery to see what Eva needed and how the set was to be constructed. They needed to sketch a schematic for camera placement, to determine where the ovens should be placed and to figure out all the small details that would make the set look as much like Eva's bakery as possible.

Eva had to make some concessions. She had to choose a new color scheme for her kitchen, foregoing the checked gingham she was currently using and was well known for. Checks have the tendency to dance on screen, so solid colors were mandatory and colors looked better on camera than the stark white aprons and toque blancs (the tall chefs' hats) that are worn in many bakeries.

Eva wanted everything to be blue. Blue mixers, oven doors, refrigerators, aprons, and chefs' hats. Everything that could be would be blue: handles on utensils, wiping cloths, canisters, and bins. Everything was to be blue in tribute to Eva's mother, Eva Sing, who had always wanted a blue kitchen. It was Eva's way of saying, "This is for you, Ma!"

Eva was a junior, but few people knew about this. And no one ever called her junior as you would a male child. Some family members called her Sing. People thought this was because Eva had a lovely singing voice, but no. Sing was her mother's maiden name.

Kacy and Eva left the Food Channel office on cloud nine. Obtaining the show was a turning point in their lives. Kacy had a driving energy in the field of marketing, while it was Eva who kept her nose to the grindstone. Baking cakes and keeping the bakery doors open had been Eva's priority. Now Kacy's new ideas were just what the bakery and Eva needed.

Kacy had many of the qualities and know-how that Eva didn't have the time or patience to unleash. The two women were going to be a dynamic duo. Get out of the way, Batman and Robin! Here come Eva and Kacy!

Before they reached the train station for their ride back to San Mateo, Eva and Kacy stopped in the bar at the Hilton Hotel.

"We have to splurge, Eva. Let's get a split of champagne to toast and congratulate ourselves," skinflint Kacy said. "We deserve it," they said in unison and slapped high fives. This time Kacy didn't flinch!

When they entered the Hoodnut Lounge on the main floor, Kacy and Eva turned more heads. The bartender and some of the guys sitting at the bar admired the beautiful Black woman and her equally beautiful blonde friend.

"Gayle and Grace were tough on us, but I think we won them over. I believe they're going to be extremely helpful," said Kacy.

The contract was going to be in six figures and would be more money coming in in two months than the bakery could make in a year.

After being served, Eva leaned forward and frowned at the bottle. "Kacy, a split is a mighty small amount of champagne. We can down this in one gulp."

"I know, Eva, but we can't afford anything bigger yet," Kacy explained.

Eva lifted her glass and Kacy followed. "Here's to success!" They clinked the glasses, toasted each other, and drank quick swigs of what seemed like a thimble full of champagne.

On the train traveling south, back to San Mateo, Kacy said, "Eva, this should be a sixty-forty proposition. You are the sixty percent, and I'll take thirty percent and we'll put ten percent in the bank to continue support of the bakery. We don't want to cut back on our bread and butter. We should be able to shoot two shows at a time and economize our time."

"Yeah," Eva agreed. "We'll be able to give more work hours to our current staff and, if we become real popular, we'll hire some new people. We'll keep the bakery going as it is now and bank some and live some. I never thought I'd see this day," added Eva.

"I know," Kacy said. "We're a far sight from where we were when we met at the party for John Dandy at Coyote Point."

Kacy and Eva also began discussing the possibility of franchising, so more people could make cakes the Eva way.

Kacy said, "Eva, I've worked up a surprise for you. We talked about it a long time ago, but I've gone a step farther. I've begun work on a companion book and videos to sell along with the show. We'll allow some colleges to use the shows for credit classes. Some of the videos will show how to make flowers and a few on how to make different types of edging. Then we'll have a few on how to make different fillings work. What types of fillings can be used? Can I use a whipped cream cake at this event? We'll have thirty-nine shows in the can in no time and, along with book sales, apron sales, everything-you-can-think-of sales, we should do well."

"We've picked a great title for the show, 'Have Your Cake with Eva' and the little blue bird logo is mo money, mo money, mo money! Thank you, Keenan and Damon Wayans," Eva chuckled and both women laughed.

Chapter 14
Reverend Davidson

Sitting at the kitchen table before going to the bakery one Sunday morning and sharing idle time and cups of coffee, Kacy asked Eva, "Have you heard from John and Dell or from Dorothy Easter?"

"Now that you mention it, I have heard from John and Dell. Haven't heard from Dorothy though. John is having a jam session at his home over in Oakland, and you'll never guess who I'm going to the party with."

"No, I can't guess," Kacy said.

"Wait! Don't tell me!" Kacy raised her hand. "Rev. Whosie Whatsit's is taking my friend out?"

"You got it, girl! The Reverend and me are an item. We're off to discover Ray Charles!" Eva and Kacy broke up laughing.

"Kacy, this is going to be a tough courtship. I hope it ends up being a courtship. How do you date a minister?"

"Umm, Eva, how does one court or date a minister? Are there any books, or how-tos?"

"That's the thing, Kacy. I've been married. I don't think he's been married. Ministers can't go slippin' and slidin' like just plain dudes. Ooh, Kacy, I think I've gone from the frying pan into the fire. I don't need this."

"Sure you do, Eva. Just think of it as taking an expedition to Mt. Everest. You're going to climb this mountain one step at a time."

"Give me a paper bag, Kacy! I have to breathe in it, I'm hyperventilating. I'm nervous. I want to kiss and hug. Can I kiss and hug a minister? Why am I doing this to myself?"

"Eva, just follow his lead. He graduated from a college and a seminary. That means he has some type of upbringing and education. He'll be cool.

"Eva, did you hear me? I'm beginning to sound like the kids. 'Cool' is not part of my vocabulary. I'm sure he'll do what's appropriate."

Eva responded, "I like being cool. I'll be cool, if he'll be cool. It's going to be fine. It's just a date. Just a date."

Reverend 'Whosie Whatsit's' real name was Reverend Clifford Raymond Davidson. Doggone, was he a handsome man! Class of '74 Howard University, School of Divinity. He was a religion major with a history minor and had an MBA from Stanford. A man tailor-made to play the lead in *Guess Who's Coming to Dinner.* Any mama's daughter would want a man with such credentials. And the Daddy wouldn't mind either. Eva didn't think she could make a good preacher's wife, but this was just an innocent date.

Rev. Davidson had been coming around quite often. He was a great carpenter and handyman. There was always something to be fixed or repaired at the bakery, and he had volunteered to fix those shelves and did a great job. He had also done a few odd jobs at Eva's house. She was glad to have this extra set of muscles, and high-ladder-climbing abilities were more than welcome. The Reverend was great at changing the long fluorescent lights that frequently blew out. It wasn't that Eva and Kacy couldn't change the lights. They had been changing the bulbs by themselves for some time, especially Eva. But the women knew that if you can talk a man into doing what is supposed to be "man's work," you'll find it a huge ego-booster for the man. *him* .

If Eva had asked the first Pid brother, Marcus, to change the lights at the bakery, he would have blown a fuse and started a fire. If she had asked the second Pid brother, Tom, to change the lights, he would have tried to sell the used bulbs to her friends or customers. The Stu's were handicapped in that area, but the Reverend was abundantly gifted in more ways than Eva wanted to talk about.

Chapter 15
The Proposal

Clifford was thrilled to get his chance to be alone with Eva. He was used to seeing her at Sunday night service or in the bakery. He made himself as handy as possible. He enjoyed all of them – Eva, Kacy, their children and the staff.

Clifford knew he shouldn't think such thoughts, but he knew he would love to sprinkle sugar on Eva and lick off every granule. Reverend Davidson was a man of the cloth, a minister, a devout man, but he was a man! He was also looking for a sweet, intelligent woman. If she happened to be a good lover and wife, too, that was going to be the icing on his cake.

Eva was good-looking; no, she was down right pretty. She had children, but they were bright, well-mannered children, and they came to church regularly. She was in business and had just landed a TV series on the Food Channel. Reverend Davidson would like to sit her down, in a manner of speaking. He knew marriage to a person so accomplished and with children already would be a challenge. She might not be a person who wanted to be set or sat down. He also knew he was a good catch. His salary at the church was adequate for a medium-sized Black congregation. And he was a tenured staff member at the Seminary. He owned his own home and had a good, if not new, car. He had an excellent education. He

[handwritten: mentioned before - ok?]

had graduated Magna Cum Laude from Howard University. He didn't talk much about his sojourn at Stanford.

Reverend Clifford Raymond Davidson was six feet, three inches tall, with a lean muscled body, flat stomach, good buns, pretty teeth, and a beautiful full head of gorgeous, kinky black hair. He was "Guess Who's Coming To Dinner" material, all right!

The day of the party across the bay, he picked Eva up at her house. She looked like an advertisement for "What the smart woman is wearing." Down the walk she came, in a deep salmon-colored cotton-knit pantsuit and white tank top, complimented by tan espadrilles laced around her ankles and a natural straw shoulder bag backpack combination. *[handwritten: early on; it was pants suit.]*

Clifford stood next to the open car door, all elegance and gallantry, wearing tan slacks, a light blue La Cosse shirt, and a navy blue summer-weight jacket.

They were going to have a leisurely drive to Oakland and this would be his opportunity to tell Eva of his intentions.

As they were crossing the San Mateo, Hayward Bridge, Reverend Davidson began, "Eva, I'd like to take you away from all the work you're doing. I'd like to marry you and make you a preacher's wife. The only hard work you'd have to do, if you marry me, is to cook, wash and iron for me. Keep the house clean, tend to your children, do the yard and maybe have one child with me. And show up at church every Sunday morning with special emphasis on the first Sundays when the Deaconesses wear their white outfits."

Eva looked at him incredulously. "Man, you've been around me long enough to know you're talking complete 'smack,' as the kids would say. Are you out of your mind? Sit me down! Me! Eva Sing Cullen Garrett. After all the time and hard work I've put into make my business grow? And with this TV thing on the horizon? You have got to be out of your ever lovin', cotton pickin' mind? Clifford, you're joking. Aren't you?"

Clifford smiled and grinned a huge "chicken eatin'" grin. A grin that said, "You know I'm lyin', and I let you catch me."

"Yes, Eva, I'm joking," he said. If I know anything about any 'sister' with a college education, good business, one who's a mom, with a new TV career, and looks as good as you do, you know I'm joking! You're one of the most beautiful, accomplished women I've ever met. I love you very much, and I want you to be my wife. You can just do da cleanin' once da week," he said, a few chicken feathers still part of his smile, feigning a street accent.

Eva swatted at him and said, "Boy, you are just plain silly."

"I know you would have some adjustments to make with me being a minister and all, but I know we could make those adjustments together," Clifford said.

"Clifford, I've been looking for you a long time. You're beautiful. Any woman in her right mind would beat every bit of competition to death to get and keep you. I wouldn't mind being your wife. I want to be your wife. You have a great sense of humor, bordering on insanity. You look good and I think I'm liking you an awful lot, too. Had you been serious about that cooking and ironing stuff, I was going to find the ejection button on this limousine and put your behind in the bay," Eva said laughing.

"Seriously though, I'm not ready to be married. I've had two unsuccessful goes at it. And now I'm on the brink of being able to live large. Yet, I want to take this chance to see if I can live comfortably on my own for a change. Not struggling and scrimping. Not depending on a man. Depending on myself. Being able to take care of Andrew and Lillian. It is mandatory that I help them with college. Just knowing I can do that will put me in a different frame of mind. If I can be successful in that area, perhaps I'll be ready to do the bride and groom thing again.

"Will you wait for me? I know it's a lot to ask. I know you have every woman in the church cooking for you and ready to do that washing and ironing. I bet some of them even think they can make a cake as pretty as I can," Eva said.

"Clifford, if I don't get these issues out of my system, I'll never be good for myself or anyone else. I know I'm asking a lot. I know I'm asking the hottest man in town to sit on a back burner and wait for a nutty person to see if she can make it on her own. But I'm asking. I know I love you, but I don't want you to know it yet. I don't want to tell you that because I don't want you to think I'm crazy, leaving you alone while Sister Piranha and Sister Slicker-Than-Grease have their eyes on you and can get their claws into you. Please wait for me. Let me try this. Let's give it a time limit and, if you don't think you can do it and wait for me, I'll die. But I would try to understand," Eva said plaintively.

Clifford stared straight ahead, his hands at three o'clock and nine o'clock on the steering wheel and gave a noncommittal grunt. It wasn't a yes and it wasn't a no!

They arrived at John and Dell's palatial, white, tri-level suburban home, parked the car, and walked down the street to the entrance and into a grand, catered affair.

"Eva, look at this spread. It looks like a church picnic. Only at a church picnic, you wouldn't see this wide array of spirits," Clifford poked at her jokingly.

There were red beans and rice with hot sausage, five types of salad, macaroni and cheese, platters of fruit and cheese and an Eva cake for dessert along with every type of liquid refreshment anyone could desire. John and Dell had ordered the cake from Eva's months ago to be delivered the day before the party.

The party was once again filled with jamming musicians and the house was rocking. Good food, excellent music, and wonderful people. Clifford was solicitous and sweet. He waited on Eva hand and foot, as if she were a piece of Dresden china. He acted as though the conversation in the car hadn't taken place. He was being very attentive and cock blocking, mainly because there were other men in attendance who were trying to wait on Eva, too, and engage her in conversation. *⤷ He was "Reverend" before.*

The music was outstanding and because there were more than a few people of the cloth at the party, the musicians played and sang some favorite gospel tunes. Rev. Davidson led the group in singing Kirk Franklin's "Hosanna." Because Clifford Davidson was a bit of a ham, he did an excellent imitation of Kirk Franklin and the crowd chimed right in. The crowd also sang "Silver and Gold" and tried to sing "Stomp." A person would have thought they were having church, because almost everyone knew the words. After the gospel session, someone sang "Early Autumn," and another singer did a medley of Ellington tunes. As the third vocalist started singing "How Long Has This Been Going On?" Eva and Clifford said their good-byes and made their exit.

How to treat songs?

ck. earlier for sp.

It had been a wonderful afternoon and evening for Clifford and Eva. On the way back to San Mateo, Clifford told her, "Eva, you're worth waiting for, but I'm not going to wait too long. Sister Slicker-Than-Grease doesn't look too bad. She wears short skirts, has great legs, and she can make a delicious sweet potato pie." Eva playfully smacked him upside his head.

"On a more serious note though, Eva. Our relationship will be a celibate one. Marriage is important to me. I've waited this long and just a little while longer won't kill me. But our relationship will be non-sexual. We have to wait to consummate our love."

"Clifford, you're more than worth waiting for, too. Ooh, now you've given me a cause to hurry the process. And you've given me a great reason to put in a rush order on my career."

Now it was his turn to playfully punch her on the shoulder.

Chapter 16
Church Sisters and Brothers

Sister Piranha, Sister Slicker-Than-Grease, Sister Don't-Sit-in-My-Pew, and Sister Mouth-Almighty are common characters and every church has a few.

One morning Pastor Ellwood and his wife were seated at the breakfast nook in the parsonage. "Oh my," he sighed. "Here comes Sister Piranha to the front door."

The parsonage kitchen nook window was situated so that people approaching the front door could be seen from that vantage point.

"I know she's interested in the new member, Mr. Courtney. She's here to get the 411." Rev. Ellwood shook his head.

"Dear," responded Sister Ellwood, a Toni Braxton look-a-like and the best first lady a church could have, "Sister Piranha was on the phone with me last night trying to get his 411. She is persistent, isn't she?"

"One Saturday when I was over in the church kitchen, I heard Sister Johnson put it in a nutshell," Sister Ellwood continued. "Sister Johnson was talking to Sister Samms, as only the two of them can talk, saying, 'When a new man joins the congregation, some sistahs will bring gifts and invite the new man to breakfast, lunch, or dinner and maybe all three.' These sistahs consider themselves to be good cooks, and sometimes they actually are. The sistahs throw big hints and attend every church service and special occasion. Sometimes Sister Piranha just shows up bringing something exquisite, like brownies or blackberry dumplings to the church secretary, because she may be lucky enough to run into whoever the new man is."

Sister Ellwood continued, "Sister Samms added, 'Those women and sometimes men, more often than not, dress inappropriately for church. Skirts too short, blouses too sheer, necklines too low, and obviously giving somebody the eye. No shame at all,' Sister Samms said," shaking her head.

"I know I'm not supposed to gossip but, Honey," Mrs. Ellwood said to her husband, "Some of our folks can be quite funny."

Sister Ellwood, being a very sharp woman and as beautiful and beautifully dressed as they come, had a solution to the short skirt puzzle at Prophet. If a woman wore a short skirt and sat in the back rows there wasn't a problem. But if and when Ms. East Behind plopped herself in the front row, crossing her legs, it became a different matter.

The church usher board met on Wednesday nights. Sister Ellwood asked the President of the board, Mr. Chancellor, if she could join them at their next meeting, as there was a subject she wanted to make the board aware of.

Sister Ellwood began, "Ladies and Gentlemen, there is a problem – literally, facing the pulpit and all of us in this congregation. I am soliciting your assistance. I've purchased fifty scarves from the 99¢ Store. In the future, if a female member sits in the front row and is wearing a short, short skirt, I would like the ushers to be instructed to bring her a scarf. It doesn't matter if the scarf is not returned. I would like you all to demonstrate what the scarf is for and please be dramatic in your presentation. The person wearing the short skirt is to cover her knees. I want laps on the front and second rows covered. Thank you for letting me speak at your meeting. I hope all members of the usher board will be informed.

"Mr. President, thank you so much for allowing me to bring this subject and the scarves to the members of this board. I have another meeting to attend this evening, so I'm excusing myself. Good night."

Mr. Chancellor, being a dictatorial sort, said, "Sister Ellwood has spoken. Is there any discussion?" Before anyone could say a word, he banged his gavel saying, "Starting next Sunday, this mandate from the Pastor's wife and our first lady will become the rule at Prophet." Bang! The gavel hit the table again.

There was no further discussion on that subject. The members of the usher board knew not to irritate Mr. Chancellor, or they'd be held hostage in the church social hall all night long. Mr. Chancellor was long-winded and felt his opinions were far more important than those of members of the usher board, and he felt he needed to push Sister Ellwood's agenda, come hell or high water.

◊

Sister Piranha, Sister Slicker-Than-Grease or Sister Mouth-Almighty might start a conversation in this way. "Rev. Davidson, I know my blackberry dumplings will just float off your fork. If you'd like more, just let me know. I'll come back to your office on Saturday to collect my dish."

"Thank you, Sister. You are so kind." Rev. Davidson responded.

"Rev. Ellwood, I have tickets to the new theater. Would you like to join me next Wednesday night?"

"Sister, I would love to, but I teach class that night." Whew!

"Rev. Brewster, being a bachelor must be a lonely life."

"No, Sister, it isn't when you are as busy as I have to be. . ."

"Rev. Walker, I hear you went to the Sonoma Inn last week on your day off."

"Yes, Sister, I did and I took my Bible and hundreds of papers that needed to be corrected, with me." Wow!

"Rev. Bannister, I hope you enjoyed the meal. I make cornbread dressing just the way my mother did. Please sit here while I clear the dishes and change into something less constricting."

"Oh, Sister, I'm going to help you clear the dishes, and I really can't stay for dessert. I just remembered I have to meet someone at the church in about thirty minutes."

"Rev. Bannister, I'm sorry to hear that. You don't have to help with the dishes, but you'll have to stay longer next time." These women are determined. And they have radar that the United States government could use.

Sister Mouth-Almighty is a church pain. She is a skinny, wrinkled old prune of a woman who wears enough makeup to pave a road. She smells of wine, cigarette smoke, and mothballs. Almighty's husband, poor Mr. Tyeskie, ran away after six months of marriage, but Sister Mouth-Almighty claims she is a widow.

Sister Mouth-Almighty joined Prophet after a falling out with Minister Bannister of St. George Apostolic Church. Sister Mouth-Almighty was a shouter. People at St. George were thrilled when she left that congregation because she would AMEN, HALLELUJAH, and SHO YOU RIGHT! so loudly through the sermons and most of the church service that it became difficult to hear Rev. Bannister's sermons. Everyone at St. George knew Sister Mouth-Almighty had gone far enough when she purchased copies of the sermon and routinely returned the tapes or CDs the next day. The engineer finally got up enough gumption to ask, "Sister Almighty, what's wrong with the recordings?"

"Baby, I don't know what's wrong with your equipment, but I shouts every Sunday and when I buys 'em and plays 'em back on my tape or CD player, I cain't hear my voice at all."

◊

Sister Mouth-Almighty also knew everybody's business wherever she went and now, at Prophet, she was working hard to build her repertoire. She could tell you what every man and woman wore to church at both services, because she came for the first and stayed for the second. She could tell you if a person's clothing was bought at Macy's, Nordstrom, or Goodwill. And if the clothes weren't purchased at any of these emporiums, she would make up a place, or could tell you about something just like something she had in her own closet.

This Sister tried to be a snob and wanted to be with the "best" people in the church. A new family, the owners of the largest swimming pool company in northern California, joined church one

Sunday. Sister Mouth-Almighty was the first person in the church to invite the new family to lunch. She made it her business to find out where Mrs. Swimming Pool had her hair done. Mrs. Almighty then paid the hairstylist to let her know when Mrs. Swimming Pool was coming in, so they could have their appointments at the same time.

Mouth-Almighty also said unkind things about people. When gossiping about Mr. and Mrs. Swimming Pool, she said, "Why, he so tall and she so short, when they go to bed, if they nose to nose, his toes is in it. If they toes to toes, his nose is in it. Hee, hee, hee!"

Most people in the congregation made a wide circle around Sister Mouth-Almighty because of remarks like that. And soon, Mr. and Mrs. Swimming Pool would, too.

Deacon Older-Than-Dirt was known for putting his arms around the young women as they exited the sanctuary on Sunday. He would wrap his arm around the youngster's upper body and finger as much of her breast as he could reach. Finally, one day, Sister Jackie Johnson grabbed his hand and loudly proclaimed, "Deacon Older-Than-Dirt, if you grab my titty one more time, I'm going to scream it as loud as I can. Get you hand off my titty!" She was screaming it anyway and everyone standing near heard what she said. *She sounds older than a youngster.*

"Now, now, Sister Johnson, you don't have to do that," Deacon Older-Than-Dirt mumbled as he ducked his head and scurried down the crowded church steps like the rat he was.

Brother Ain't-I-Still-Young-and-Handsome was about seventy-five and had already outlasted two wives. He was looking for a nurse or a purse. So far, he had managed both. Because he had a little money right now, thanks to the demise of the first two Mrs. Handsome's, Brother Handsome was on the prowl around the church for his next spouse.

Rev. Ellwood had invited the Mills/Peninsula Hospital's Health Advisory Committee to put on a seminar about older women and the new rise of A.I.D.S. among that population.

The disease was on the increase because men in Ain't-I-Still-Young-and-Handsome's age group were Viagra, Cialis, and Lavitra

Hiv   AIDS

users. In their haste to try out their new/old toy, they often hired prostitutes off the street, contracted H.I.V. and A.I.D.S., then, not so inadvertently, shared it with their women friends at church. Some of the scoundrels were on the down low, too, sleeping with men and contracted the disease in that manner, Thus, sharing the virus with the hapless, older, and sometimes piously sanctimonious church sisters.

Because of the seminar given by Mills/Peninsula Hospital, Brother Ain't-I-Still-Young-and-Handsome's supply of church sisters began drying up. The information from the seminar reached more and more ears and bolstered the whispers going around about Brother Ain't-I-Still-Young-and-Handsome and some of his ilk. And one Sunday he was absent from the congregation. Word was that he had relocated to Arizona and was moving in with one of his adult children who owned a large home.

Chapter 17
No Better Than Mine

Kacy was working furiously at one of the two new computers she and Eva could finally afford. Not only did she have a complete Hewlett-Packard set-up at the bakery, she also had a laptop and a printer at home. Kacy She had turned one corner of her bedroom into an office. Kacy was constantly coming up with new advertising and marketing ideas for the bakery. She was way ahead on the show, "Cake Decorating With Eva," and was also working on Eva's biography.

Kacy was happy and beginning to put money in the bank. She knew that a home for Tina and herself wasn't too far away. Kacy had come to love Eva and her children, Andrew and Lillian, as much as she loved her own daughter Tina. They had all become family. No one noticed that anyone was Black, white, green or grisly gray. They were not unaware of differences, but differences weren't the driving force of their relationships. They were a family. When racial issues came up, they were discussed, dealt with, and put to the side. With the passion concerning race in the United States, opportunities for discussion were many.

Kacy was a neophyte where ethnicity and bias were concerned. Her parents didn't often discuss these subjects in their home, and

Kacy couldn't believe some of the stories Eva, Lillian, and Andrew told her.

One evening, Eva placed her fist on her hip, as she often did when telling a story. "I walked my best friend home from school and was waiting on the back steps for her to come out and discuss our homework assignment. I overheard her Uncle Bobby say, 'Don't you ever put your arms around a nigger again!' Marilyn and I had come down the street with our arms around each other's shoulders. Those words cut me like a knife. I just slunk home. I was so hurt . . . I'll never forget that day," Eva remembered.

Andrew asked, "Mom, tell Kacy about the time that kid was using the 'N' word in my kindergarten class."

"Kacy, you won't believe this story. Andrew didn't know what was being talked about exactly, back when he was a kindergarten student. But he knew enough to tell me, his mama, that something was going on in his class. I called Mrs. Taylor to find out about the incident Andrew tried to explain to me - something about an animal and the 'N' word.

"Mrs. Taylor, Andrew's kindergarten teacher, was one of the first Black teachers to come to San Mateo and one of the best. She came here from Dallas, Texas and over the years, her reputation for giving children a great start had become legendary.

"The very day of the incident, Evelyn Taylor sent a note home, commanding all the parents of her class to come to an evening meeting. Even though Evelyn Taylor filled me in, I went to the meeting. Inquiring minds want to know," Eva joked. Several evenings later, when the parents had gathered, Mrs. Taylor explained that a child in the class had asked, "Mrs. Taylor, can you give me that 'black nigger?'" Pointing at an animal in the cage.

"She, as only Mrs. Taylor could do, and after recovering from the request and the statement this child made, asked, "Tommy, what are you talking about?" The little one pointed to the black guinea pig in the cage. Mrs. Taylor was stunned but, after his explanation, she wrote the note for the parent/teacher meeting. Everyone showed up, too.

"Mrs. Taylor doesn't play," Eva continued, hand still on her hip.

"Mrs. Taylor lectured all of us. 'Parents, when children as young as yours use that type of language, it means that they are parroting what they've heard at home. I will not have that type of language in my classroom. Shape your children up, or they will no longer be students in my class,' she sternly told us.

"Kacy, Mrs. Taylor had the top kindergarten class in the city. People were moving into our neighborhood just so their children could attend Evelyn's class. No one wanted the shame of knowing his or her child could be kicked out of her classroom.

"The poor child had heard the words 'black nigger' somewhere, but he wasn't sophisticated enough to know it was not a phrase to be used, ever - and especially not in front of his Black kindergarten teacher. In his five-year-old mind, he wanted that black thing and the word 'nigger' went with it. That's the way Tommy had heard it. I'm sure his parents were mortified.

"I didn't learn what was discussed after that because during the time I was in attendance, everyone just looked at each other guiltily. I had cakes to get out the next day, so I ducked out."

"Mom," Andrew interjected, still looking every bit like the golden mask of King Tut, "The parents probably weren't mortified. Some of the kids from that kindergarten class are still in school with me. They didn't get it then, and they don't get it now. That same phrase is still used liberally at school. But with some of the rap stuff reinforcing it, I don't know what to tell a person to do. I just tell them. Don't use that bull around me."

◊

There was more than one occasion when Lillian had her outbursts. But Kacy was learning to step around those land mines and, because of those land mines, Kacy learned even more about race relations. Kacy's background had been as white bread as was possible, and she found Lillian to be an apt teacher, although sometimes the lessons stung.

Kacy stated one day. "I've been looking at houses in the Baywood neighborhood."

Lillian sneered, "Yeah, everyone wants to live in that neighborhood. It's so much better to have all white neighbors."

Kacy winced. She said, "Lillian, you know I didn't mean it that way. The Baywood neighborhood is just a lovely place to live."

"Yeah," Lillian said with a liberal sprinkling of ice. "Nobody means it that way. But, I said what I meant, and I meant what I said." Lillian had grabbed that line from her favorite book, Brian Lanker's *I Dream a World*. Lillian had that page of the book dogeared.

Kacy didn't make many more moves down that road, but another incident with Lillian and the family stuck with Kacy for a long, long time. This was a discussion at the dinner table, one of the rare times the family of Eva Andrew, Lillian, Tina and Kacy had a chance to sit down at the table together.

Kacy was extremely upset that evening because two young Black men who were being tutored in a program through the church had become dupes in a robbery. San Mateo had instituted this program to help with the huge drop out rate among Black students at San Mateo High School. Kacy loved tutoring in this program and had come to know the two boys.

The two young men's grades were improving. Their attendance at school was on the upswing, and they had grades high enough to keep their positions on the basketball team. But, they also admired the "gangsta" life style and thought that was the life they were supposed to copy.

The boys had allowed two neighborhood thugs, Junebug and Skeet, to talk them into committing a robbery. "Just this one time," Skeet had assured the two dodos who were unfortunately caught in the act and suspended from school. Now they were going to watch their futures go straight down the drain.

Kacy lamented, "Why couldn't they have seen they had a great life in front of them? I was tutoring in the program to help them. Junebug and that Skeet person told the boys that I was the enemy, and that they shouldn't listen to anything that I had to say."

Lillian commented, "What you're asking, Kacy, reminds me of a quote from Harriet Tubman. She once told an interviewer,

*"I could have saved hundreds more
if I could have convinced
them they wasn't slaves."*

"The type of crap that is spewed from the mouths of people like Junebug and Skeet," Lillian continued, "Comes from a twenty-first century slave mentality."

Eva, nodded and said, "Those boys didn't realize that robbery could turn into a life of slavery."

Andrew chimed in, "Uh huh, they could have been free by staying in that program with you, Kacy."

"Now they are going to be slaves in the 'system' most of the rest of their lives," Lillian concluded.

Kacy sighed, "I read a report about how many Black men in this country go to prison. More money is spent on building prisons than is spent on building schools. There is something racially upside down about statistics like that," Kacy sighed.

"When I heard about the boys being arrested," Kacy continued, "I called that fellow, Conrad Caines, the new City Attorney for the City of San Mateo. He said he couldn't handle the case, but that he would call one of his Hastings Law School buddies, Rick Zanardi. He was sure that Rick would take the case. Mr. Caines was also quite sure that Rick Zanardi could win any case. I'm going to keep in touch with Mr. Zanardi to see how things go. I can't stand by and see those two boys' lives nipped in the bud."

Eva was so touched by Kacy's extra effort to help young people from the community that she felt she had to do something special for Kacy.

The next day at the bakery, Eva announced, "I have a new cake to add to our line-up. It's the old Blums coffee crunch cake. You know I've been working on the recipe for a couple of weeks, and it's ready to go into the case now. I think I've perfected the taste. It's just like the Blums cake and the new name is going to be Kacy's Krunch Kake."

All the staff member's thought it was a terrific idea and Kacy was flattered at having a cake named in her honor. And of course a new PR gimmick began running through her mind.

Several days after the big announcement about the new cake, Kacy, who now owned a car, returned to the bakery after a visit to the Department of Motor Vehicles. Pulling Eva to the side, Kacy whispered, "Eva, I'm so darned embarrassed. I went to the DMV to get a vanity plate for my car today. I filled out the papers and indicated that I wanted KKK on my license plate. The Black man at the counter kept looking at me in the oddest manner and told me that those letters were restricted. I told him about the crunch cake, but he still wouldn't let me have KKK. He asked me where I was born. I told him Boston, and he gave me a funny smile and said, 'Lady, go get a book and read about the Ku Klux Klan.' Eva, what's the Ku Klux Klan?"

Another history lesson was in order for one of the sweetest and most innocent women in the United States. Eva had laughed through the entire story.

◊

Children had said mean things to blonde, blue-eyed Tina at school because Andrew, whose complexion was as dark as night, would pick her up after school sometimes. Or brown-skinned Eva would be there when Kacy couldn't pick up her daughter but the blended Murphy/Garrett family dealt with the issue of students being mean to Tina on a level that her elementary school psyche could understand. They let Tina know she was an important person and loved.

Most of the kids at school already knew they would get a butt whuppin' and possibly a bloody nose if almost-white-looking Lillian ever heard any "bovine excrement" about color or race.

"We're all the same race," Lillian would say, in a superior tone of voice her light face flushing red. "Your ethnicity is no better or worse than mine. In fact, mine is better than yours, because I'm two things - American of African descent and as Irish as Paddy's pig! You are unfortunate to just be whatever it is you are!"

Chapter 18
Dr. Ozzie Hutchinson

There was nothing wrong with the Lutheran Church, but Prophet Baptist had something special that made Kacy feel at home.

She was attending church regularly now, and she volunteered to help edit the church bulletin, as well as to serve in the tutoring program. There was also the new guy, a redhead, who had recently joined church and he looked as though he needed her to pay more attention to him.

This fellow was really something. He was learning to sing gospel as well as Luther Vandross sang those sultry soul tunes.

Smiles, friendship and hugs every Sunday were normal parts of the church service. And the congregants were especially accepting of Tina. Everyone treated Kacy and Tina so warmly.

Hundreds of people were members of the congregation. It wasn't a mega church; rather it was a good-sized church. There were Latinos, Fiji-Islanders, Filipinos, Vietnamese and a sprinkling of whites while the majority were Americans of African descent. It was turning out to be a great church for Kacy and Tina. Now this redhead, who just happened to be a physician and in the right church at the right time, had the potential to make life more interesting for Kacy. Dr. Oswald R. Hutchinson. He was a Urologist and his practice was a few miles to the south in Menlo Park. He was tall, handsome, and single.

Ozzie Hutchinson had heard the minister, Rev. Hubert Ellwood, on the radio one Sunday morning. He had flipped through the dial on his way home from the hospital on an emergency visit to one of his patients. Ozzie had continued to listen to the station after he heard the unusual lyrics of a song, an old hymn:

> *Be strong! We are not here*
> *to play To dream to drift:*
> *We have hard work to do and loads to lift;*
> *Shun not the struggle: face it – 'tis God's gift.*
> *Be strong, be strong!*

Dr. Hutchinson had just said those words to his patient. "Be strong. Be strong!" And he found the phrase "We are not here to play," to be oddly modern words in such an old tune.

Intrigued and rather absent-mindedly, Ozzie continued listening to the station. Then, on came the next program featuring the deep, mellow voice of Rev. Hubert Ellwood. The sermon began:

"Imagine the NCAA championship game: Illinois versus North Carolina. The Edward Barnes Arena is packed and the referee is ready for the tip-off. But something's missing: there is no basketball."
Basketball was one of Ozzie Hutchinson's favorite sports. This sermon had an unusual beginning he thought. What a way for a preacher to start a sermon?
"Super Bowl XXXIX, Jacksonville, Florida. They are ready for the kickoff, but something is missing: there is no football.

"What type of minister is this, talking about basketball and football to begin a sermon? Ozzie's brow wrinkled.

"You just received your favorite game – Xbox or PlayStation. But something's missing: there's no game cartridge. You are all set to shop, but something's missing: there is not a "50 Percent Off"

sign anywhere. How about this: You are starving and the table is set with fine china. But something's missing: there is nothing in the pots. You are sixty-five, all set to retire, and something's missing: there is no Social Security money left. That's not funny, is it?"

By the time Rev. Ellwood said, "That's not funny, is it?" Ozzie, by now, was paying strict attention. After he pulled into his driveway, he sat in his car and listened to the entire sermon. At the end, Rev. Ellwood announced where his church was located. He told the audience, "The sermon you have just heard is titled "Peter's Power Source, Part I, and the next two sermons will be Peter's Power Source Part II and Peter's Power Source, Part III."

Courtesy of Rev. Larry Wayne Ellis, Sr. Pastor, Pilgrim Baptist Church, 217 N. Grant Street, San Mateo, California.

Ozzie found this preacher was appealing and decided that next Sunday, he would go to the church and hear the next two sermons in person.

During the following two Sundays, he fell in love with the preaching, the choir, and the location. Those factors helped him decide to become a member of Prophet Baptist Church. Ozzie was a lapsed Presbyterian and that Sunday he made the decision to join Prophet. The congregation whooped as this tall, white, redheaded man became a candidate for baptism. Ozzie was stunned at the response, but laughed later when he learned that the congregation did that for every candidate for baptism.

Several Sundays later, Ozzie protested to choir director Larry Corley, "Larry, I think you're barking up the wrong tree entertaining any notion that I can sing gospel."

"Oz, take these CDs and tapes home. I want you to practice in your car and in the shower. Come half-an-hour early to choir rehearsal on Wednesday. The two of us will run through some drills," Corley encouraged. "Some of the members who have been standing near you during service have heard your voice. They told me that you have to add your baritone to the choir."

From Larry Corley and Stephen Hackett, the ministers of

(and

music, Ozzie learned to use his voice in ways he hadn't known he could. After a few months, Ozzie was even given a couple of solos to sing. The first time Ozzie sang alone, he turned pale, sweaty and started gasping. By the second time though, he had calmed down and let the music flow. The congregation called out, "That's all right, Brother Ozzie." "Just sing it Brother Ozzie," and "Amen, Brother Ozzie!"

Kacy wasn't really looking for male companionship, but her eyes met Ozzie's one Sunday as the congregation was going through the meet, greet, and hug session. When Ozzie and Kacy hugged they felt electricity between them. Her heart started doing the back beat for Kirk Franklin's *Stomp.* Ozzie leaned close to her ear and asked, "Where'd you get those blue eyes?"

At the bakery on Monday morning Kacy asked, "Eva, have you noticed that redhead in the choir? Sunday was my turn to make eyes at someone. I'm going to ask him out. He likes the color of my eyes."

"How could you not see Brother Ozzie in the choir?" Eva chuckled. "He's at least six-three and marches in next to Brother Dewey who is five-two. And, your eyes are something to look at! You do it lady!"

"If I wasn't into tunnel vision with Clifford, I'd give you a run for your money."

"I'm glad you're occupied," Kacy grinned.

"What do you know about him? Tell me! Tell me!" Eva teased.

"He's comfortable and cute. Not cute like my ex-thug husband, Michael - but handsome. Like a white Harry Belafonte."

"I knew he reminded me of someone. Belafonte! That's exactly right!" Eva agreed.

"To me he looks wonderful and that's all I care about," Kacy sighed.

"What do you mean, 'to you'? I've seen Slicker-Than- Grease and Piranha giving him the eye. Girl, he looks good to everybody. Me included." Eva laughed.

"He dresses well, drives a neat sports car, has an office in Menlo Park and practices at Stanford. None of that's bad!" Kacy said.

"What did you do to get so much information? Did you put a trace on him?"

Kacy continued, "And Eva, he goes to the same church I go to. I never realized that a man being a churchgoer would mean anything to me. But it does."

"Don't avoid me," Eva probed. "How'd you find out so much about him?"

"I asked him after church last Sunday," Kacy giggled.

"Humph, you're moving fast, Miss Kacy."

You're darn right, I'm moving fast and you just confirmed why I should. Slicker-Than-Grease, Piranha, and even my roomie? I'd better put the pedal to the metal!"

Ozzie and Kacy's first date was at the rose garden in Central Park. He picked her up at her and Eva's house on 37th Avenue in a metallic blue Porsche. He wore blue jeans with a soft, light blue, tucked-in Polo shirt and a white cable knit sweater tied around his shoulders.

Kacy wore a lavender halter-top, eyelet sundress. She came to his shoulder with her long-legged, sylph-like frame.

They parked at the 9th Avenue entrance to the park, exited the car and slowly walked in, holding hands and listening to their shoes crunch on the composite lane that led to the iron dog landmark. The lane branched off to a gazebo surrounded by rose bushes. They entered this perfumed-filled space and sat on a bench inside the bower.

"We held hands and drank in the aroma of the flowers in full bloom. There were shrub roses, English legends, Hardy's heirlooms over a hundred different types. The fragrance was divine and so was he. I leaned against him and we talked for hours." Kacy confided to Eva the next day.

After the initial date, Ozzie and Kacy attended church functions together and squeezed in as many private dates as they could. They fit each other like a glove. Yet, Kacy wasn't looking for anything except a good future for herself and Tina. And that rosy future was already on the horizon.

The TV segments were going well. The ratings were as high as

Emeril's, The Contessa and Iron Chef. Eva and Kacy were showing the world how to have some cake and eat it, too.

The two good-looking, accomplished, equally compatible friends were moving to a niche on top of the world, the very place they had talked about being when they first met.

Chapter 19
Lillian

In her junior year at San Mateo High School, Lillian had blossomed into the school's top female jock. She was taller than her Mom and Kacy now, with a lean, muscular, Tyra Banks body, and she wore her dark curls short and close to her head. She could hit a softball out of any park. Lillian was the pitcher on the team, along with being a commissioner on the girl's athletic league. She played tennis, soccer, flag football, and golf, along with being the top swimmer on campus.

Lillian, just like her brother Andrew, earned excellent grades and was ready to choose a college. She felt that she didn't want to be in high school much longer. She had taken all her requirements and was considering early graduation. She was well liked by all of her friends, although her elementary school reputation of using her fists continued to follow her.

Lillian Garrett had always been as pretty as the day was long. Now she had grown into a beautiful, lanky, light-skinned version of her mother. But her reputation for kicking ass and taking names if her boundaries were crossed was never going to leave her. Don't get in her face on issues of ethnicity, race, gender, sexual orientation, or civil rights if you didn't want your nose bloodied and bruises or lumps to appear somewhere on your body.

85

Lillian was well read, followed CSPAN, CNN, and all news programming. She devoured newspapers and newsmagazines and went to the news outlets on line almost every day. She wanted to go to Harvard or Yale upon graduation, and even though she wished to leave high school early, she still had a little time to select between the two.

One Saturday, Lillian and Kacy gave each other an opportunity to have a day to themselves. Kacy suggested they go to Sushi Sam's Endomata, on Third Avenue for Sam's Specials. Sam takes a large, fried, crispy battered prawn, places it in flavored rice and teriyaki sauce, then rolls the concoction in seaweed. It was one of Lillian's favorite dishes.

Kacy adored Lillian and always wanted to know her better and understand what it was like to be Lillian.

Kacy parked her car in front of the restaurant. Walking toward the front door, Kacy and Lillian made a striking pair. Both women were about the same height. They were tall, long-legged, and had great Tyra Banks, Naomi Campbell, and Elle McPhearson figures. Lillian was the taller of the two and had tight thighs and muscled calves showing below her thigh-length khaki shorts. Her Birkenstocks and short cap of dark curls added to her scrubbed, athletic look.

Kacy, in contrast, wore her soft, blonde locks shoulder length. Her startling blue eyes and long sweeping lashes always commanded that people look straight into them. Kacy wore form-fitting blue jeans with blue, jeweled back pockets and a blue sweater set that helped her blue eyes reflect even bluer.

Entering the restaurant, they were shown a back booth, and were seated and served hot tea. They put in an order and waited for their entrées to come. Kacy began the conversation, saying, "Lillian, I know sometimes it's difficult for you. You have almost the same coloring as Tina and me, although your hair is dark. You remind me of an old neighbor who was very kind to me at a time when I needed a friend. You remind me of Mrs. Lomie Collins. I know you suffer, but I don't ever want to be the cause of that suffering. Your Mom told me to watch out for you a long time ago. Eva told me sometimes you have negative reactions and verbalize them, due to the ugly racial comments and situations you've been forced to endure because of your light skin. But I want you to know I love you, and I would never, ever intentionally hurt you, Eva or Andrew. You are my family. There is nothing but love coming to you from this corner of the world."

The Sam's Specials were served along with an order of California Roll, Dragon Roll, a salad, and more hot tea. They talked about clothes, Tina and school and were on their way to solving all the problems of the world.

Lillian nodded her head. "Kacy, it isn't easy being me. I have brown eyes, brown hair, a complexion like yours, but I like being me. Probably, because Eva is my mother, I haven't had the problems some light-skinned Black people have had. I don't want to be white. I haven't found what is supposed to be so advantageous about being a white person. I know there is still discrimination and that it's still because of the color of one's skin, but I'm happy being me."

"I'm glad to know that you're happy being you," Kacy responded, picking up a piece of the Dragon Roll with chopsticks. "Much of your positive attitude has rubbed off on Tina, my little girl who's not so little anymore and who admires everything you do. She's a freshman in high school! Where did the time go? But Lillian, you don't seem to respond to racial discrimination the way some others do. Well, you used to use your fists more often and teeth too, if I remember."

"No, Kacy, I don't think I do either, anymore. But, maybe just a little... But, I don't know if we catch hell because we're Black or because we're women. Women, period, are still having difficulties all over the world. They want to kill a woman in Nigeria for having a baby out of wedlock. What's that all about? It took a man to make that baby, too. Why isn't he being persecuted? And why do they want to kill her?"

"Lillian, you don't have to guess why they want to kill that woman. Men are still running the show. And you understand the lack of evolution when you hear stupid news stories like that one."

"But Kacy, the baby is going to need a mother and, of course, the method by which they propose to kill her is gross. Putting her in the ground, with only her head exposed and stoning her. How primitive! Why is it that the men of the world feel they can solve problems and issues by going to war and killing? That's nuts to me. No, some men haven't evolved."

"No, Lillian," Kacy said with sorrow in her blue eyes, "Some men, it seems, will never evolve. But you don't have to go to a third-world country to find that out. We're not doing much better in this country when it comes to broadminded and forward-thinking men. Many men still want to be the 'uterus police.' And a lot of foolish women, even in this day and age, go along with them."

The waiter interrupted, bringing them more hot tea. He said to Kacy, "Ma'am, please excuse me, I'm not flirting, but I have to tell you, you have the prettiest blue eyes I've ever seen."

"Why, thank you, sir!" Kacy blushed, nodded her head, and sipped her hot tea self-consciously.

"Kacy," Lillian continued after the waiter had left, "that was a lovely compliment but where was I? I have a slight, permanent tan and don't have to use tanning lotion or bake in the sun to achieve this great color. I don't have to wear a padded girdle; I have a butt. I'm not Jaylo, but it's my ass! I don't have to run lipstick off my mouth: I have lips. I'm not going to have to worry about osteoporosis because I have good African genes and sturdy bones."

"Lillian, I understand the ass part," Kacy said, "but what are you talking about with the lipstick and the mouth?"

"Kacy, haven't you seen some older white women with thin lips? And it's not just the older women. Some young ones do it, too. They don't have lips, so they put lipstick all up under their noses to make it look as though they have lips. Black girls and women don't have that problem. There's even a woman on one of the 'soaps' who has injected collagen into her lips. She looks horrible. Large lips are in vogue now with many white women, but artificially enlarging lips is just awful! Some people are even accusing Angelina Jolie of enhancing her mouth."

"What do you propose those of us with thin lips do?" Kacy laughed.

"I'm not talking about you, Kacy. You have a nice mouth. In fact, I can't find anything wrong with you. You're just a very kind, very loving soul. And you're pretty, too. I just love Kacy, because Kacy's Kacy."

"That's sweet, Lillian, and I love you because you're you, too."

"I had a great opportunity at Indian Wells a few years ago, Kacy, as a volunteer ball girl. One afternoon, Venus Williams pulled out of the match because she was ailing.

The crowd at that tennis match became so hateful. When Venus entered the stadium and walked down the stairs to sit by her father, Richard Williams, the crowd started booing. Normally, tennis fans are among the most polite in the world, yet I've seen them treat the Williams sisters and the Williams family differently than I've ever seen any other players or their families treated."

"Yes, Lillian, I follow tennis too. I saw that match on TV. I was so embarrassed by the way the crowd acted. I was glad that John McEnroe, Cliff Drysdale and the other announcers found the crowd reaction quite unsettling."

"I believe that bad reaction is because the Williams family is Black," Lillian said, "and it's only because they're Black that they're treated so poorly. I've been around tennis for four years now. I started in middle school with the youth tennis program through the Rec Department. Now that I'm a junior, I've been around enough to know how other controversial players have been beat up on by the crowds. However, I've never seen anything like what happens when the Williams family is involved. Venus was obviously hurt and shaken by the crowd's reaction."

"You could see on TV the amazement and confusion on Venus' face. When the booing became so loud, she dropped her head. I felt so bad for her," Kacy said.

"I've been in locker rooms and have heard nasty reactions from some of the players, and I've heard racial slurs from the audience. But, to boo a player as that player walks to her seat is unheard of," Lillian said. I put some of the blame on the organizers of the event. They should have gone to the mike or had Mary Carillo or Mary Jo Fernandez tell the audience in no uncertain terms to be quiet! They should have asked the crowd to be civil."

"Lillian, did you know that after that incident, the Williams sisters vowed to stop playing at Indian Wells?"

"I think that's wonderful! Venus and Serena knew it would be tough duty. Their mother, Oracine, told them it would be. Yet, it still makes you cry when you see an entire audience turn on a player for racial reasons. The audience often comes down on players and boos, hisses, and whistles, but those fans at Indian Wells, in my opinion, went beyond the pale with the Williams sisters."

Kacy sighed, "Well, they're millionaires. No other women in tennis have made so much money so fast. I agree with you, Lillian; yet, if the organizers had asked the crowd to quiet down, it might have incited them even more."

"You're right," Lillian said, exhaling and gazing. "It could have gone that way, too. You also have to realize that I get to hear what the other players and the audiences say when they don't know or realize who I am. I'm in an interesting position, you know."

"Lillian, you're not the Lone Ranger in those instances. I hear awful garbage come out of people's mouths, too. They don't know I live with a Black family. They don't know how I love Eva, Andrew, and you. But I don't have the courage or the tools to fight them with. I just cringe and get away from the bastards."

"I'm fortunate in the fact that I come from the same stock as Nelson Mandela and Rose Kennedy," Lillian bragged. "Two people who are at the tip-top of my most-admired list. I have to also admit though, that Ms. Serena has a lot of attitude. She's had to cover herself with it like Patti La Belle sings, 'I got a new Attitude.' I feel this deeply, because the crowds don't really root for Serena, or Venus either, until they've almost won the match."

"Yeah, I've noticed that, too." Kacy chuckled, "I wasn't sensitive to that fact until I moved in with you folks. My awareness about such issues is far more acute these days. I wish I could change the whole darn world. But it's too hard to do all by yourself."

"I remember being at Stanford, Kacy, for a Bank of the West Classic. The majority of the crowd was cheering for the Russian player, Anna Kornakova. The fans would rather cheer for the foreign player than to root for a Black American player. Especially if her last name was Williams."

"Anna Kornakova was always an oddity to me in the world of tennis, Lillian. She never won anything. The men just loved to see her on the court. And it wasn't just white men either. I've heard some Black men from church drool over Ms. Kornakova. I guess when you look like her, you don't have to play good tennis."

Lillian laughed. "You're right! She didn't!"

"There's another thing, Kacy. I also have had the problem of white kids thinking I'm too Black and Black kids thinking I'm too white. I just have to be Lillian. I can't serve anyone but God and myself. I have to do what I know is right. Mom has taught me to be true to myself."

"That's the right attitude, Lillian. I had to learn that, too, about being true to yourself. Michael, my ex-husband, had my self-esteem smack dab in the toilet. Living with you guys has helped me get it back. I believe in myself now, and I know I'm going to be a success. Your mom and I are the salt and pepper of the cake world! It took guts to get us started, and we're just about ready to reach the top."

"Yeah, Kacy and all of us are proud of you and Mom.

But I want you to know, too, that I love my country, but my country hasn't always been good to people who look like Mom, Andrew, Andrew's dad, the Williams sisters, and me when they learn I consider my Black heritage to be paramount."

"Yes, Lillian," Kacy agreed. "We have to work harder on the woman thing, the Black thing, and every thing. Look at tiny Iceland. They have more women in government than we do. India and Israel have both had women presidents. In many respects, we have not 'come a long way, baby!'"

"Lillian, do you think we should change the name of our country to Inited States? Iceland, India, Israel are all countries that start with I. Perhaps that 'I' will help us elect a Hillary or a Barbara Lee of Oakland, California, to be president."

"Ooh, Kacy, look at the time," Lillian said. "I have to get back to the house. We should have treated ourselves to more lunches, sooner. I'm almost ready to go away to school, and now we finally sit down and have a real good talk."

"Everything in its time, Lillian. Everything in its time." Kacy shook her head.

Chapter 20
Tina

Eva's children, the handsome, dark-complected, King Tut look-alike, Andrew, and the tall, pretty, light-skinned, jock, Lillian, looked after Tina like over protective older siblings would, even though they weren't related by blood. They tried to make sure Tina was always where she was supposed to be and that nothing out of the ordinary ever happened to her.

One of the reasons Andrew and Lillian looked after Tina so closely was because of something that had happened when the twelve-year old Tina had been in Middle School. Her teacher gave the class an assignment on World War II. Tina chose the Holocaust as her subject. She wrote a paper that was far beyond her years. She had done all the research online and found forgotten information in some very old encyclopedias that Eva had stored in the garage. Tina added music and made the report into a multi-media presentation.

Tina's favorite book was *The Diary of Anne Frank* and that's why she chose the Holocaust as her subject. She didn't know any Jewish children in school, but she had been to Temple Beth El for a Bar Mitzvah and had become intrigued by the Jewish religion and the World War II era in history.

The Bar Mitzvah had been for Donald Karp, the son of one of

Kacy's friends. Tina bubbled after the ceremony, "I want to be able to learn all of the Hebrew ceremony and make a speech, too. I want to stand in font of an audience and recite the way Donald did. One of the best things about the ceremony was all of that food in the social hall. I've never seen so many different kinds of chocolate desserts in my whole life. Then, Donald's relatives and all of his friends gave him tons of envelopes with money in them. It was a wonderful ceremony."

After Tina delivered her multi-media presentation to the class, some of the students taunted her after school and called her a Jew-lover.

Lillian heard the news and after school, when she went to pick up Tina, she had Tina point out two of the class tormentors. Lillian caught up with the kids just as they were leaving campus. She had put her books on the ground and she walked quickly over to the two boys, grabbed them by the back of their necks, turned them toward each other and knocked their heads together.

Letting go of the boys she leaned close to them shaking her finger in their faces, fist on hip, Eva style. She growled, "In the future, you little bigots, you'd better leave Tina alone and you'd better learn how to treat people! Plus that, I'd better not ever hear you say anything against Jews again. You hear me!"

The boys nodded their heads and scooted the hell out of there.

Tina had learned about the Quinciñeras at the bakery. Many Mexican families bought the cake for that glorious rite of passage from Eva. Tina was lucky enough to be invited to two lovely Quinciñeras and became hooked on that concept, too.

Tina told Kacy, "Mom, the only thing I can compare the Bar Mitzvah to is the Quinciñera that they give for the Mexican girls on their fifteenth birthday. There is so much love given to those kids at their parties. And lots of money, too. I want to be Jewish and Mexican. I want a Quinciñera and a Bat Mitzvah combined."

Chapter 21
Questions on Religion

Tina loved going to church with her mother and her new Garrett family. The people at Prophet treated her like she had always been a member. Yet, some things about Prophet Baptist Church bothered thirteen-year-old Tina.

Tina and Kacy had long conversations about the subjects that unnerved the curious child. Kacy didn't have answers, but she encouraged Tina to question and read.

In Sunday school, Tina, blonde ponytail bobbing animatedly, asked, "Why is it only Christians can go to heaven? I read Anne Frank's diary. She was a good girl and a smart girl. terrible people killed her. Anne Frank didn't hurt anybody. Why isn't she going to heaven?"

Later, in a private conversation with Rev. Ellwood, Tina said. "I don't want to go to heaven, Pastor."

"Why is that, Tina?" Rev. Ellwood asked gently.

"My friend, Joy Yoshimoto, goes to the Buddhist Church. She doesn't believe in Jesus. Joy is a nice girl. She has been very kind to me at school. If Joy can't go, I don't want to go either."

Rev. Ellwood said, "Tina, I know about the Buddhist religion and many other religions that don't believe as we do at Prophet. Our belief is spelled out. But a good thing is that this country is founded on freedom of religion. Your friends can believe what they want to, and you can believe what you want to. We are a teaching church, and I hope when you're able to decide what church you want to belong to, you'll choose a church like Prophet. I hope you will become a Baptist, Tina. I mainly hope you will always be a good person and believe in God. And when you get to college, Tina, I hope you will study comparative religions. That should help you with the answer about how Baptist people and this church learn about going to heaven. I'd also like you to go to the Bible and read John 14:6, Acts 4:12, and Timothy 2:5.

"Another thing about being a Baptist and a Christian. We believe in the Trinity, The Father, the Son, and the Holy Ghost. We believe in the Bible and, as you grow older, you can read the Bible and understand it for yourself. We believe in baptism by immersion, and we believe that all good people will go to heaven not just 144,000 people as some religions do. I also want you to go to the office and ask Mrs. Griffin for a copy of *The Responsible Christian Guidebook*. Okay, Tina?"

"Okay, Pastor."

Tina had a similar conversation with Rev. Davidson. He was at the bakery putting Freon in a refrigerator one Saturday afternoon. Tina bounced over to him and asked, "Rev. Davidson, who runs heaven?"

"Tina, God runs heaven, I guess. God, Jesus, The Holy Ghost. God runs heaven with some help from St. Peter and the angels."

"Well then, why can't my friend Ali go to heaven? He believes in Muhammad. He goes to the mosque all the time. He seems to be a really neat person and even won the county spelling bee. Why can't he go to heaven?"

"Tina, Muhammad is a prophet. He's not God."

"But Ali talks about God. He told me the Koran is like the Bible. And why is it always he?"

"You ask good question, Tina," Rev. Davidson smiled.

"Rev. Davidson, I like church, but before Halloween, Rev. Ellwood told the Sunday School, 'Don't wear ghost costumes or devil costumes to the trick or treat party at the social hall.' I don't understand. He talks about the devil almost every Sunday, and he talks about the Holy Ghost. Why can't I be a ghost at Halloween? I could be the Holy Ghost. This religion stuff is confusing to me." And, she added, as a child would, "But I love church!"

"Tina, when you get to college," Rev. Davidson responded, "you're going to have to take some comparative religion classes. But keep asking those questions. Keep going to Sunday school. And I want to continue to talk about this subject with you. I'm going to call you tonight and give you some Bible passages to read. You might start with John 3:16. Unfortunately, I have to get back to the church right now. I fixed the refrigerator." Packing his tools, he waved, "See you later."

That evening, Rev. Davidson called Tina. "My little friend, I want you to know that worship, fellowship, and learning stimulates growth. Keep coming to church and Sunday school and hanging around good people. Your willingness to learn and your interest in others will help you mature and become more Christ-like. Keep yourself open to learning, Tina. I believe God has a plan for you. You're inquisitive. In the New Testament, all that God does for us in Christ is summed up by the term Salvation. Salvation has a past, a present, and a future aspect: we have been saved. You'll find that in Ephesians 2:8-10; we are being saved, Philippians 2:12-13; and we will be saved, Mark 13:13. I think that's enough homework for now. Goodnight, Tina."

"Good night, Pastor." Hanging up the phone, Tina said to herself, if my friends can't go to heaven, I'm not going.

Chapter 22
The Octopus

As good a shield as Andrew and Lillian were for Tina, they couldn't buffer her from everything. A new kid entered the junior class at Hillside High School and became immediately enamored with Tina. His name was George Rumsfeld, and he seemed okay on the surface. He was white and lived in the Baywood Park area of San Mateo. His family was well-to-do and he appeared to be very nice. A school dance was coming up and George asked Tina if she would be his date. She was ecstatic. An upper classman inviting a freshman to a dance was a coup for the freshman. "Yes, I'd love to be your date," Tina answered. *I loved*

George, known as Geo, picked her up on time. They went to the dance and had a great time. After, they went to Dave and Buster's, a video arcade on steroids, to have sodas and kick back with the rest of the kids.

In a couple of weeks, the young man called again and asked Tina to go to the movies with him.

"Sure," Tina said. "I'd love to."

They arrived at the movies in downtown San Mateo and entered the darkened auditorium as the previews were flickering on the screen. They were barely seated when Geo, all of a sudden, became an octopus. His hands were flying all over the place. He was becoming too, too, familiar!

Tina demanded that he stop. "Would you please get your paws off me! What's wrong with you?" But her "stop" wasn't being heard or understood by the eager Geo. He was working with all his might to get his hand inside her blouse. Tina leaned as far away from him as she could, finally she jumped up and said, "Excuse me! I'm going to the restroom."

In the restroom, Tina looked in the mirror and gasped at the way her blouse was golly wonkers. She straightened herself up, pulled out her cell phone and called home. Lillian answered. "Just the person I need to talk to," Tina whimpered.

Lillian asked, "Girl, what's wrong with you?"

Tina whined, even though she was angry, "This boy doesn't understand the word 'NO!' He's giving me a bad time and won't keep his hands to himself!"

Lillian said, "Okay, Tina, take your time getting back to your seat. I'll be there as quickly as I can."

Lillian sprinted out of the house, jumped into her Volkswagen and flew down El Camino Real. Turning right on Third Avenue, she almost played bumper cars on the way to the parking lot three blocks west at the railroad tracks. She parked her car taking up two spaces and dashed across Second Avenue, down Main Street, into the theater. Thank goodness San Mateo had a grid pattern downtown. She wouldn't have been able to move that quickly in a city that was laid out like San Francisco or Redwood City.

Before she left the ladies room, Tina splashed water on her face and in her eyes so no one could tell she had been crying. She went to the concession stand, bought some popcorn and a couple of boxes of candy and drinks. She took her time returning to her seat. She had a bundle of stuff under her arms and on the flimsy cardboard tray. She was juggling everything and fumbled around, trying to keep the items from spilling. Arriving back at the seat, she urged the goodies onto Geo, who had become an octopus. It was important to divert him and keep something in his mitts, beside her.

"Here. Here's some popcorn for you, a box of Milk Duds, and a Pepsi."

Geo greedily accepted the popcorn and candy, placed his drink in the hole in the armrest, and tried to resnuggle with Tina.

She refused to use the hole in the armrest of her seat to put her drink down. She held onto the cup of liquid to use as a type of armor. She continued to juggle popcorn, candy, and soda. Geo, the octopus, didn't get the hint.

The Octopus said, "I didn't think you were ever coming back."

"Well, I'm here now, but I do wish you'd keep your hands to yourself," Tina whispered harshly.

As long as the octopus had the boxes of popcorn and candy, he was fairly well occupied. His hand and elbow moved in piston precision: hand-to-mouth, hand-to-mouth. But as soon as he had popped the last piece of chocolate-covered-caramel between his lips, he started to reach for Tina.

All at once, someone was standing in front of Tina and Geo. The row of seats in front of them had no patrons and the figure looming in front of them was illuminated and backlit by the screen, making it hard to distinguish. The figure said in a low, gruff voice, "Move over, Tina." Tina scrambled over one seat rather flustered while trying still to balance her drink and popcorn. Then long legs stepped over the chairs and a young white girl, Geo thought, placed herself in the space that Tina had previously occupied.

The person who had loomed over them, barking orders in a harsh whisper, was Lillian. Lillian sat between Geo the octopus and Tina. Tina was now relaxed and finally unloaded some of the diversions from her hands.

Lillian leaned over to Geo, as though she were going to nibble his ear. She whispered to him with her lips touching his ear, "The movie is called the Pianist, not the Groper. When you go out with Tina, you keep your damn hands to yourself or you're liable to draw back a hand that will not be able to play a piano." Then Lillian chomped down on the poor kid's earlobe with teeth as sharp as a cat's.

Geo let out a scream that caused other movie goers to look in their direction. The Octopus exploded from his seat and beat it to hell out of the movie theater. He was holding his ear, as a trickle of warm liquid oozed down his neck.

Lillian grabbed a napkin from Tina and spit in it. She grabbed another one and wiped her tongue and mouth vigorously. "Let's go home Tina," she said.

In the car, on the way home, Tina asked, "Lillian, what did you say to that jerky boy?"

Lillian said, "I said what I meant, and I meant what I said!"

For the next few days at school, Tina didn't see the Octopus. But on Wednesday, he appeared behind her while she was standing in line at the cafeteria.

He declared, "Why didn't you let me know you lived with niggers? And a white nigger, too?" He didn't say it low or in a confidential voice. He said it so almost everyone in earshot could hear. "That nigger told me to keep my hands off you. Well, you don't have to worry about that again!"

He shoved by Tina so hard with his elbow that he knocked her down, causing her tray to spill. She fell to her knees, the food and tray went skidding across the cafeteria floor. Several students, who had heard the verbal assault and saw what Geo had done, rushed over and helped Tina to her feet.

Tina was stunned and disheveled but didn't respond to the assault, although tears brimmed in her blue eyes. Some students helped her to clean up the spilled food and smoothed her rumpled hair and clothes. Other students who had heard what Geo had said to Tina, immediately went to find Andrew and another group went looking for Lillian. After Andrew heard what had happened to Tina, he went looking for Lillian, too.

Lillian was out on the quad surrounded by a chattering group of students. "Sis, let me handle this dude this time," Andrew said, after drawing his sister away from the crowd.

This was unusual. Everyone knew of Lillian's volatility, but Andrew never bothered with things of this sort. Andrew was easy to get along with. But this time, as a male, he knew what it would take to get even with Geo the Octopus, and Andrew was determined to handle the situation his way. No one had the right to invade Tina's space or to hurt her.

Andrew had fifth and sixth period gym. Any student who played on an athletic team did. This gave the students a chance to get ready for their various after-school games and to manage the heavy schedule of sports activities they were involved in.

The octopus was in these classes, too, but he was a new student and on the volleyball team. Andrew and his friends played football. Andrew walked over to the gym and into the locker room where he found his friend Robert. Robert was a teenaged entrepreneur and always had wads of money in his wallet.

Andrew asked, "Robert, I need to borrow a hundred dollars from you, right now, and I want you to get Alan, Eddie and Reacie. Meet me here in half an hour. That's two o'clock, right here at these lockers."

Robert knew that if Andrew made a request of him, for anything, he'd be good for it. No questions asked. Robert went into his wallet and forked over two fifty-dollar bills. *Check order of names.*

"Okay, homey, I'll be back with the posse in half an hour."

Reacie, Alan, Eddie and Robert showed up promptly at two o'clock sharp in front of Andrew's locker, where Andrew was seated, putting on his cleats for a scrimmage. "What's up, man?" Robert asked Andrew. *repeat what's first used.*

"Yeah, blood, whatcha got cookin'?" Reacie asked.

"Here's the deal," Andrew said.

Andrew asked, "Did you guys hear what happened to Tina at lunch time?" They all chorused, "Yeah!"

Andrew stood, placing his arms around the shoulders of Reacie and Robert as they, with the other guys, formed a huddle. Andrew whispered something and they all cracked up.

"Man, do you think you can get away with that?" Alan asked.

"Watch me!" Andrew responded. "Just watch me!"

After a minute or two, Geo the Octopus entered the locker room and headed in their direction, going to his own locker.

"One hundred dollars!" exclaimed Eddie loudly.

"One hundred dollars!" repeated Reacie. "Man, let me do it. It's worth it. I'll be suspended for a week, but it will be worth it. One hundred dollars!"

Eddie piped up, "Are you sure it'll only be a week's suspension?"

Andrew said, "That's what it was the last time it happened. It's just what the OG's you know, the original gangstas, principals, teachers, parents, call a 'spring time prank!'"

"Yeah, springtime prank! I gotcha. Springtime prank," echoed Alan.

"What you guys talkin' about?" asked Geo, as he passed the posse.

One might have thought Geo would have been reluctant to approach a group of Black kids on campus, but young men look at each other differently. They wrestle, tussle and are in constant combat on one playing field or the other. Geo was not suspicious, nor did he hold any outward animosity toward his fellow gladiators, Black, white, or in-between. There was a mutual understanding where testosterone was concerned. They may not like each other, but the world of jockdom hid a multitude of sins.

Lillian had not only humiliated Geo. Geo had learned that Lillian was a light-skinned Black bitch. Black, a bitch and female, too. That was more than Geo's ego could tolerate. He couldn't kick the ass of the school's top female jock, but he thought he could knock Tina around to get even. Tina was nothing but a freshman. Unfortunately, the classmate who filled Geo in on Tina's family circumstances had neglected to mention the young man whom Tina considered an older brother. That person never mentioned the dark-as-night, handsome, King-Tut-look-alike brother, Andrew.

Before Andrew and the gang responded to Geo's question. The did a little small-talk to really rope Geo in.

"Man, what team you on?" Asked Reacie.

"Volleyball," answered Geo, the new kid.

"Who hit you upside your head, dude?" inquired Alan.

"A mosquito bit me on my ear and it got infected," Geo lied.

Andrew, Reacie, Robert, Alan and Eddie all knew he was lying about the bandaged ear and knew that he'd be a perfect candidate for Andrew's plan.

The young men formed a huddle again and let Geo in on the way to make one hundred dollars, quick, fast and in a hurry.

Intentional

dupe
STet

The new boy loved the idea and asked to be the one to make the money—although he had to fight with Eddie for the privilege. Geo immediately became the eager beaver and one of the guys.

"Where do we meet? What time? Do you think the thing will fit? Who's got the money?" Geo couldn't ask enough questions.

Andrew held up two fifties with President Ulysses S. Grant's face emblazoned on them. He said, "My man, these little bits of paper with dead Presidents on them, will be all yours tomorrow morning at nine A.M. You do the deed at eight-forty-five and we'll be waiting for you, right here in the locker room, with your clothes and the other picture of Mr. Grant. Here's a fifty in advance."

Greedy, lecherous Geo scrunched the money into his pocket and left the guys, continuing on to his locker, acting as though he didn't know Andrew and the gang. The posse slid their hands into their pockets and slowly sauntered out of the locker room, whistling, eyeing one another and trying not to laugh out loud.

The next day, Hillside High School was all abuzz. Geo Rumsfeld had been suspended! He had been caught running around the campus stark naked—and told the principal, Mr. Miller, that he didn't know what had happened to his clothes.

"Some kids from the PE class promised me a hundred dollars to streak the campus in a pair of flesh-colored tights. But when I got undressed, some guy I didn't know took my clothes and threatened to chop off my penis if I didn't start running and not look back. The guy had a meat cleaver in his hand and was making chopping motions."

"Continue," Mr. Miller said calmly. Geo was shaking and covered his privates, embarrassed. "I don't know who the guys were. I hadn't met them before. But I know their names were Joseph, Cleatus, Jerome and CJ. And I can't think of the other kids' name."

Fred, the head custodian, called Mr. Miller to the quad, where Geo had been stopped in mid streak. Fred told Mr. Miller to bring a blanket.

Mr. Miller flew out of the office yelling over his shoulder to his secretary, Mrs. Douglas, "Mrs. Douglas, grab a blanket and follow me."

Mrs. Douglas went to the nurse's office, found a blanket and ran like a track star to keep up with Mr. Miller. When the two of them arrived at the quadrangle where Fred was standing with the student Geo Rumsfeld, Mrs. Douglas threw the blanket over the naked, hapless Geo and hustled him off to the office. The head Counselor, Mrs. Swann, checked the entire 1,500 plus names of the student body and found no students with those names in that PE class. And there was no one with the name Cleatus or CJ on the entire campus. Mrs. Swann's next task was to call Mr. and Mrs. Rumsfeld.

Normally, Mrs. Rumsfeld didn't answer the home phone. This was a chore usually done by the housekeeper, Mrs. Pickens. But today, Geo's mother answered, "Hello, Rumsfeld residence."

"Mrs. Rumsfeld, this is Mrs. Swann, Counselor at Hillside High School. Could you and your husband please come to Mr. Miller's office immediately? There has been a mishap. George has not been injured, but he has somehow lost his clothing and needs something to wear. But Mr. Miller, our Principal, wants me to emphasize that you and Mr. Rumsfeld get here quickly."

Mrs. Rumsfeld speed-dialed the office of her husband, Carl Rumsfeld, shouting, "Carl, drop what your doing, something has happened at Hillside and the principal says it's urgent that both of us get there at once."

Andrew saw Robert later in the day and said, "Blood, here's fifty. The little jerk must have left the other money at home. It wasn't in his pants pocket. I'll give you the rest of the money on the weekend - and thanks for the loan."

Robert countered, "Man, you don't owe me a thing. Consider it paid. For the laugh, the intrigue, and the payback to slimy Geo, it was more than worth fifty bucks. Buy me a soda, man!"

Reacie had changed back into his regular clothes. He had thrown the disguise into several garbage bags and distributed them into dumpsters around the campus and across the street at the City Park.

When Reacie met up with Andrew, Robert, Alan, and Eddie after school, Reacie whooped, "Wham, bam, thank you Ma'am! That's what I'm talkin' 'bout!"

Reacie, Andrew and the guys slapped high fives, bumped chests,

and
∧ exchanged complicated "dap" handshakes, grasp, shake, grip, and tap. They left the campus, to return to their normal routines of jobs, homework, and class the next day.

Chapter 23
Andrew, Lillian, and Tina

Andrew jumped into the bakery, yelling, "Mom, I'm going to Stanford! I received my acceptance letter today."

This drop-dead-gorgeous young man, whose skin was the color and texture of black velvet, had the world in the palm of his hand. He was bright, good-looking, and kind – although a little bit of a dickens could be found if you looked hard enough. He had been the quarterback for the football team, the captain of the debating team, an agile skateboarder, and popular with all the girls, Black, white, and in-between.

"Talk about your dreams being answered," Eva grinned, placing her fist on her hip. "I wish my Mom and Dad were here to see this. Daddy wanted to play golf on the Stanford course. He could have done it at no cost, if a relative had been a student. Maybe he – they are hovering overhead somewhere. Andrew, I'm so proud of you!"

"Mom, I'm going to work my butt off. I know I'm going to like 'the farm', but I also want to graduate early and get a job. In these next three to four years, I will have had enough school. I want to find a 'po-sition,' and buy my Mama anything she wants. You busted your hump for Lillian and me. And you opened our home to Kacy and Tina. I want to give you something. Fur coat, big fine car. Mom, what do you want?"

"Andrew, I want what every mother wants for her children. I want you to have peace and happiness. And I guess what I really want," Eva chuckled, "is for you to marry, settle down and make me lots of pretty grandbabies.

"You know your good looks never made waves with me. All I wanted you to do was to be a good kid, a decent human being and to excel. You've done all that. But," Eva added, "no grandbabies before that mortarboard and your graduation day. And if you can't do that, give your mama a call, and I'll provide all the condoms you think you can use."

Andrew blushed and gave her a hug. "Nobody would say something like that but my mama." While still hugging Eva, he kissed her on top of her head.

◊

Kacy had been at the back desk deeply involved in paper work. When she heard the boisterous commotion at the front of the bakery, she closed her books, put down her pencil and came up to Eva's table.

Andrew left his mother's side and went to Kacy, hugged her too and pecked her on her cheek.

Kacy smilingly questioned, "Andrew, how is it that you never stepped out of line?"

Still hugging Kacy but looking straight at Eva, Andrew said, "I love Eva too much to cause her heartache and pain. And Kacy, you already know she'd take her fist off her hip and pop me with it if I even tried to step out of line."

"Yeah, yeah," Eva jumped in, laughing, "You weren't afraid of me, Andrew. Still, I do appreciate the respect you always showed, not only to me but to your sister, Kacy and Tina, too."

"Mom, I had no choice. You've pounded that stuff into me since before I could even speak. You inoculated me before I got my first vaccination for measles. But enough of this serious talk," he said as he let Kacy go. "Now I'm off to conquer Stanford. I'm going to enjoy non-stop dating and make good grades."

◊

Lillian was even prettier than anyone had predicted. She had her mother's good looks and Halle Berry shadows in her face. Her complexion was a lighter shade of pale, but she knew how to enhance her good looks with the right but light makeup.

Lillian graduated high school early, as planned and four years later, upon graduating Yale, she was being considered for a position with the International Olympic Committee. She had racked up some good jobs while in college - Assistant Athletic Manager to the Dean of Athletics at Yale, an internship with Nike, and had made assistant to Steve Kinney, Regional Director for the National Consortium for Academics and Sports. Mr. and Mrs. Kinney had taken Lillian under their wing. One reason was because Mrs. Kinney was also a very light-skinned Black woman and she enjoyed comparing notes and incidents with Lillian.

Other notches on Lillian's belt included the track and field organizations she consulted for and the work she'd done with an athletic equipment company. Her internship with Dr. Harry Edwards, the noted sports sociologist, also held her in good stead.

One morning, Lillian made a telephone call. "Mr. Kinney, this is Lillian. I'm calling from Colorado Springs. I'm now in the office building at the Olympic Training Center. I arrived early and have a couple of hours to kill before I meet with the hiring panel. I've ridden all over Colorado Springs, so I thought I'd just come here, park my car, and enjoy the atmosphere of the campus. But now I'm nervous and need to talk to a friend. I've studied and studied, but can you chat with me awhile? I want to get rid of my butterflies."

"Lillian, you know that I'd be happy to talk to you! The Olympics are my passion, you've called the right man."

Steve Kinney had been a professional football player with the Detroit Lions and Chicago Bears. But when he was in college, he had been one of those football speedsters who could run the forty-yard dash at breakneck speed. He had also been involved with San Jose State University and San Jose City College when those two schools held the title "Speed City, USA." Because of that unique distinction, decathlete Bruce Jenner gave his name and prestige to the San Jose City College track meets for about five years.

Steve Kinney was six-feet five, caramely-brown, with a voice as big as his size. He was tickled to get this call from a young woman he adored and mentored. When he heard Lillian's voice, he shooed his secretary out of his office, leaned back in his leather chair and put his huge feet on the desk.

"Lillian, if I were you, I think I would remind the interview committee how the top brass of the International Olympic committee is having big trouble. I don't think they'll want to hear it, but you can do it in a lady-like way."

With a low soft laugh, Lillian said, "I've rarely done anything in a lady-like way, Mr. Kinney. They may throw me out of the office, but I'll try to do it gently and with no animosity."

"If I remember correctly," Steve said, "the situation went all the way back to the Juan Antonio Samaranch regime. That would be from 1999 to the year 2000, when the committee had to defend itself against charges that some members and their families accepted gifts form officials in cities bidding to host the Games. I believe ten members were expelled or forced to resign during the investigations. And you can tell the interview committee, Steve Kinney of San Jose, California, said you, Lillian Garret, are the person who can help them move forward and get out of that mess."

"Okay, Mr. Kinney. I'll lay out some guidelines I feel the IOC can use to get back in sync with their basic concepts. In my research, I learned that going back as far as 1998, China accused the IOC of unfair treatment during the bidding process and that some countries were involved in vote buying. There was corruption everywhere."

"Oh, yes, Lillian, I remember all of that, too. The newspapers were filled with reports on how corrupt the Olympic Committee was and about how many countries were paying off officials in order to try to guarantee that the Olympics would come to their country."

"Mr. Kinney, even though I'm nervous, I can't wait for the

interview." Lillian picked up her Starbucks cup and took a long drink of the cooling coffee. Her stomach was doing little flips.

Lillian continued, feeling that talking about issues that were dear to her would make her feel calmer. "Anita DeFrantz, the former rower, is serving on the interview committee. I love that woman. You know she was the first Black woman who threw her hat in the ring to become the CEO of the International Olympic Committee."

"You're not the only one crazy about DeFrantz, Lillian. I remember her winning the bronze medal in the 1976 Montreal Olympics. Who'd ever heard of a Black person rowing⊙and not just a Black person, a Black woman!"

"Yeah, Mr. Kinney. She's now a lawyer and she was the president of the Amateur Athletic Foundation. Talk about your average over-achiever."

"Lillian, maybe if you get the position, you can be influential in Anita De Frantz's next bid at the top seat."

"Wouldn't that be fantastic! Ms. DeFrantz could achieve her dream, and I'm sure her becoming president would put a smile on the face of almost every female athlete in the world. Wouldn't it be ironic though, if the International Olympic Committee could elect a woman President before the United States elects one?"

Lillian's left ear was becoming numb, so she switched the phone to her right ear and took another sip of coffee. This marathon conversation with her mentor Steve Kinney was putting her apprehension to rest. She'd applied for jobs before, but the significance of this job somehow sent stable, aggressive Lillian into a mild frenzy.

"No, Lillian, that would be sad," Steve Kinney laughed. The United States had better hurry though. They don't know Lillian Garrett as I do. You'll probably help Anita DeFrantz's election happen, to the shame of the United States."

"Well, I'd sure like to help Anita," Lillian said.

"I think it's over the top that you have a hero in Anita DeFrantz," Steve said. "There is a lot of brainpower in that family, going all the way back to her grandfather Faburn DeFrantz. Parents of some of my colleagues told me how the YMCA in Indianapolis was known as the DeFrantz YMCA. Anita's grandfather broke many color line barriers while being the president of the Senate Avenue YMCA."

"You know, Mr. Kinney, I learned about Faburn DeFrantz myself when I was studying about Anita DeFrantz. I was astonished to find so much information about her online. In a side article, I learned that Grandpa Faburn had helped a young Black man named Bill Garrett. Because the last name was the same as mine, I devoured the articles—there were several. It seems that Faburn DeFrantz changed the color of basketball at the University of Indiana back in 1947. I'm going to do more research on that subject later."

Lillian looked at her watch and made a low whistle. "Mr. Kinney, darn! We've talked for almost an hour. Thanks for the encouragement and the great conversation. If you can stand it, I'll call you when my interview is over to let you know how it went. I feel I'm going to get the job."

"Lillian, I have no doubt you'll be fully employed by the International Olympic Committee before the day is over. Talk to you soon. Glad I was able to help you relax a little."

"Okay, Mr. Kinney, and please give my best to Mrs. Kinney. Bye now."

Steve Kinney, true to form, had been there to help bolster his mentee, Lillian Garrett. In his career as Dean at Notre Dame de Namur in Belmont, California, Steve had held similar conversations with other students, but never one from the Olympics headquarters, and never with a student as bright as Lillian.

◊

Blonde, pony-tailed Tina was on her way to Columbia University. She was going to write for the best newspaper in the world and author the great American novel one day. It was predestined. She was going to be like her mother Kacy. "No, I'm going to be better than my mother." That became her mantra. And she had to find time, while at Columbia, to add classes in comparative religion. She felt Rev. Ellwood and Clifford looking over her shoulder.

Tina said to anyone, who would listen, "I have to solve the question of heaven. If I go to heaven, I want everyone else to go, too. I've learned enough about segregation, and I'll be darned if I'm going to a segregated heaven."

The professors at Columbia were going to have their hands full when educating Tina Murphy.

Chapter 24
Jump the Broom Time

Kneeling at the back of one of the five commercial refrigerators in the bakery workroom – the one closest to the sink, wrench in his hand and tools strewn about the floor, Clifford said, "Eva, the time is up. We didn't name a day, but I think I've gone as far as I can go. I've repaired every appliance in the bakery, twice or more, and there are repair people from reputable companies all over the peninsula on call for every freezer, refrigerator, and oven in the place. I no longer have to fix anything. It's time to get married."

Eva was standing at the sinks, dropping the supply of pastry bags she had used into hot water. She turned away from the sinks to get a clearer view of Clifford because from where she was standing, she could only see his hand with the wrench in it and his toolbox.

As Clifford was making his statement, Eva eased her fist to her left hip and said, "That was a big jump. From fixing appliances to a wedding day, but I'm with you, Clifford. You're right. You've been an excellent date. Going to the Black and White Ball last week, with you, Kacy and Ozzie and watching them smooch, was when I knew our wedding shouldn't be too far away. This celibacy routine is going to drive me crazy. Celibacy is okay for teenagers, but I'm an old girl, and I want to put my hands on you and have yours on me, too."

Eva looked off dreamily into space. "It's been almost six years. The kids were in elementary school when we met. Now mine are on their way to college, with Tina right behind them. It's past time."

"Eva, those are my sentiments exactly. But that's why we had mostly communal dates. I didn't trust myself being alone with you all the time. We needed to be around a lot of people. Scripture says, 'the flesh is weak.'"

Clifford, while shoving the refrigerator back into place, stated, "We've gone out with the staff at church, the staff at the bakery, the kids and some dates on our own, but most of our dates were, if you'll excuse the expression, 'gang bangs.' I want and am ready for a wife in every sense of the word." Clifford grinned, as he walked toward Eva.

"Yep, it's time, my dear. Time, as our ancestors would say, to 'jump the broom.' Do you want to call Ellwood or should I?" Eva asked.

"I don't have to call him. I'll see him tomorrow at breakfast. He's going to be as happy as I am."

"And why's that Clifford?" Eva inquired.

"Rev. Ellwood thought we were shuckin' and jivin'. He didn't think we'd ever set a date. He's ragged me many times about it."

"Tell him he was wrong." Eva walked over to the calendar on the wall and pointed. "How about August twenty-second? That's my good friend Elizabeth Courtney's birthday and as fine a Sunday as any. I know it's a Sunday because she keeps hinting that she wants me to bring her a cake that day."

Clifford tidied the area in front of the refrigerator and finished with the job. Then he walked over to the sinks where Eva was working. He washed his hands, dried them on a towel that was draped over the edge of the sink, and then encircled tall, brown, curly-headed Eva with his strong, warm arms, leaned into her, burying his head in her neck.

In soft tones, Eva whispered, "Clifford, thank you for waiting, and dating, and repairing everything at the house and the bakery. I knew it was time, too, when there really was nothing left to repair."

She was now turned around and looked lovingly into his soft

brown eyes. The heat from their bodies was radiating as though someone had cracked open the door on the convection oven, "Now I can tell you that I love you with my whole heart and soul and can say it out loud."

"The kids are on their way to college. The TV shows are going well and Kacy is house hunting. I've done all the things I wanted to do. My life is in pretty good shape, and now I can work on being a great wife to a wonderful man."

"I love you, Eva Garret! But I'd better back away, before this celibacy strategy becomes a sham," Clifford said.

Clifford and Eva kissed and it wasn't an altruistic, friendship kiss or a stage kiss.

Back in 1944, Hollywood turned out a movie starring Humphrey Bogart and Lauren Bacall. The film, *To Have and Have Not*. It was thirty-year old Bogie's and twenty-year old Bacall's first time acting together. Her famous line, in that sultry voice, is, "If you want something, just whistle." Moments later, she kisses him.

He says, "What did you do that for?"

She says, "I've been wondering if I'd like it."

He says, "What's the decision?"

She says, "I don't know yet." They kiss again and she adds, "It's even better when you help."

That second kiss had the critics using more ink than is contained in the body of a giant squid. Audiences went wild and the sexiness of the scene had the Hayes Office – film lands official censors – condemn the kiss. According to some columnists, there was saliva flying everywhere in the Bogart, Bacall clinch.

Clifford and Eva almost put Bogart and Bacall to shame. Eva and Clifford were both panting when they stopped kissing and backed away from each other, holding one another by the elbows. Eva said, "I love you even more, Rev. Clifford Raymond Davidson!"

Once again, they kissed, and Clifford had to step back from Eva again, heart pounding and on a low, slow expulsion of breath, he whispered, "No more kisses like that one, until August 22. I am made of flesh and blood."

Chapter 25
The Wedding

Eva and Reverend Davidson were ready to have a wonderful wedding celebration at Prophet Baptist Church. They invited the entire congregation. It was going to be one of the biggest weddings the church had ever had. Clifford and Eva had all the ingredients to become a model couple but Eva already knew she was not going to be a model preacher's wife.

In a fit that might be construed as cold feet, Eva declared to Clifford one day, "I'm not going to completely give up my career, you know." She said this to Clifford as they were on their way to do some shopping at Hillsdale Mall.

"I'm not going to wear those stupid white suits or dresses and those flying saucer hats that so many church sisters are fond of. They are out of the question where I'm concerned," Eva continued. "I'm marrying you, Clifford, not the church."

Clifford gave her a side-long glance and sighed. He knew this was nothing but pre-wedding jitters and would pass. But he said, "Little crazy lady whom I love with all my heart, please calm down. Little Eva, the white hats, dresses and suits are worn by the Deaconesses. I already know without your suggestions, nudging and snide remarks that my beautiful wife-to-be will not – wear – white!

And Eva, baby, they only do that on First Sunday, Communion Sunday. Relax, Eva. Please, relax!"

◊

Clifford was still the assistant pastor and very well thought of by Pastor Ellwood and the congregation. He was a good preacher and the only one the congregation really liked to hear when Rev. Ellwood was out of town.

On their way back from shopping, Eva was in a better mood after a chocolate milkshake and now teased Clifford about Sister Piranha and Sister Slicker-Than-Grease. She recited this ditty to the good Reverend:

"They eye's may shine,
They teeth may grit,
But none of you,
They gonna git."

Clifford just looked at her, shaking his head and Eva broke into gales of laughter.

◊

The congregation volunteered for many jobs around the church; and Mrs. Samms and Mrs. Johnson, along with keeping inventory in the kitchen, also tended the flowerbeds in front of the church. One Saturday morning while weeding, watering and putting in new plants, Mrs. Samms, one of the church mothers, remarked to Mrs. Johnson, "Reverend Ellwood is an excellent preacher, counselor and scholar. There are two things he does better than anyone, though. He can do a wedding and a funeral. And if I have to tell it myself, he's been a good all-around minister, too."

Samms and Johnson were a sight to behold in dirty, cutoffs, over-sized shirts, rubber shoes, gloves, and dirt smudges everywhere.

Mrs. Johnson agreed, "Mrs. Samms, you're right. Rev. Ellwood helped this church grow by leaps and bounds, but the reason I like him so much is that Rev. Ellwood can do a wedding and a funeral."

"Mrs. Johnson, everyone knows that. Isn't that just what I said? He is so forward thinking and not like some of them old "jack legs" who call themselves preachers. Every year Rev. Ellwood goes on sabbatical to Oxford, England. Sometimes he takes a deacon or two, but the trip is mainly to educate, meditate and rejuvenate. When he returns, he just soars for a few weeks. You know he's a Doctor of Divinity."

"Mrs. Samms, you don't have to tell me that. We all know that," Sister Johnson said.

"I wasn't trying to be a know-it-all. I was just emphasizing the fact." Mrs. Samms was trying hard to keep her Christianity, so she just smiled sweetly and only thought to herself, "No Mrs. Luetta Johnson, you weren't trying to be a know-it-all. You ARE a know-it-all!"

Mrs. Samms and Mrs. Johnson were quite the pair. When people saw them coming, they knew church history was going to be recorded - rightly or wrongly. These two ladies knew chapter and verse about the church history. Chapter and verse! And they made sure they were going to keep recording the history as eyewitnesses. They, as some of the other sisters, Sister Don't-Sit-In-My-Pew, Sister Piranha, Sister Slicker-Than-Grease and Sister Mouth-Almighty didn't want to miss anything, especially if it had to do with Prophet Baptist Church. There was always going to be the gospel, according to Samms, Johnson and some of the others.

Sister Johnson was a tall, dark-skinned, amply-built woman with a large derriere that always made her skirts hike up in the back. She kept her hair dyed red, which did not complement her dark complexion, but she wasn't going to let a gray strand appear on her head.

Sister Samms was a short, taffy-colored dumpling of a woman who wore her dyed-black hair in old-fashioned finger waves, although one rarely saw the finger waves because Sister Samms owned a large wardrobe of hats. And yes, some of them were of the flying saucer variety that Eva hated.

◊

Clifford was crazy about Kirk Franklin's music. One evening, Eva stopped by his office at the church. They sat together and chose the music for the wedding. Actually, Clifford chose the music. Music was not where Eva dared to tread.

"I'm going to sing at the wedding, Eva. Is that okay with you?" Eva's eyebrows raised. Clifford had a decent voice, but he was also a ham and Eva kept her mouth shut on that subject. "I brought some CD's so you can hear my choices. If there's anything you want, make a list, okay?"

Eva could see the little boy in him and indulgence was going to be her byword. "Clifford, whatever you choose will be fine with me. I'll stick with the cake and the caterer. You are welcome to do the music. Plus, as much as I admire our ministers of music, I think you'll do better working with them than I will."

"Okay, Eva, but listen to this. This is what I'm going to sing to you."

He hit the play button and the strains of "Love Song" from Kirk's Christmas CD spilled into the room. When that song finished, he slipped in a new disc and said, "This is what the choir will sing." The tune was "Real Love" from the Kirk Franklin and the Family CD and video.

"Those are beautiful, Clifford and so appropriate. They give me goose bumps. I thought people had stopped writing love songs, but Kirk Franklin has touched a nerve in me. Look at my arm," Eva rolled her sleeve up and shoved her arm right in his face. "I've got goose bumps."

Clifford kissed her arm and playfully bit it, then shoved her arm back at her, saying, "No more kissing, remember?"

Eva giggled, rolled down her sleeve and placed her arm across her thigh, as she leaned toward the desk. "I love the pieces you've chosen, Clifford and no more kissing, I promise," Eva said with an impish grin on her face.

Clifford continued, "Brother Larry Corley and Brother Kenneth Hackett have consented to do the rest of the music, and you'll come down the aisle to the traditional wedding march.

"Eva, I had lunch at Spiedo's, over on Fourth Avenue, with Larry Corley and Kenneth Hackett last week. Their conversation about our music was so funny. They always try to best one another, you know, like playing the dozens, only churchified. Those two men really know their music, but they'll have you cracking up in minutes if you hang around them long enough. Larry picked at Kenneth and Kenneth gave it right back to him. It was all I could do to keep a straight face."

"Larry, most people don't know much about the wedding march. They tell me they want Lohengren's Wedding March. I guess it can be called that but 'Lohengren' is the opera. What some people call *Here Comes the Bride* or *The Bridal Chorus* was written by Wagner for the opera, and it became famous during Civil War days."

"Kenneth, as always you have the answer. I didn't know that, but I did know that the recessional is by Felix Mendelssohn and it comes from *A Midsummer Night's Dream*. It also came from a performance of the piece at the wedding of the English Princess Royal after Mendelssohn's death in 1851. There, we're both even."

"Man, you need to hush your fuss," Kenneth said.

Larry countered, "Man, if I hush, you'd never learn anything," Kenneth emitted a humph and snapped his fingers twice in the air. From the three men, Rev. Davidson, Larry and Kenneth, laughter poured through the restaurant. Many of the restaurant patrons stopped with forks in mid-air to see what was causing the three men seated at the table near the window to become so boisterous.

"Once again, Clifford," Eva assured, "It's in your hands. Hackett and Corley can do no wrong in my book. And I promise, no more kisses until August 22."

◊

Mrs. Samms and Mrs. Johnson were never at a loss for words, and while they were taking inventory in the church kitchen one day, Mrs. Johnson said, "Rev. Ellwood has a touch that is uncanny at weddings. Do you remember the couple he gave shoelaces to? The couple was to keep them tied and always think of the tie that binds. That was so romantic."

"Mrs. Johnson, that's not the one I liked. I liked it when he gave that other couple light bulbs. The bulbs were to keep the love-light in their marriage shining. Tears came to my eyes when Rev. Ellwood did that."

"Mrs. Samms, the very best one was when Harry McCorkle married Siseretta Ferguson. He gave them batteries. Some of the folks said Mr. McCorkle was so old that Siseretta was going to have to shove them batteries up his butt to get him going in the evening. But that was before Viagra. Rev. Ellwood said the batteries were to give their marriage that extra charge if it seemed things were cooling down. That was romantic, too."

"It certainly was, but I'll never get the image out of my mind of Siseretta shoving a battery up the old geezer's butt," Mrs. Samms agreed.

The two old ladies laughed and laughed.

◊

Eva selected a cake of eight tiers, all heart-shaped. There were eighteen, eight-inch, satellite cakes branching off from the twenty-inch base. Those satellite cakes followed a Tongan tradition. Each of the assistant ministers, deacons, and their wives would be given one of the satellite cakes. Each cake had the scripture from First Corinthians 13:4-8 inscribed on it. Love is patient, love is kind. It does not envy, it does not boast, it is not easily angered, it keeps no record of the wrongs. Love does not delight in evil but rejoices with the truth. It always protects, always trusts, always hopes, always perseveres. Love never fails. Love never ends."

The wedding was beautiful. Prophet Church had been built to look like the inside of Noah's ark, rustic and hand-hewn, with turquoise upholstered pews and carpets and a simple cross in the nave above the baptismal pool. The wedding coordinator, Essie Green, had decorated all of the pews with large pale blue bows and placed blue candles on the altar table.

Eva walked down the main aisle wearing a blue silk suit and a small spray of blue flowers over her right ear. Clifford wore a black traditional cutaway coat. Lillian and Tina were the attendants and wore blue silk, sleeveless sheaths. Kacy, matron of honor, wore a long blue off-the- shoulder, body-hugging Oscar de la Renta that made her eyes appear even bluer. And Andrew, the best man, was dressed the same as Clifford.

Except for the outstanding music, the wedding was short and simple. The congregation was charmed as Rev. Davidson sang to Eva. And they clapped heartily as Clifford kissed the bride. This time, they exchanged a shorter, less passionate kiss than the one at the bakery.

Mrs. Johnson and Mrs. Samms were disappointed because Rev. Ellwood didn't give any gadgets to Clifford and Eva. That omission from the wedding ritual put a crimp in the soon-to-come Johnson and Samms gossip session.

Because there were so many people attending the reception, it was held at King Center. Clifford and Eva had rented the large auditorium as well as the three rooms in front of the building and the lobby.

Mrs. Johnson and Mrs. Samms had arrived at the center before the wedding and enjoyed the pleasure of watching Lesli Mack and her crew decorate the hall. Samms and Johnson had actually had Redi Wheels pick them up early on purpose, as they didn't want to miss one detail of the day's proceedings.

Lesli and her Epicurean Dimensions staff had transformed the auditorium into an oasis. There were topiaries and potted palms standing like sentries along every wall and the bright fabric transformed the large assembly room in a recreation center into a Moroccan tent.

With the wedding and reception over and even though Rev. Ellwood hadn't given Mrs. Johnson and Mrs. Samms ammunition by giving Clifford and Eva ceremonial wedding gifts, there had to be a gossip session by the two church biddies.

While sitting on a bench in front of King Center, waiting for Redi Wheels to pick them up and return them to their homes, Mrs. Samms asked Mrs. Johnson if she had enjoyed the wedding and the reception.

Mrs. Johnson answered, "I wouldn't have missed this wedding

for anything in the world. When I heard Lesli was doing the food, I just had to be here. I love the way

Epi . . . you know what, puts on a party." Mrs. Johnson couldn't get her dentures to cooperate with the words Epicurean Dimensions, the name of Lesli's company. "I guarantee a party by Lesli will always be different and special."

"You're right about that, Mrs. Johnson. It's always going to be extra special. Lesli does make an event unusual."

"Mrs. Samms, isn't that what I just said?"

Mrs. Samms ignored the comment and continued, "Did you ever see hors d'oeuvres like those at the last wedding she did? Stuffed grape leaves. I never thought I'd ever eat a grape leaf. They taste like vinegary collard greens."

"They was okay," Luetta Johnson responded, "but I liked the stuffed eggs, they had something special in them. I don't know what the ingredient was, but I've never tasted stuffed eggs like that before. I only eat the tried and true. You can't go wrong with stuffed eggs," Sister Johnson said.

"Only one thing though," Alberta Samms said, "I wouldn't eat that caviar. It tasted like crunchy bb's drenched in manure." Sister Samms cupped her hand and whispered into Luetta Johnson's ear. "They tasted like shitty bb's. And there was too much food, I thought."

Sister Johnson said, exasperated, "Would you please be quiet! You're never satisfied. If there hadn't been enough food, you would have complained about that. Girl, hush! When you get to heaven you're going to tell God the sugar's too sweet. And how do you know what manure tastes like?"

"I know, cuz I gardens," Sister Samms defended. "How'd you like that carved watermelon? It looked like a rose. I wonder where they found those carved eggshells? It was just too elegant."

"And that tent-look in King Center. Never saw anything like that before."

"You're right, Luetta! It was just nice and I never went to a wedding where they gave you a piece of the cake in a box. Did you see how the Deacons rated? They got a whole cake."

"Yeah, girl, that must have been expensive. I could hear the cash register go ka-ching, ka-ching. Davidson had better get another job."

"I heard that! I also heard they do that in England, give you the cake in a box; it's supposed to be a souvenir. You keep it for years."

"Not me, I'm going to eat my cake. You're right about the English tradition, but I think they use a different kind of cake. Something like a fruitcake, because it lasts for thousands of years. You can have fruitcake. This is just plain cake. If I were you, I'd keep the box but eat the cake."

"You didn't have to say that to me, I was going to eat my cake. And they had enough food this time."

"Girl, would you please hush. They always have enough food. Didn't you just say there wasn't enough food?"

"Eva and Clifford are going to make a lovely couple."

"Yes, they are. But did you think when they started the first dance that they danced too close?"

"It was a bit close, but they are grown folks and they're young. They're supposed to dance close!"

"He was even doing the boogaloo. That dance went out years ago. And I was so glad they did the 'electric slide.' I didn't think I'd ever get a chance to get on the dance floor, but after the 'slide,' the young men kept coming over and asking to dance. That was very sweet of them," Mrs. Johnson smiled.

"It was, and they didn't get fresh or try to do them vulgar bumps."

"Mrs. Samms, you know full well that Jeff, Thurman, Dennis, 'n them ain't gonna try to get fresh with no old girls like us. You just wishful thinkin'."

"No, I'm not, Mrs. Johnson. No, I'm not! But it was nice that they asked us to dance. They was brought up right."

"I wonder where Eva and Clifford are going to live?"

"I hear he bought a new house."

"What type of present did you give them?" Mrs. Johnson asked.

"What do you give a couple who has everything?"

"Girl, I just came to the wedding and slipped them a small envelope."

"They will make a nice couple."

The Redi-Wheels bus arrived and Mrs. Samms and Mrs. Johnson clambered on.

Riding home, they were silent for a time when Mrs. Johnson said, "You know, Mrs. Samms, I have mixed emotions about any wedding. When I reflect on Mr. Johnson, I don't know why anyone would get married. That old coot kept me on my knees. I had to keep God close to keep my sanity. That man almost drove me crazy.

"There was many a day that I could have righteously killed him. You know what that bum did to me one day? He was going out of town on a hunting excursion to Alaska. He and about ten other guys were driving up to Alaska in two motor homes. I had had a little sweet tooth and baked myself a cake. There was too much for just the two of us so I said I'd freeze it. He said, 'No, you ain't, I'm going to take that up to Alaska with us in the motor home. The guys'll love it.' Well, I didn't complain, that was a good idea.

"Then he said he wanted to take some chicken. I told him to get some out the freezer and I'd fix it for him. That simpleton reached into the freezer and pulled out a bag with four little ole pieces in it. Now, Mrs. Samms, if he was going to share the cake with the guys, a whole half of a cake and more, you know four pieces of chicken wasn't going to go very far with ten men. I went to the freezer and added twelve more pieces, baked the chicken, and put it in a bowl. Now, remember he only took out four pieces for me to cook.

"When he got ready to go, he took every piece of the chicken and put it in his cooler. I asked, 'Mr. Johnson, are you going to take all the chicken?' Girl, don't you know he got mad! He got huffy and put most of the chicken back in the refrigerator. Well, we had our usual fight. Later I took the chicken, put it back in his locker and gave him all but four pieces to take with him. Mr. Johnson was one of the most selfish, evil Negroes on the face of the earth."

"Mrs. Johnson, you ain't got nothin' on me. You know Earl Samms was the devil incarnate. And you don't have to tell me a thing about getting married. If any man looked cross-eyed at me talkin' bout gettin' married, Rev. Ellwood and Rev. Davidson would have to come visit me in San Quentin. Sister Johnson I could beat you killin' anything. The day I liked to have killed Earl is the day I went to move his big old brown truck. You know on street cleaning day we have to move our cars or get a ticket. I went out to move his truck, and I couldn't get the door open. I went in and asked him what was wrong with the door my key wouldn't open it. Earl said the ignition had broken, and he had to get new keys.

"'Okay'. I didn't quite buy it, but 'okay', I said to myself. Then a few weeks later, he was in a snit about something else and blurted out, 'I didn't have no trouble with the ignition. I had all the locks changed cuz you never gave me no keys to your car.'

"Sister Johnson, I just counted to ten and asked the Lord to keep me away from the knives in the house cuz slittin' his throat at that moment would have been too good.

"Mrs. Johnson, I hope Clifford and Eva will be happy. After about five years of marriage, I simply hated Earl. But I didn't have nowhere to go."

"Mrs. Samms, you ain't tellin' me nothin' I don't know. My marriage was no bed of roses. With the help of Jesus, I hung in there. If times had been different, I would have left his sorry butt long years ago. But that wasn't in the cards and I was not about to be out on the streets. Mrs. Samms, we both did the right thing. We out lived both of them ole goats. Hee, hee, hee!"

"One thing you must know, Mrs. Johnson, most people think we had ideal marriages and ideal husbands, but no one knows where the nose goes when the doh close!"

They laughed so hard they scared the driver who was also laughing at Mrs. Johnson's comments.

When Mrs. Samms regained her composure, she said, "Driver, this is my house coming up. The one with the yellow shutters. I'll see you next week at church, Mrs. Johnson. Good night, now!"

Chapter 26
Confession

Clifford and Eva didn't have time for a honeymoon. That big event was put off for a future date, but the first weekend after the wedding, Eva invited Lillian to spend the night with her in the new digs. Eva also wanted Kacy to have the house on 37th Avenue to herself, A little peace and quiet for a hard-working woman.

Saturday morning, Clifford had arisen early to go down to his gym. This new home sported a three-car garage. Clifford had converted the third garage into a state-of-the-art gym. Treadmill, rowing machine, barbells, AB-lounger, jump ropes, mats, flat screen TV, telephones, and a refrigerator for beverages.

After Eva made sure Clifford was downstairs, she went to the guest bedroom and wakened Lillian. "Lazy Mary, get up. I have some hot coffee and goodies in the bedroom. When you get washed up, come and join me for some mother-daughter time."

"Did you sleep well?" Eva asked.

"Oh Mom, did I. That mattress is like the commercial says 'I was sleeping on a cloud.' Where's Clifford?"

"He's down in the gym working out."

On a table near the window, Eva had brought up a tray of hot coffee, sweet rolls, and fruit. They drank, ate and chatted, remembering highlights of the wedding.

Eva finished eating first and crossed the room to sit on the white suede chaise. Then Lillian joined her mom, by sitting at Eva's feet and placing her head on Eva's lap. Lillian started, "Mom, I have a confession. You're lucky and blessed that I'm a good girl. Thank you for raising me that way. Because you are who you are and I love you so much, I was able to put the brakes on before I went stone cold crazy. I was going to take Clifford away from you." Tears welled in Lillian's eyes. "I thought I was hope-to-die in love with Clifford and I probably still am. He's so damn good-looking. I just knew if he loved you and because I was a junior version of you, I had it goin' on! I thought I could just saunter in front of Clifford in a bikini, shake my groove thing, snap my fingers, and Clifford would be mine."

Lillian raised her head to look at her mother. Eva's hand left her hip. Eva sat up a little straighter, letting Lillian know she had her mother's attention. Eva began smoothing Lillian's hair, a knowing look on her face.

"Mom, Clifford knew I was flirting with him. He was very aware of what I was doing. I was trying to be a *femmé fatale* and just knew with my 'brick-house-body,' my youth, and supposed beauty, I was going to sweep this good man off his feet and cause the scandal of the year. And Mom, I didn't care! All the morals you taught me, all the good sense you pounded into me, went in one ear and out the other, onto the floor."

Eva sat in mock surprise, listening intently and continued to smooth Lillian's hair, while looking lovingly and sadly at her daughter.

"What happened, Lillian?" Eva asked. "What stopped you?"

"Well," Lillian continued, "That good-looking ole stuffed shirt you chose to be my stepfather, took me for a ride. I thought it was going to be the beginning of a big romance. Mom, that ride was the beginning of setting your dumb little know-it-all-daughter straight!"

Eva smiled knowingly, "What happened, Lillian?"

"That fine dude, the Rev. Davidson, took me to the new Indian Springs Park, that new park up near Community Hospital. Mom, it is the most romantic place in the whole city. It has a fabulous view, and those great little streams flowing off stones into a pool -- it is just the greatest place in the world for a *rendezvous*. I knew I was on my way to the adventure of my life. We had a blanket, a picnic lunch picked up from Draeger's, a bottle of wine, and all the accoutrements. Romance was in the air, and I was going to steal my Mom's man! I was going to be lewd, lascivious, raunchy, and sinful. Me, little Lillian Garrett, was big enough to step into my mother's shoes. Me, Mom! I was going to step into the shoes of the cake baker, *par excellence*, the TV cake show host, the local female entrepreneur of the year. I was going to take my mother's man, because I thought I was all that. The same woman who nurtured me, taught me to be a good person, a church-going sister, who taught me to earn good grades and be the best Lillian I could be. I, Lillian Garrett, was going to steal my mama's man. Mom, I thought I was all that and a bag of chips. But the Reverend Clifford Davidson gave me the lecture of my life."

Tears flowed from Lillian's eyes. "Mom, Clifford was so kind and gentle. He didn't put me down. He didn't tell me I was stupid. He didn't say what a jackass I was being or how much all of this would hurt you if you found out.

"He told me about my future and about his future. He told me how important his life was to him and how much and how hard he had worked and struggled all his life to choose the profession he had chosen. He told me how difficult it was to be a man of the cloth and about how hard the line was that he had to walk. He iterated how hard it was to be a good man and to avoid all the temptations including me that come his way. He ran down a list of the sisters in the church who laid in wait for him and the other pastors with sweet potato pies, short skirts, and more.

"But most of all, Mom, he told me how he admired you and all your accomplishments and how much hell you had to go through to make a way for Andrew and me. He told me how difficult it was in college for him to even go to the school of divinity. He'd wanted to be a professional football player and was All State at Grambling, but transferred to Howard's School of Divinity." Looking wistful, Lillian said, "He sure has the body of a football player, even today."

Eva interjected, "I will agree with you on that body, but go on, Lillian. Tell me the rest."

"And you know what, Mom, I still love him and I still wish I had whatever it is you have, because I would sweep him off his feet in a minute if I could. Clifford told me what love is. He read some poems that made me weep. Then he had his Bible and opened it to First Corinthians 13:4-9. Mom, you even put that on your cakes for the wedding. It was beautiful." Lillian was sobbing.

Eva continued to pat Lillian, saying, "Baby, my heart hurts for you."

"Then he talked of how much he absolutely adored you and how he would die before he ever did anything that would hurt you. Clifford told me, 'Lillian, you are going to be my daughter one day, and I don't have to explain incest to you.' He didn't!"

Lillian's tears were abating, "Mom, what I'm going to do in my future is make sure I find a man just like the one you've found. And Mom, I'm even going to be luckier than you, because I will have Clifford for a step dad, and I'll find a husband like him, too."

Eva leaned forward and put both her arms around Lillian. They both shed tears of love, respect, and admiration. Eva had already known every word that Lillian told her, because Clifford had previously revealed every syllable of the conversation the day the *rendezvous* had taken place. Eva never let on that Clifford had told all.

"Lillian, you'll get over this. I'm glad Clifford was able to share with you how much he and I love each other. You'll find one day that this was just a crush. You'll find someone to love just the way you think you love Clifford. Only it will be better, because the person you really fall in love with is going to love you right back, the same way you love him. Or her," Eva added.

The "her" comment made Lillian look up at her mother and smile. "Mom, you're never serious."

"Yes, I am. We never know what the future might hold."

When Eva and Lillian pulled themselves together, Eva continued, "I'm going to have to get up to that Indian Springs Park and see if Clifford will share any of that good stuff with me. Lillian, I love you, and all the sense I pounded into you still exists. Sometimes we need others in our lives to help us put into action what we already know is right."

The thumping of footsteps could be heard coming up the stairs. It was Clifford, returning from his workout. He walked into the bedroom, wearing cut-off sweats and an old sleeveless sweatshirt, smelly and damp. Lillian's back was turned to him, with her head still on her mother's lap. Eva held her nose and waved him away, emphasizing Clifford's aromatic condition, and she gave him a big wink. He said, "Good morning, ladies," and hurried to his shower. He needed no explanation; he knew Eva would fill him in later.

Chapter 27
Word Worm

Kacy was ready to buy a house. She had saved her money and had been looking all over town for the right place. She and Eva would do house hunting every spare moment they could find. When they were out delivering cakes or just running errands, a house for Kacy and Tina was always in the back of their minds.

"Kacy, I have a friend named Charles Lax. He's a realtor and has some new listings in Baywood. Here's his number. Call him when you get a chance, will you?"

"Eva," Kacy said, "Put the card on my desk, please. I'm delivering a cake in that neighborhood tomorrow. I'll check out some of the signs and let him know if I'm interested. Have you heard about Janice King with Coldwell Banker? I hear she also has some listings."

A week after the glow of the wedding wore off and people were back into their routines, Kacy rose late for work and was savoring the peace of being alone in the warmth of the house on 37th Avenue. She went to the bathroom, washed her face and brushed her teeth, then went into to the kitchen to start the coffee.

Peace, wonderful peace! Not that Kacy didn't love all the kids, but the empty house was a treat. Yet, it wasn't hers. This was Eva's house. The plan was to rent this one out after Kacy found something suitable.

Kacy was making residual money from the TV show, the manuals, and Eva's biography. She was also making money from several freelance writing and editing jobs that had come her way. The bakery was bringing in decent money for both Eva and Kacy. Who'd have thought two women who had had their backs against the wall some fifteen years ago would be where they are now?

Kacy sipped her hot cup of coffee and padded back to the bedroom for a welcomed shower. While soaping, Kacy passed her hand over her left breast and felt something that she hadn't felt before. There was a lump. Where in the heck had that come from? To be sure her fingers hadn't betrayed her, she went back over the spot several times and, yes, there was a lump.

Kacy went yearly to see Betty Calvin and staff when they had the Breast Cancer Awareness Day for the Church. Everyone went to Mills/Peninsula Hospital. Both men and women signed up for breast screenings. After fifty or sixty people had been examined and this was done on a Sunday afternoon everyone would assemble in the hospital auditorium and listen to people such as Dr. Max Roach or Mark Turbow, two of the top oncologists in the Bay Area.

Kacy was prompt and punctual about going for her annual exams. Where in hell had this come from and how had she missed it? Don't panic, she told herself. Call Betty Calvin's office at the Breast Center.

Betty Calvin was a member of Prophet, too. She was also the lead radiological technician at the San Mateo Breast Center. Kacy and Betty had worked on several projects together at Prophet and Kacy was quite fond of Betty.

"Betty, how'd you become involved in this type of work?" Kacy asked one day when they were pasting labels on envelopes for a big mailing for the church.

"I used to be a receptionist and records clerk for the hospital. Then my husband, Sam, discovered a lump in his breast one day while showering. Of course I was concerned and beside myself, not knowing what to do. Coincidentally, Mills/Peninsula had just opened a course for radiology technicians because they were planning to open a breast center for women. I immediately signed up. That was in 1992. I became a technician and although it was too late for my Sam, I've worked myself up in the office and now am in this position. You never know where God is going to lead you, Kacy. You just have to be ready when the call comes."

"Betty, I wish we could clone you. God Bless you, my friend!"

Because of that conversation, Kacy knew of Betty's dedication to her field and knew that if there were anyone at the center who could help her, it would be Betty.

Kacy almost broke her neck stepping so quickly out of the shower onto the tile, with wet feet. Hurriedly, she made her way to the desk in the bedroom to get her phone. The Breast Center phone number was on a white-barreled pen with pink lettering. It was at the ready in the plastic pencil holder made for Kacy by a friend. Kacy punched in the numbers with lightning speed.

"Betty?"

Betty's warm voice responded, "Hi, Kacy! Good morning."

Kacy didn't really hear Betty, she burst out saying, "It's Kacy Murphy. I have a lump. I'm concerned! It's 8:00 A.M. What are you doing there so early? I expected to get your answering machine."

"Whoa! Slow down, Kacy. We open at 7:30 A.M." Let me calm her down, Betty thought. "Our clientele requested the early time. People have busy lives these days and want to get started early, good news or bad news. I like the early hours because I miss most of the traffic when I cross the bridge in the morning. You say you felt a lump?"

"Yes, Betty and I'm beginning to shake."

"You're supposed to be concerned, Kacy. How soon can you get in?"

"Is it possible for me to come right over?" Kacy asked in a voice that now was trembling.

"Come right now." Betty urged, "We'll fit you in."

In a dither, Kacy pulled on a light blue velour jogging suit. She quickly locked the house and jumped into her new white Cadillac Cetera. She zoomed over to Mills/Peninsula Hospital and went straight to the back of the building where the Breast Center was located. The receptionist was waiting for Kacy and took her to the dressing room where she had Kacy slip into an ill-fitting hospital gown.

Betty Calvin walked into the dressing room reached for Kacy, gently placed her hand under Kacy's elbow and ushered Kacy into one of the mammography rooms with the squishing machine in it.

There was a lump. Betty had already felt it with her fingertips. "Don't breathe, Kacy. Okay, now you can breathe."

"Kacy, something's there but let's get the physician in here. She's going to take you across the hall so you can look at the pictures yourself." Betty pushed a button on the wall and, after a few moments, Dr. Harriett Rofsky, Director of Breast Imaging, joined Kacy and Betty in the examining room and walked with them into the viewing room.

Dr. Rofsky lowered the lights in the room and brought up the lights that illuminated the images of the breast that were on x-ray like sheets. It clearly showed a tiny nodule with what looked liked tentacles in the left lower side of the breast.

"Dr. Rofsky, is it cancer?"

Doctors don't normally give an answer to that question until there has been a biopsy. They tell the patient that they will be called the next day. But Kacy was so insistent and demanding in her question and tone that Dr. Rofsky gave an affirmative answer.

She was aware of what had been pointed out, but Kacy was in a haze. She also heard what the doctor was saying, but Dr. Rofsky's words seemed to be filtered through mufflers. Dr. Rofsky was talking to Kacy, but the only utterances that seemed clear was something like, "Cancer is a word, not a sentence." And Dr. Rofsky sensitively suggested several alternatives to Kacy. The word that stuck in Kacy's brain was lumpectomy. Lumpectomy – lumpectomy – lumpectomy. The word was becoming a word worm, a word she couldn't stop her brain from repeating.

Someone, Kacy didn't remember who, escorted her back into the dressing room. Betty came in saying, "When you're dressed, come into my office. I'll leave the door open for you. It's the first one on the left as you leave this room."

Kacy already knew, there was just something that let her

know, the lump was cancer. Sometimes lumps are just tumors, but this lump in her breast was cancer. She was going to have a lumpectomy.

"Dammit! Why me?" Kacy repeated out loud. "Why me?"

Chapter 28
Bakery Love

"What are my options, Betty?" Kacy asked almost inaudibly.

Betty Calvin reiterated what Dr. Rofsky had all ready [*already*] said. Hearing Betty repeat Harriett Rofsky's words seemed to remove the muffled sound. Now, every word became clear and concise to Kacy: "Chemotherapy" and "lumpectomy" burned into her brain.

"I have to go to the bakery and tell Eva first. Then I'll share the news with the staff. I have to call New York and tell Tina and then call Ozzie. Boy, I have a lot of people in my life to share my misery with." Tears rolled down her cheeks.

I'm a damn sight better off than I was fifteen years ago when I was out on the street with no place to rest my head, Kacy mused. Stop crying and get this show on the road!

Kacy changed her strategy just a little, calling Ozzie first. She called him from the parking lot of the hospital. His voice, at this moment, was what she needed to hear.

The phone rang at Ozzie's urology office in Menlo Park. Nurse Practitioner Marion York answered, "Dr. Hutchinson's office."

"Hi, Marion. This is Kacy. It's an emergency. May I speak to Ozzie, please?"

"Kacy, what's wrong?" Marion asked, concerned.

"I don't want to be rude, Marion, but I have to talk to Ozzie."

"Okay!" Marion answered, "I have to interrupt him, he's with a patient."

"Interrupt him please, Marion," Kacy said with a voice that was becoming husky.

Excusing himself from his patient in one of the examining rooms, "Something horrible must have happened, Marion. Kacy would never interrupt me while I'm with a patient," Ozzie murmured as he dashed down the hall.

Ozzie snatched the phone from his desk, with none of his usual bedside manner. This wasn't one of his patients. This was his number-one lady, his main squeeze. "Kacy, what's wrong?"

"I'm sitting in the parking lot of the Breast Center in San Mateo. I found a lump." She blurted out. "I've opted for a lumpectomy and chemo. I'm upset."

Cancer! Ozzie felt a chill go through him, "Repeat what you just said, Kacy."

She did.

"Whatever you want to do, and whatever you need, I'll be right there for you. I'll close shop early. Marion can handle the rest of the lineup, and I'll be in San Mateo as quickly as I can. Where will you be?"

"I hope I'll be at home by the time you get here. I'm going to the bakery to tell Eva and the staff. Gotta let the crew know what's up. I'll call Eva the minute I get off the phone with you. I went straight to the Breast Center when I felt the lump, didn't even call Eva to let her know I'd be late. Ozzie, I've lost my mind. I'm not thinking."

"You're not supposed to be thinking. But cancer is a word, not a sentence. I'm going to smother you with all the love you can handle. I'll be there for you, Kacy. See you soon."

"Ozzie, funny you'd say that 'sentence' thing: Dr. Rofsky just said that to me, too. She also explained that it might not be cancer, but after they aspirated the breast they learned what I already felt in my gut. You're so sweet." Kacy's eyes were brimming, and she started to cry again.

Tears came to Ozzie's eyes, too, but he didn't want her to know it. "See you in a few, Kacy," Ozzie said and they both clicked off.

Kacy let more tears drop, then pulled herself together. She dialed the bakery.

Jason answered. "Eva's Bakery. May I help you?"

"Yes, Jason. This is Kacy. May I speak to Eva, please?" Her voice was muffled.

Jason put the phone on hold and went to Eva. "It's Kacy and she sounds funny."

Eva snatched the phone from Jason and almost shouting, "Girl, where are you? Is everything okay?"

"No, it's not," Kacy said. "But I'm safe, and I'll be there in a few minutes. I'm sorry I didn't call earlier, but I wasn't thinking. I'm okay. I'll be right there."

"Girl," Eva pleaded, more insistently, "Are you okay? What's the matter?"

"Eva, I'm okay, kind of. I'll be there in a few minutes. Again, I'm sorry I didn't call earlier, but I wasn't thinking. I'll be right there," Kacy repeated.

The phone went click in Eva's ear.

Before pulling out of the parking lot at the Breast Center, Kacy fumbled in the consul between the two front seats and attempted to apply some makeup.

At the bakery, she pulled around to the back alley and parked her car in one of the stalls. "How can I talk to Eva and the crew without falling apart?" Kacy asked herself.

She got out of the car and walked in the backdoor. Kacy's heart pounded with every step to Eva's workstation.

Eva looked up. It was obvious that her blonde sister was crying. Red nose, red cheeks, recently applied eye make up was pooling under Kacy's lower lids, which were also brimmed with red. Something was wrong, definitely wrong.

Eva hopped down from her stool and ran toward Kacy, flinging her arms around her. "Kacy, what's wrong? What's the matter?"

Eva, in her excitement, pushed and shoved Kacy backward, not hard, but they retraced Kacy's path back into the room where Kacy's desk was located. Eva slid the door shut and once again embraced Kacy.

Kacy attempted through heart-wrenching sobs to talk to Eva.

Eva could barely understand Kacy but when she could make out the words "breast" and "cancer," Eva started crying, too. Both just stood in each other's arms sobbing. Eva tried to say something through jagged breaths and sobs, too.

Eva began thinking about her mother, Eva, the woman she was named after. Her dear sweet mother and how awful it had been back in 1969, when she died of uterine cancer. No one told the five children what their mother's illness was. All they knew was that their mother was sick. Eva's mom spent endless days in the hospital and would make the medical authorities bring her home, so she could be with her children as often as possible.

Eva had been just twelve years old and remembered how she and her younger sister and brother would jump up and down when they saw the ambulance turning the corner at Cypress and El Dorado. "Mama's coming, Mama's coming!" The three younger children loved it when Mama came home, even though it meant they would have to be quiet and give their mother shots of morphine. Taking care of their mama made them feel like they were big kids.

Yet, no one in the family nor in the community mentioned the "C" word. It was taboo. When the adults did talk about the "C" word, it was done in whispers and hushed tones.

Here was Kacy sobbing about this dreaded disease and talking about it out-loud, in front of God and everybody. Good for Kacy! Still, the word "cancer" opened up a deep wound in Eva's heart again, these many years later.

◊

Jason beckoned to the staff, saying, "We have to find out what's going on. Kacy's been crying."

"Why didn't you tell me sooner?" Eva begged.

Both women were gasping and sobbing, then they started to laugh, through snotty noses, wet tissues and faces.

As they were trying to console one another, Kacy's slick-soled shoes and emotional state, helped the two of them lose their footing. Whump! They hit the floor. It wasn't a hard fall, but it made a noisy thud. They ended up in a heap on the cement floor.

Kacy and Eva were crying and laughing like two crazies. It was a sad moment, but it was funny, too. They were trying to talk to each other, but they also saw how funny they looked. Eva in her apron with frosting-stained hands, trying to comfort her best friend who was crying and laughing so hard she could hardly talk or breathe, and who was now smeared with green frosting on her face, in her hair and on her blue jogging suit.

The staff was standing on the other side of the sliding door. All of them rushed the door and with Jason in the lead, they slid it open. "Are you two all right?"

"Eva? Kacy?"

The whole staff was talking at once. Jason ran back into the decorating room, where the sink was and retrieved wet towels and more tissue. Makeup was dripping, and frosting from Eva was all over the two of them. They did look funny. The staff positioned chairs so the two women could get off the floor. There was patting of hair, wiping of noses, giggling and still more tears.

They were both disheveled and distressed but were now seated. Eva finally composed herself enough to say, "Staff, Kacy has something to tell you."

Kacy eased into it. "Everyone, I'm going to be all right, but I discovered a lump in my breast and I'm going to have a lumpectomy and chemotherapy. I'm going to be okay."

A collective intake of breath came from the group. When they recovered, through their own tears, the staff quickly became a cheerleading squad.

"That's all right, Kacy!"

"We know you can make it."

"We're with you!"

Different people kept chiming in. Mary, Rai, Lupe, Maria, Justina and even Jason encouraged one moment and cried the next. This news was about one of the family becoming sick. The bakery staff was crushed, and they were experiencing a roller coaster of emotions. The crew, except Jason, trickled back to their workstations, but not much work was done the rest of the day. No one was very productive, but they tried.

Kacy, Eva and Jason sat in the back a while longer. Jason, being the only man on the premises, wanted to make sure they were okay as he, although younger than both women, tried playing the role of Papa Bear, consoling and offering testosterone-ladened assurance. When he felt they were as okay as he could arrange, he went back to his table to finish decorating a basket-of-flowers cake.

When Eva and Kacy were coherent again, Eva said, "You'd better call Tina. I'll call Andrew and Lillian; I'm also going to call Rev. Ellwood and Clifford. Friend," Eva offered, "we've been through a lot together. We'll make it through this, too. You're strong and you have a lot to live for."

"I know, Eva. It's just the initial shock. I called Ozzie and he's going to meet me at the house.

"It's not that I didn't know quite a bit about breast cancer already. I've attended the seminars every year that are given by the health advisory committee. But it's a shock when it's you. Dr. Rofsky and Mrs. Calvin from the Breast Center gave me tons of information. What the hell if I lose a breast? They're not that big anyway. Maybe I can get implants and become a 44D! Watch out, Dolly Parton! I'm not going to lose a breast, I'm opting for a lumpectomy"

"You'd look just about like Dolly Parton, too, only you're taller. Breasts aren't the most important part of a woman's body," Eva confided.

"I know, but they are an erogenous zone and Ozzie is warming up." Kacy grinned.

"But he's so cute and he seems to be understanding. Kacy, I bet he can work with a gal who's a oner."

"That's easy for you to say, Eva. You've still got two, even though they're only mosquito bites."

"Would you please leave my flat chest out of this!"

"Aha! Hurts when it gets close to home."

"Girl, most men will tell you they don't need more than a mouthful. And girlfriends, too!"

"Yeah, it's just a fantasy to have 44D's. But, I don't want to die, Eva. I haven't lived long enough."

"No one wants to die, Kacy. I don't believe that anyone wants to die. Unless they're very old and infirm."

"I want to be here to see Tina win the Pulitzer. I want to own my home."

"You will! Relax. It's going to be a tough haul for awhile, but we're going to look at this like a minor discomfort, a bump in the road. You said you are going for a lumpectomy. That means the breast will remain intact. You'll have a scar. But what the hell! When it comes to scars, even the best diamonds have a few infractions."

"Yeah, who wants a flawless diamond? I'm a rarity as I am and a scar will only enhance the territory."

"You know, Kacy, a scar for me would take me out of the 'itty bitty titty committee,' of which I'm now the president."

"Eva, stop! You're making me laugh."

"Are you familiar with a man named Norman Cousins?"

"Yeah, I've heard the name," Kathy remembered.

"About twenty years ago, he wrote a book called *Laughter Is the Best Medicine*. Brother Cousins' philosophy is going to become our philosophy. We're going to laugh, go through chemo and we're going to survive. We can and we will. Do you understand, Kacy? This is about 'we.' We shall overcome and all that," Eva emphasized by waving her hand. "You're going to make it; we're going to make it. Just you wait and see!

"I have to share a joke with you that was attributed to Billie Holiday. Billie said, 'I hear they are going to try to replace gasoline with manure. That will go a long way to stop the siphoning of gas!'"

Kacy's face broke into a huge smile. "That's funny! But people don't siphon gas anymore."

"No, they don't, but you're messing up the joke. It's an old joke. Now, go home. I'll see you later this evening."

Eva finally rose, made sure Kacy looked fairly decent, and ushered her out the back door. "I'll call you soon. Don't forget to call Tina!"

"I won't, Mother Hen. See you tonight." They kissed each other's cheeks. Kacy went back to her Cetera, pulled out of the back alley, and was on her way to 37th Avenue.

143

Chapter 29
Preparation

Tina fell to pieces when her mother reached her on the phone. "Mom, I'll be on the next plane home. I'll just have to drop some classes, but I'll take care of the details later."

Kacy countered, "Just wait a second, Tina. I have everything covered. You're going to stay in school. We're as close as the phone, and I'll send you daily pictures on the net to let you see what I look like as I go through chemo. You'll be on break pretty soon and that will be time enough for you to come home. I'm going to be just fine.

"Do you remember Mrs. Calvin? She's that wonderful woman who runs the Breast Center in San Mateo, and she goes to Prophet Baptist Church, too. She has me headed in the right direction. Eva isn't going to let me want for a thing. Ozzie is coming to be with me tonight, and Eva has even called Rev. Ellwood and Uncle Clifford. I'm going to put this into the hands of a higher power. God hasn't let us down so far, Tina. As they say at Prophet, 'He has brought us a mighty long way.' I'm going to be all right."

Tina was crying, her words hard to understand. "I'll try to be strong Mom, but you have to promise to call me at least twice a day. I'm so sorry. My wonderful, wonderful mother has cancer.

Momma, oh Momma!" Tina dissolved into deep, gut-wrenching emotion.

"Tina! Tina! Please, don't cry. I'm going to be just fine. Cancer research and treatments are so much better now."

"Yes, but how do we know, Mom? People still die from cancer."

"You're right and a lot of people don't! The statistics are in my favor. We have the best oncologists in the world connected with the Breast Center, and Ozzie, as sweet as he is, won't let anything happen to me. Tina, please don't take this so hard. I promise you, I'm going to be okay."

"Mom, I'm coming home."

"Tina, no you're not. School is far more important and the support group in San Mateo will call you daily. Please do your studying and your break will be here before you know it."

After assuring Tina that she was going to be well taken care of, the two finally hung up. But the minute Tina said goodbye to her mother, she called Eva.

"Eva, you have to promise to let me know if anything changes. I'll be home so fast that Michael Johnson, Maurice Green, and Marion Jones won't be able to beat me in the 100-meter dash."

"Tina, your mother will be taken care of just as though she was one of the Tsar's famous Easter eggs." *nice!*

Even without the reference to the Tsar, Tina knew that her mother was going to receive the best of care.

"Eva, I just think I should come home."

"Tina, if this was 1969, I'd tell you to come home. It's not. These are the 1990s. Your mother is going to recover from this. I've already promised her that. And now I'll do the same for you."

Tina felt better after talking to Eva, but it was going to take days for her to get on track again. Tina felt the same way about Kacy that Lillian felt about Eva. However, Tina had never bloodied anyone's nose over it.

Chapter 30
Ozzie Wakes Up

Eva had similar conversations with Andrew at Stanford and Lillian at Yale. Both of them offered to drop what they were doing and come home. Andrew was the most realistic though. Because he was just down the Peninsula at Stanford, he could be at home almost immediately if there was anything he could do. Eva assured both of her children that things were going to be okay and that both of them would be wise to come home on their scheduled breaks from school. Andrew said, "Mom, I'll be home after my last class today."

◊

Late in the afternoon came the knock Kacy had been waiting for. She flung the door open knowing Ozzie would be on the other side.

"Ozzie, I almost broke my neck getting to the door because I knew it was you. Did I ever tell you how handsome you are with your Harry Belafonte face and red hair?"

In Ozzie's arms was the biggest bouquet of flowers Kacy had ever seen. After blushing from the compliment that had just flowed over him like warm honey, he dropped the flowers and grabbed her. He hugged and kissed Kacy, as though she might disappear.

"Kacy, baby, I couldn't get here fast enough," he said, as he looked deeply into her blue eyes. They kissed and hugged for a long time, on the front steps of the house.

When they finally pulled apart, "Dang!" Kacy said, "I think I'll concoct another illness for next month to see if I can get the same rise out of you. I didn't know you cared," she said, tongue in cheek.

"I didn't either, Kacy. Well, I mean, I, I, cared," Ozzie stammered. "But now I know I really do care. This upset has let me know I have deeper feelings for you than I thought I had. I'm in love with you, and we need to do something about that. We need to be Dr. and Mrs. Hutchinson, yesterday!"

"Hold on, Junior G-man! Can we wait just a minute here?" Kacy asked with mock resistance.

"Kacy, I'm not trying to rush you, but darn it, it hit me that I might lose you before you are truly mine. I don't want that to happen. I want to be yours, and I want you to be mine. I love you with my whole heart Kacy Murphy," Ozzie breathed into her hair.

"As Eva says, 'Ain't this sumpthin?' I've been ready to be Mrs. Hutchinson for quite some time. Is getting sick or telling you I was going to be sick all I needed to do to get you to propose? We could have made wedding plans a long, long time ago," Kacy said laughing. "What date shall we choose?"

"How about April 26, next year?" Ozzie said. "The twenty-sixth is my mother's birthday." She was in a joking mood, but Ozzie was as serious as a heart attack.

Realizing Ozzie was serious, Kacy furrowed her brow. She answered seriously, too. "Okay, Ozzie. That's the date then."

"I'll tell Clifford and we can start preparing."

"It's a date," Kacy repeated.

After picking up the gigantic bouquet and sweeping away the dropped buds and leaves from the porch, Kacy and Ozzie walked into the kitchen.

"Where will we find enough vases to put for these beautiful flowers in?" Ozzie asked.

"Knowing Eva, I'll bet she has tons in the garage."

They found shelves lined with vases. Kacy and Ozzie gathered some in their arms and returned to the kitchen. They cut asters, mums, roses, and ferns, birds of paradise, and flowers they didn't know the names of. There were enough flowers to fill five of the largest vases.

"Did you leave any flowers in the shop?" Kacy asked

"Not many," Ozzie laughingly confessed.

Chapter 31
Bless Us

Eva arrived at the house on 37th Avenue at five o'clock. Then Rev. Ellwood rang the bell. Deacon Henry stopped in with chicken that Mrs. Henry had fried. Sister Prothro and Deacon Prothro came in with a big pot of greens. Sister Curry showed up with a sweet potato pie and potato salad.

Eva slipped into the kitchen, quickly tossed a salad and put on a pot of coffee. Clifford, Eva's husband, was the last one to arrive.

No, he wasn't. The last person was Andrew who rushed in with a bouquet of flowers for Kacy. He surveyed the room, kissed Kacy on the forehead and sputtered, "I, I, I could have left my sorry little flowers in the store. It looks like a florist shop in here."

Everyone laughed, as Kacy assured Andrew, "Your flowers are beautiful, wanted and appreciated. Anything you bring me, Andrew, is special."

After Kacy thanked them all for coming, Rev. Ellwood led everyone in prayer. They prayed for the healing of Sister Kacy and that she would have a speedy recovery. They prayed for everyone in the room and for others who might be sick or afflicted. They prayed for peace, blessed the food and fell into warm fellowship.

Sister Prothro and Sister Curry received the food offerings as they appeared and arranged them on the dining room table, buffet-style on the white linen tablecloth. "This table looks like a groaning board," Eva commented.

Rev. Ellwood had blessed the food in his initial prayer so one and all helped themselves and continued their lively conversations.

After the group finished eating, Deacon Prothro moved to the piano. They sang *Jacob's Ladder, Blessed Assurance, Steal Away, This Little Light of Mine,* and other old standards. With the friendship and spiritual love floating around the room, Kacy felt like the words in *Jacob's Ladder. "Every rung goes higher, higher . . ."* I'm climbing a ladder, this gathering is one of the first rungs. I'm going to go higher and higher, Kacy thought.

During the evening, Kacy hadn't had much to say, but she found her voice just before everyone prepared to leave.

"You know, I've been a part of similar gatherings in other homes, usually when someone has died. I'm so glad and grateful that you all did this for me, but I hope it's not an omen."

"Oh, no!" everyone chorused. "That's definitely not the case."

"I didn't know the church held these types of gatherings for people who were just sick," Kacy said, sheepishly.

"This is business as usual for Prophet Baptist Church," Rev. Ellwood explained. "We try to meet all of our congregation's needs. Everyone has to pitch in, to do for one another. Kacy, you just call and we'll be there, twenty-four-seven."

As people collected their bowls and platters and left, Eva told Kacy, "I'm not about to clean up this mess. I'm calling Geraldine Kirkland. Let's hope she's free to come over tomorrow, even though it's not her regular cleaning day. She looked closely at Kacy, by now stretched out on the sofa. "How you doing', good buddy?"

"I think I'm going to make it. With an assemblage like this one, I have no choice but to make a full recovery. I'm feeling much better than I felt this morning. I'm on *Jacob's Ladder,*" Kacy reflected.

Chapter 32
We're With You
Vignettes

Monday morning at eight sharp, Kacy was at the Crystal Springs shopping center. A group of doctors had just opened a new oncology center that practiced Western and Eastern medicine. It was one of the most beautiful medical offices Kacy had ever seen. The office featured the most whimsical paint job one could imagine. The reception area's main wall was painted dark blue with large orange dots. Other areas were painted similarly, with sea-green walls and large red dots, and chartreuse walls with large pink dots. Inviting, overstuffed chairs and cherry wood tables and bookracks complimented each room. The office sat in a lush garden at the corner of the shopping center. It had glass windows from floor to ceiling on the top floor, bringing a view of the garden inside.

The patients oohed and ahhed about being in such pleasant and zany surroundings. One patient even joked, "If I can come to an office like this, I don't mind being sick."

Doc Turner, one of the partners in this practice, always gave his new patients a personal tour.

"You've already seen the top floor. Let me show you what's downstairs.

"The first floor has smaller rooms for aromatherapy and massage. Here are the offices of Dr. Sung and Dr. Miyamoto, who are with us from Korea and Japan. We try to keep our office as upbeat and cheery as we possibly can for an oncology clinic," Doc Turner told the new patients.

◊

"Mom, AT&T is making Fort Knox dough off the two of us."

"That's true, Tina, but at least we can space the calls and we're not talking at the peak hours." Mother and daughter had become inseparable on the phone.

"How are your studies going, Tina?" Kacy asked.

"Columbia is a breeze, Mom. The words are flowing and I'm sailing. Nothing seems to be difficult. Mom, I'm just looking forward to my break, so I can come home and take care of you. New York is great, but I want to be home," Tina whined in a baby voice.

"I know, Tina, but believe me, everyone is taking good care of your mother. You'll be home soon."

Kacy was energized by Andrew and Lillian calling her as often as they could. She felt fortunate to see Andrew often, even when he visited the house on 37th Avenue with one or two of the many young women who were constantly at his side.

"And what's your name, again?" Kacy asked one young lovely.

"Phelicia Jones, Ms. Murphy."

"Oh, what a lovely name," Kacy responded. Thinking to herself, poor dear, you're the fiftieth young woman I've met since Andrew's been down at Stanford - if you only knew.

Andrew was thinking, I hope Aunt Kacy doesn't slip up and give me away.

Kacy gave Andrew a knowing look and a wink. She would try not to betray the fact that her handsome, dark-skinned nephew was in great demand. Or was he just a gigolo? Well, if he was, his Aunt Kacy and his mother Eva turned a blind eye to his dalliances.

◊

Kacy's treatments at the oncology center were going well. When people or customers approached her, now that she was back at work, in self-defense Kacy would stretch her arms out chest high in front of herself, stating, "Hi, I'm so glad to see you, but I have to be careful how I let you hug me. I'm a little sore post-surgery, you know." People appreciated Kacy's straightforwardness.

One of her most joyous days after the surgery was when Kacy and Eva's friend, Maryanne Saylor, showed up at the bakery with a big Bloomingdale's bag for Kacy. "What's in it, Maryanne?"

"Open it and see, you Kookoofish!" A Maryannism.

Kacy tore into the bag that was stuffed with tissue- paper-wrapped tams of every hue in the rainbow. "Maryanne," Kacy grinned, "These tams are a kick! The perfect thing for a bald head. Thank you so much."

Maryanne headed for the door. "If you don't like them, let me know. We can always go to the Wig Palace over on Fifth Avenue." Maryanne waved and was gone.

Kacy spent the next half-hour modeling a red tam, a black, a blue. "Oh, the tan tam will go with everything. Nobody but Maryanne would have thought about my bald head."

◊

Dorothy Easter and not-so-little Claudia began visiting Kacy, too, and that thrilled her. "Claudia, do you remember when you were a tiny one out at Coyote Point and I just about kissed every inch of your skin off?"

"No, Ms. Kacy, I don't, but Mama tells me about that incident all the time. I wish I had been older. But Ms. Kacy, I'm in middle school, and I want to be a writer because of you and Tina. I love to write, and I'm going to win the Pulitzer Prize one of these days!"

"Well, Claudia, I'm so glad we inspired you to write. I'm going to recommend that all little children get kissed for inspiration. I plan to be there when you win the Pulitzer."

"Kacy, we're going to have one big cheering section on that day. But Claudia and I had better boogie. That traffic across the bridge is going to be hell in just an hour," Dorothy lamented.

Dorothy, Claudia, and Kacy kissed and said goodbye.

◊

Kacy came to the bakery as often as her strength allowed. It was better for her to keep busy. And now that she was more aware of breast cancer and the crusade to find a cure, she became involved with the Mills/Peninsula Health Advisory Board. One of the speakers at an awareness meeting was the Assessor of the City and County of San Francisco, Doris Ward.

Doris told the audience at one of the seminars, "If you want a life with no stress and no trouble, I have a perfect place for you: it's called Colma, California. Colma is a city in California with a good-sized population - most of them dead. Colma is a city of cemeteries." The audience roared.

◊

A way Kacy found to avoid stress was to do paperwork at the bakery. For her it was fun.

"Eva, how was that cake-decorating seminar you went to?"

"It was okay, but you know I'm not into using those air brushes. I still think freehand is the best way to decorate cakes. But to each his own. I started out free hand and I'm going to stay freehand. You know - teaching old dogs, et-cet-era, et-cet-era." She dragged out the words like Yul Brenner in *The King and I.*

"You know, Eva, it sure is a pleasure to work on the books these days. We're in the black! You're on top of the trends and people are still ordering our cakes. Seven years ago, who'd a thought it?"

◊

Kacy was still bald-headed and still in the midst of her chemo treatments. One morning, as she entered the bakery, she stopped mid-step when she saw that all of the staff were bald. The entire staff had gone to Quan Lin Beauty Salon after work the night before, to have Paula Sutgray, hair stylist extraordinaire, shave their heads.

Mary, one of the cake decorators, had said, "I need a stiff drink before I get my hair cut off."

Rei said, "I don't drink, but I need something to give me some courage, too. I've never been bald before."

Paula produced wineglasses and a bottle of Chardonnay on ice, reserved for special customer. Jason opened the bottle and did the honors. When Paula learned why the bakery staff had all wanted shaved heads, she gave them a discount.

And for those who didn't imbibe in alcohol, Jason disappeared out the back door and appeared shortly thereafter with a tray of Haagen-Daz cones from Baskin and Robbins over on Third Avenue.

When Kacy entered the bakery, the first person she truly focused on was Ozzie, without his beautiful red hair. He was flanked by Eva, who was sporting a head that looked like a truffle in a box of Godiva chocolates. Eva had big gold earrings swinging from her ears. Jason was bald; Mary, Rei and all the staff were shaved clean. That included Justina and all the Latina staff members, too. They had shaved off all their long beautiful black locks.

"Don't worry, Kacy," Jason chirped, "The hair didn't go to waste. There's an organization that takes the hair and makes it into wigs for young cancer patients undergoing chemo. Paula Sutgray knew how to cut the hair so it could be used for that purpose. Ain't we cute?"

"Cute isn't what I'd call it," Kacy laughed. Then she burst into tears and so did everyone else, but these were happy tears this time.

The bakery staff was a family. They all wanted to do something, anything for Kacy. Each time Kacy looked at the naked heads of her bakery family, she felt cheered, warmed, touched, strengthened and loved.

The baldheads at the bakery startled the customers, too, but when they learned the reason for the tonsorial display. The customers gained another reason to shop at Eva's Bakery.

155

Chapter 33
Junebug and Skeet

Junebug's parents, Scott and Hattie Gonzales, were hard-working, honest people. They were also members of Prophet Baptist Church, and they were the parents of eight children.

"Mama? Daddy? Tell us how you met?" One or more of the eight Gonzales children frequently asked to hear this story.

"Well," drawled, Mr. Gonzales, "me and Hattie met when we was cuttin' 'cots at the cannery down off Tully Road in San Jose. Someone threw a rat on the belt to scare your Mama. I was the foreman that day and I just happened by when Hattie took off runnin' and ran straight into my arms. I hugged her tight as I could, with a little extra hug thrown in. It was love at first hug. She was a looker back in them days. Fact is, she still is."

"Yes, and your daddy was slim and trim and had the most beautiful, black, wavy hair I had ever seen. That Mexican-Black mixture made him into a regular Don Juan. I knew he was giving me an extra squeeze, but he was so handsome, I didn't care. I was scared of that dead rat, but forgot all about that ole messy thing when these big warm arms grabbed me. Daddy thought he was slick, but I knew what he was doin', and I let him do it."

The Gonzales children never heard enough of that story from their now-retired parents. After the cannery and raising her family,

Mrs. Gonzales, who had been an elementary school aide, and Mr. Gonzales, after having been a carpenter for over twenty years, retired.

Junebug was the nickname the family gave Scott Gonzales Jr., the oldest boy. Nobody called him Junior.

June was the name the dudes in the hood called him because it took too much energy to call him Junebug. Cool people don't have the time or energy to call people by two names.

The girls in the neighborhood called him J-o-o-o-n-e - B-u-u-u-g-g. They dragged out both words and made it sound like something you wanted to squish under your foot. The girls thought June was cute. He was six feet tall, wore his hair in braids, and had a mouth full of gold and decay. His wardrobe consisted of baggy clothes, not because it was stylish, but because that's what he was used to. In jail, the authorities rarely issued clothes that fit, and Junebug had been in and out of jail most of his life.

June wasn't into steady work and didn't really want a job. Weekly, he had to appear at the Human Development Department, formerly know as the Unemployment Office. He was fulfilling the obligation of an interview, so he could keep his checks coming.

During an intake review with a clerk, she asked, "Mr. Scott, what's your former occupation?"

"Ah was a camoonity leadah," June snickered, half high. He enjoyed being a "community leader." Not a leader in the normal sense. June was intent upon leading people astray and he was being a smart-ass with the clerk.

◊   *Readers may not understand.*

During another command meeting, at SMPD, Officer Cannon said, "Skeet makes me think of 'Wrong Way Corrigan.' Corrigan's that pilot who wanted to be famous back in 1938. He was supposedly trying to make a non-stop trip from New York to California. Taking off at dawn, puzzled onlookers watched him do a 180-degree turn and vanish into a cloudbank. Twenty-eight hours later, Corrigan stepped out of his plane in Dublin, Ireland, saying, "Just got in from New York. Where am I?"

"Those in the know feel Corrigan knew what he was doing. But he stuck to his story that he got turned around – read his compass backward – meant to go to California, he claimed. The only people who were fooled by that story wanted to be fooled. Case in point: Skeet!"

"What's on his sheet?" Chief Mann asked. "Do you still own that Cessna, Cannon?"

"Yeah, Chief, I park it down at San Carlos. Do you want to go up?"

"No, thanks, Cannon, but I'll take the info from that sheet."

"Chicken!" Cannon smirked at the Chief, "Now, let me see, Skeet Wainwright's illustrious history: petty theft, larceny, car jacking and crank. Mainly, throwing rocks and hiding his hands. And, according to word on the street, good at getting idiotic young dudes to do his dirty work."

Officer Petrie added, "Word is, some youngbloods were sent to jail for something Skeet put them up to. Skeet walks away clean and pockets the profits. If there was a wrong way or an underhanded way to do something, you can count on Skeet."

◊

"Hey, baby brotha, Ah gotta job Ah wants you do fa me. Get a couple other dudes and you can make a little change on tha side, ya unnerstand." That was part of Skeet's rap.

He was a dirty, dirty dog, with plenty of neighborhood stains on his hands. Yet he and his partner, June, somehow managed to fly beneath the radar.

As a younger man, Skeet had spent many a day at juvenile hall and then made frequent visits to the county jail as an adult. How he missed a trip to the federal prison was a mystery.

◊

Three girls and four boys in the Scott Gonzales family managed to graduate from college. They held good jobs and made good homes for themselves. But not June!

"I learned evvything I need to know in juvvey. Ain't no need to go to high school. Them teachers ain't got nuttin' fah me." He dropped out and stayed out.

"When Ah needs a little change, Ah do days work at da car wash. Ah help out paint contractors and work with Mr. Webb, the tile man. Keeps me off welfare. Ah eats lunch at St. Vincent De Paul's. They gives out brown bags. Sometimes I likes it, sometimes I don't. When it's brown bread samages, I throws it away. And at nights, Ah dines at West Side Chuch. It don't cost but a quarter. They's lots uh us dat goes dare ta eat," June explained himself.

"Hattie, what did we do wrong?" Mr. Gonzales asked shaking his head.

"We have to look at Scott Jr. as though he is a bad dream. We didn't do anything. Little Scott has chosen his own life. We have seven others who are doing fine and that's what we have to think about. We have to pray for Scott and love him, but we can't let him taint the rest of this family." Tears rolled down both their cheeks.

Scott Sr. regained his composure and winked at Hattie, "But baby, you know, Scott Jr. takes after your brother Sammy."

Hattie Scott playfully smacked her husband on his arm, "Now don't you go talkin' about my relatives! Your gene pool ain't all that high falootin'. Don't you have a Uncle Benny who spent some time in the Big House?"

◊

Skeet was also a boy from a good family. Skeet's father was Rev. Thaddeus Wainwright.

Seated on picnic tables near the basketball courts at King Center, "Skeet, you ain't nothin' but a bad ass PK," Bucky, a neighborhood scum bucket, commented. "Most every damn preacher's kid in this neighborhood been in some kina trouble, cept fah the girls," Bucky chuckled.

It is a generalization and a stereotype, but many preachers' kids display errant behavior. Some of them want to prove to the bad boys that they can be one of the crowd.

"An' you know what, Skeet? We jes laughs at your dumb ass.

Sometimes in ya face, sometimes 'hind ya backs," continued Bucky. "You always trying to be sumpin' you ain't!"

"Where ya mama playing piano at these days?" Bucky changed the subject. Jerome "Skeet" Wainwright's mother, Dotty, was a homemaker and an all-around nice person. Mrs. Wainwright was known for her gospel piano playing.

"Now, you getting ready fah me to kick the shit outchew Bucky. Don't go talking bout my mama."

"Nah, nah, man, Ah ain't talkin' bout yo mama. My mama axed me to axe you that qurstion cuz she wanna go where ya mama be playin'. She like the way yo mama play. Sheet man, Ah ain't talkin bout yo mama. Lightin' up, man!"

"Aight man, cuz Ah wuz getting' ready to put leatha on yo ass. You wuz gonna have my size twelve's up yo ass. Ah dunno, Ah gotta axe her."

◊

Skeet had his share of the female population, too. Lacy Williams, one of the girls he dated, commented, "I just love me some Skeet. He's brown and smooth like a Hershey candy bar. If he shaves, you can't tell. Even though his hair is thin, I love it slicked back and that ponytail turns me on."

Lacy's father didn't like that she went out with Skeet. Mr. Williams described Skeet this way: "Five feet nine inches tall and well built. His physique shows that he's done time in jail pumping iron. Him and his buddies are all buff, as you girls call it. If me and my golfing buddies spent as much time pumping iron as those idiots do, we'd be buff, too. When they're in jail, it's a bigger crime to pick up a book or read a newspaper than to pump iron. These dufuss brothers spend their time in jail cooking up what crimes they'll commit when they get out. And then they pump more iron."

"Daddy, you're too critical. I only date Skeet sometimes."

"Lacy, I know you can do better than to hang around that scum," Mr. Williams huffed.

"Daddy, may I say something?"

"In defense of that jerk? No! Hell, no! I get the last word. I buy the groceries around here!"

◊

Skeet owned an endless wardrobe of warm-up suits in every color and fabric – jersey, satin, terry. "Skeet," his mother commented in dismay, "you must have ninety-nine of them ugly things. Don't you own one decent shirt and tie?"

"Mama wud I need dat fah? I ain't gown ta no chuch," and he'd laugh. Mrs. Wainwright wanted to cry. "Jerome, may I ask you one more question?"

"Shoot, Ma."

"Why do you insist on talking that incoherent gibberish?"

"Mama, I have a constituency. If I spoke as though I was educated, I'd be suspect."

Mrs. Wainwright shook her head, "Jerome, that logic is lost on me."

◊

Skeet and June were ace boon coons. Wherever you saw one, you saw the other. June lived in a small cottage on Claremont Street, just off Mt. Diablo and Skeet lived in a single-room-occupancy hotel with the toilet facilities down the hall.

"Mama, I wants to thank you and daddy for payin' da rent fah me," June would often comment when he visited his folks.

"You're so welcome, Scott," Hattie Gonzales would reply. The Gonzales' paid the rent for him because they didn't want Scott Jr. living on the street, and they definitely didn't want him asking if he could stay in their garage.

"Dis and Dat, Bad and Baddest, Itch and Ouch. Two people nice people don't want to be around," Officer Cannon sneered.

Chapter 34
Trash

At Seventh and Railroad Avenues in San Mateo stands a silver-painted electrical box. There are similar structures at almost every crossing, to automatically control the red and white barrier arms at each crossing to halt traffic.

The structure stands on a concrete slab and is partially hidden by oleander bushes, tall weeds, and trash. This isolated spot had become a hangout for drinkers, dice-players, dopers, and ladies who work hard for their money, doin a lil' sumpin' sumpin' on the side.

Another afternoon, during a command meeting at the Police Department, seated around a long, mahogany table are Chief Mann, Lieutenant Petrie, Captain Scanlan and Captain Hammerman.

"Chief, Caltrain has to help us out a little bit. That crossing-control box at Seventh and Railroad has become a magnet for human and other types of debris. The city's underbelly has started hanging out there, and they're giving our staff a headache."

"I know," Chief Mann agreed. "I got a call from Tyrone Robinson, the new director at Caltrain. He promised that he'll have that spot cleaned up while installing the new suicide barriers. It will be done by the end of this month."

"That's great news, Chief! Sergeant Haney and his crew on

the midnight-to-five shift find needles, rubber tubes, and tons of condoms in and around that area all the time. The Saturday morning street sweepers keep it fairly clean, but that's only once a week. Those sweepers deserve hazard pay," Lieutenant Petrie chuckled.

"One of our problems," Chief Mann added, "is the people in the surrounding area. They know what's going on at that spot, but they won't call us. To a person, they say, 'I thought someone else would do it. Ain't nuna my business.'"

◊

Out for a night of up-to-no-good, Skeet and Junebug went to Zuppie's, a working-class bar that featured darts and billiards, on South B Street. They dropped in for a few beers, although they usually did business east of the tracks. This bar wasn't their usual hangout, but fate put them there that evening.

Two young rookie cops, out to flex their muscles, stopped Skeet and June as they were leaving Zuppie's. Not too many Black guys frequented bars west of the tracks.

"What are you guys doing out here tonight?" the driver yelled, pulling his cruiser over and flashing a light on the two uglies.

"Show your ID!" the second officer barked.

The cops exited their vehicle. The larger officer hiked up his gun belt and stuck out his chest. The shorter one, hyped by now, scooted around the back of the patrol car, hand on his billy, to join in the harassment.

Skeet complained, "Man, what chew messin' wid us foe? We ain't done nuttin. Y'all twisted mafukkah's ohways messin' wid somebody."

As Skeet and June were giving as good as they got, they pulled out their ID's.

"Face the wall! Hands on the wall! Spread um!" One of the officers brayed.

Junebug spit, "You two fuckin' puhvuts jus ain' got nuff to do. Wyant you jes go back an finish mastabatin'? Y'all got nuttin' on us. Sheeeit!"

The two officers checked Junebug and Skeet's wallets and patted them down. But with the fountain of profanity coming the officer's way, and because they knew the two scum buckets weren't really doing anything, they didn't do the best pat down in the world. Finding nothing, they gave the ID's back to "Dis and Dat," sending them on their way.

The stop by the two cops sent Skeet and June into a rage. The two miscreants knew they had been violated. Racial profiling!

As ignorant and low-down as Skeet and June pretended to be, they had rights, too. Hot as firecrackers, they headed toward the railroad track, cussing every step of the way. In the trash-strewn haven where people didn't go to say their prayers, three men were already embedded. Nestled among the refuse were Snake and Bucky, two aborigines from the hood and a homeless Asian mute named Shoji.

"Shoji," Bucky tittered, wyant you go to De Paul's and get you a new sumpin'. That raggedy-ass suit you wearin' so dirty, it can stand by itself."

"Yeah," Snake added, "An wyant, you gitchew a storage box? You got nuff shit in that cart to take care ov a army. You got that thing piled to the gunnels."

The three men were in various stages of repose, passing around a 40-ounce can of Red Stag Malt Liquor in a paper sack.

Skeet and June entered the mess, "Man, those two mafuggin' cops jacked us up. They ain't got no right doin' that kina mafuggin sheeeit like dat. Stawhm troopahs, dat's what dey is. This Uhmuraca, they ain't sposed to do dat sheet to Muracun citizens. Go fuck with dem dam Messicans!"

"Dat's what Ahm talkin' bout, dirty azzhole, mafuggin' cops!" moaned June.

Bucky watched Shoji pull out a pair of dice, "Why you damn fools wanna go an let Shoji take all ya money? You know dat wud he gone do!"

Bucky and Snake didn't care about losing to Shoji; they only had chump change and mainly came to drink from the 40-ounce can provided by Shoji.

Adding insult to injury, Skeet and June were quickly relieved of the twenty dollars left in their possession. After several passes with Shoji in the lead, June and Skeet crapped out, both throwing snake eyes to Shoji's 'Cadillac does, a pair of foes.'

Bucky stretched out and laughed, "June so hot, you cud light a match on um. Pass me mo juice. Ahm medicatin'. Tole you not to mess wid Shoji!"

Being jacked up by the cops and now losing their money to that "slant-eyed mafuggin' bastard" Shoji, according to June, just made things worse.

Skeet had become so angry that he put his hand down his pants and pulled out a small caliber midnight special - a junk gun. They had so intimidated the rookie cops with their gutter mouths that the cop who patted Skeet down, didn't go high enough on his inner left thigh.

"Mahfuggin cops didn' fine dis," Skeet waved the weapon toward Shoji.

Shoji ignored Skeet completely and kept his gaze on the dice.

As Skeet was mouthing off and waving the gun, Shoji rose from the ground very slowly, not looking at Bucky, Snake, June or Skeet. Then like a mongoose going for a cobra, Shoji made a silken tai chi move that turned Skeet around, with Skeet's gun hand pinned to his back. Shoji now had the gun.

June started backing away and Skeet screeched, "Aight man, aight! I wuz just playin'! I din mean nuttin! Leh me go, Shoji! Leh me go, you mean kung fu mafuggah!"

Shoji shoved and kicked Skeet in his butt, pushing Skeet out of the trashy recess, and threw the Saturday night special after him.

"Shoji, man, next time ah see you, Ah'm gone kick yo gahdam Samurai ass!" Skeet blistered the air, scrambling back on all fours, crablike, to pick up his gun. *hice!*

Muffled laughs from Bucky and Snake and wheezing sounds from Shoji, could be heard as the three men stayed inside the weedy mess. Skeet fumbled the gun into his pocket.

"What chew doin', Skeet?" June wanted to know.

Skeet was holding his right hand and crunching his fingers into a pulsating claw. "Tryin' to get da blood circalatin' back into mah han."

People on the street knew Shoji was homeless, but they also knew he wasn't stupid. Word was that Shoji had earned a black belt, back somewhere in his other life.

"Dayum," Bucky snorted, "Evvybody out hyeah know they ain't supose to mess wid Shoji. Take a fool like Skeet to try it. Ain't da fust tahm Shoji done whupped some brothah."

"Ah guess dose two dummies gone on home. It so quiet 'tween um, you cud hyeah ah rat piss on cotton. . . He he he he," Snake laughed. "Pass da fouty."

Junebug and Skeet had been violated by the cops, then beaten out of their money and humiliated by a homeless, lowlife foreigner, to hear them tell it. The next person to cross their path was going to catch pure-dee-holy-hell.

◊

Kacy had stayed at the bakery to get some paper work done. Looking up at the clock, midnight, it was late. She put the paper-work away, cleaned her desk, grabbed her belongings, and headed for the back door.

Locking the door, she remembered, "Oh, heck! I'm parked in front of the store." Rather than go back in, she headed down the dark alley. The store was one block away from the railroad tracks and sometimes there were unsavory characters hanging around, but Kacy wasn't afraid. She knew most of the people in the neighborhood and fear wasn't part of her personality.

As she turned the corner out of the alley and headed along the sidewalk toward her car, two men came up behind her.

"Hey, baby, you got some change?"

She turned around slightly and said, "No, I'm sorry, I don't have any money."

"Baby, aincha got some change?"

Again she explained, "I don't have any money on me! Sorry!"

A searing hot pain went through her back. Then another pain, higher in her abdomen. Kacy jolted forward, grabbing her stomach. She tumbled like a rag doll, landing face down on the pavement.

Space out

Kacy Murphy felt her life slipping away. Her last words were –
"Tina . . . My house...!"

Over nothing, two of the slimiest, most lowdown characters in town, had ended an innocent and beautiful life.

Chapter 35
The Funeral

At 4:00 A.M. the Dean of the School of Journalism knocked on the door of room 233 in Collette Norman Hall.

Tina called out, "Who is it?" She was seated in front of a muted TV, writing a script on her laptop for tomorrow's class.

"Ms. Murphy, this is Dean Courtney. May I come in?"

Tina stepped to the door. She peered through the peek hole and made sure it was the Dean. It was Dean Brian Courtney, but he was accompanied by two uniformed police officers. She unlatched the door chain quickly, letting the Dean and the officers in.

"What's going on?" Tina blurted, questioning. But the Dean spoke first.

"Ms. Murphy, I have bad news. Please call Mrs. Eva Garrett in California. We've been told there has been a serious accident at your home, and you're to call immediately. I'm informed that because of the nature of the accident, these two officers will accompany you to La Guardia."

Tina's eyes became as big as saucers, every hair on her arms and the back of her neck came to attention. She thought, "Mom. Cancer? Not yet! She told me it was under control! Not my mother. Eva? Lillian? Andrew? Something has happened to one of them." She bolted for her purse that was on the floor next to the chair she had been seated in. Although her purse was a typical female jumble, she was able to hone in on her cell phone. Grabbing the phone she hit two buttons, the code for the house on 37th Avenue, in San Mateo. The phone rang, "Eva," Tina almost screamed. "What's wrong?"

Eva said in a tiny voice, "Come home, Tina. Your mother's been killed."

Tina slumped to the floor. Officer Joe Passinissi and Officer Toni Klinger rushed to pick her up. They eased Tina into the large chair that she had been seated in earlier, pounding out her script.

Officer Passinissi picked up the phone that slid out of Tina's hand. Placing the instrument to his ear, he said, "Mrs. Garrett?"

The barely audible voice answered, "I'm Eva Garrett. Who is this?"

"I'm Officer Passinissi, Ma'am. NYPD was contacted by the San Mateo Police Department earlier this evening about the tragedy. Our Bereavement Department sent Officer Klinger and me to contact the college and break the news to Ms. Murphy. We'll accompany her to the airport and have officers meet her at SFO to make sure she gets home okay."

"Oh," Eva said. "Is she all right?"

"She's slightly faint. We have the Police report from our city, so we will fill her in on the details. We have a ticket waiting for her at the airport, and we will help her get home," he repeated himself.

"Thank you so much, Officer Passinissi. Thank you. Could you please put her back on the phone?"

"Yes, Ma'am. Here she is." The officer handed the phone to Tina.

"Eva, what happened?"

"Seems the police feel somebody or somebodys tried to rob your mother and she didn't have a cent on her. The police say it looked like a random robbery, or . . .," Eva began to cry. "Oh Tina, just come home as fast as you can."

Through her own tears, Tina cried, "Okay Eva. I'm on my way."

Tina was numb, but went to the bathroom, washed her face and brushed her teeth. She went to the bedroom, threw some clothes in a duffel, turned out the lights and locked the apartment. She floated to the police car parked at the curb, not remembering her feet touching the surface of anything. Through a blur she was whisked to La Guardia Airport. Officer Passinissi stayed in New York and Officer Klinger, the female Officer, because of a change in orders from the top, flew to SFO with Tina.

At SFO, there were two uniformed officers and <u>Chief Susan Mann</u>, to escort Tina to the house on 37th Avenue.

Normally, the Chief didn't take part in this type of operation. <u>Captain Snodgrass</u> dutifully handled the section of the department that took care of helping families in time of need. But Mann happened to be at the station after doing ride-alongs with people from the Citizens Academy. The Chief participated in this unfortunate duty because Eva and Kacy had always made delicious, zany cakes for city events. She, too, wanted to reach out to the Garret and Murphy family. Death was bad enough, but even the police weren't inured to murder.

◊

Telephones had been ringing all night at the home Kacy, Eva and the kids had shared on 37th Avenue. Lillian was on her way home from Yale. Andrew had already driven up from Stanford, and the house began to fill with church friends, the bakery staff, neighbors, and police officers. Although it was about 2:00 A.M. the news of this tragedy had spread fast.

What was going on? What had happened to Kacy? Someone had taken her life. Snuffed it out in an instant. They had eliminated the life of one of the most beautiful souls God had put on the face of the earth. Eva's friend was gone.

Who did it? Was it "they?" Was it "him?" Was it "her?" Who did this to my wonderful friend? Eva's thoughts tumbled.

◊

Ozzie was lower than a snake's belly and could not stop his tears. In an era of men not being able to cry, he didn't care who saw him. His grief was Vesuvian!

◊

The funeral had been put off for two weeks because there had to be a criminal investigation. But the police could find no clues. They ran into continuous dead ends. The downtown denizens and the folks in the know were as mute as Shoji and the Sphinx.

When the coroner finally released Kacy's body, Eva made the funeral arrangements. During the two weeks of intensive investigation, Eva was too numb to think about burying her friend. In a way, the wait was good because it gave her a chance to take time off and grieve for Kacy.

Because she knew this would be a big funeral, Eva ordered large-screen TV's for the social hall at Prophet so everyone who couldn't be accommodated in the main sanctuary would be able to see and hear the service from that venue.

When Kacy was taking chemo treatments, Eva had become her chauffeur. She and Eva would have deep conversations about their longevity. It was during those long talks that Kacy told Eva about her love of Baptist funerals, especially those at Prophet Church. "Eva, I want the pomp and circumstance, along with the warmth and hominess. I don't want a sterile, cold, sad funeral."

Sitting in the kitchen at the 37th Avenue home, giving instructions to the funeral director, Mr. Snieder, "Kacy always told me that if she died first, I was to plan a big funeral for her at Prophet Baptist Church. It should be the biggest funeral I could afford, and it had to have all the good singing and music and tributes we could come up with. Little did either of us know that Kacy's request would be granted so unexpectedly," Eva reminisced to Mr. Snieder.

Clifford walked into the kitchen to hear the end of his wife's conversation with Mr. Snieder. "I called Rev. Ellwood. He'll have to do this one. I don't believe I will be able to hold up. And anyway, he can do a better service than anyone in the world."

The next call was to the Minister of Music, Kenneth Hackett. Kenneth was down in Houston, Texas, at the Gospel Music Workshop of America. Larry Corley answered the phone.

"Hi, Eva. How are you? You know Kenneth's not here. How can I help you?"

"I'm working on Kacy's funeral. You know how she loved going to church at Prophet, not just because she met her fabulous redhead Ozzie there, but she loved the music and, and . . ." Eva had to stop because tears started to flow.

"Larry I need you to bring in some people for Kacy's funeral. It will be next Wednesday. Can you put it together for me?"

"Eva, you know I'll do that for you. Pull yourself together and don't worry about a note. Kenneth and I will do you proud. Don't you worry."

"Thanks, Larry. Turn me over 'cuz I'm done. You take it from here!"

"If you need anything else, just call us. Bye, Eva."

Because Larry and Kenneth had been in the world of gospel music for so long and were board members of the GMWA, Gospel Music Workshop of America, in the space of just five phone calls, Larry had the crème de la crème of the Gospel world locked up.

"Hello, Tremaine Hawkins? This is Larry Corley at Prophet Baptist church in San Mateo. A very important person in our congregation has died, and I've had a request to get you and some other people to sing at the funeral. Are you available next Wednesday?"

"For you, Larry, and only for you. Fax or email me some information and a map and I'll be there. Tell me about the person who died."

Larry explained who Kacy was and the circumstances under which she died.

"Larry, I don't believe it!" Tremaine said in dismay. "I was at John Dandy's last party and met the lady from that bakery. They did the greatest cake for John. Their coffee crunch cake is my favorite, though. That's too bad that someone killed her partner. I'll be glad to offer my services."

"Thanks, Tremaine," Larry said. "I have others to call. You know Kenneth Hackett from the Gospel Workshop? He's the head minister of music at Prophet; he knows your charts. And this is a paid gig, Tremaine. Can you believe it? So many people want us to perform gratis. Not this lady; she's class all the way! You get paid!"

Larry made similar calls to Donnie McClurkin and Billy Preston. Both also said yes. And with the help of Producer Derrick Wade out of Los Angeles, an entire package was put together that would have made any gospel promoter envious.

Prophet Baptist Church had enough good voices and musicians to fill in the rest, and the choir stand would be filled to capacity.

Larry dictated this message into a tape recorder, so he wouldn't have to repeat everything to Kenneth. "Tremaine will sing *Precious Lord Take My Hand, Christ Is All,* and *The Potter's House*. Willie Swann, one of the locals, will sing *Well Done* and *What A Friend We Have In Jesus*. I'm going to sing *Deep River* and *Soon I Will Be Done*. Billy Preston, the greatest gospel organists in Christendom, will do what Billy Preston is known to do. The coda will be *Just a Closer Walk With Thee* not the jazzy New Orleans version but the sacred, slow, religious version, with all the verses. When the words from *Just a Closer Walk with Thee* are listened to, that song becomes one of the most sacred on earth."

Next, Larry called Eva back and repeated the roster to her. "I left a message for Kenneth, and I'm sure he'll get back to you. Do you like the lineup, Eva?"

"Wow!" Larry, that was quick," Eva exclaimed. Everyone you've chosen has won Grammy and Stellar Awards. Do you think we can afford them?"

"Eva, just leave it to me and Kenneth. This will be some home-going."

"It's in your hands, Larry. Spare no expense. For Kacy, we won't worry about the checkbook. I'll talk to you later, and thanks."

◊

Eva made another call to the funeral home. "Mr. Sneider, I want a white hearse, white limousines we will probably need three. Family and the bakery staff will fill three vehicles. White flowers and a white casket. Since we've done most of this by phone, I'll stop by the mortuary Sunday to pick out a casket. And, of course, the flowers will be the concern of the florist, not yours.

"I would also like the funeral home staff to dress in white. White tuxedos, I think."

"Ma'am, we would like to do that, but it would be an expense for our staff," Mr. Sneider hesitated.

"Can you do this, Mr. Sneider? Go to Selix Formal Wear, over on Third Avenue. Just order what you need for Wednesday. Send me the bill."

"Okay, Mrs. Garrett. We can do that."

Eva requested that all of the pallbearers dress in black. The pallbearers were able to grant that request.

In the living room of the family home, Ozzie said to Tina, "I can't stop crying."

"Neither can I, Ozzie. There is hollowness in my soul. I'm just empty. A ticket home wouldn't have cost that much. I should have come home when my mom first called." Tina was kicking the hell out of herself because she felt she should have insisted on coming home when she first received the call about the breast cancer.

"My mother's dead. Not just dead, but killed! Killed by who or whom, nobody knows. The police have no clues."

"Tina," Ozzie sniffled, "I didn't know how much I loved her. The light didn't come on until she told me she had cancer. We dated, we went places together. I knew I loved her, but I didn't say it enough. I showed it in my actions. We didn't date other people. . ."

"Ozzie, I guess our lesson is to let people know how much we love them. You can't just show it. You have to say I love you. Don't wait. Tomorrow isn't promised to any of us," Tina murmured, wiping her nose.

◊

At 10:15 A.M., Wednesday morning, pulling up in front of Prophet Baptist Church, the family and friends piled out of the white limousines. Their arrival was early for the 11:00 A.M. service. They had time to mill around, talking to early guests like Sister Piranha, Sister Slicker-Than-Grease, Sister Johnson, Sister Samms, and Sister Don't-Sit-In-My-Pew. They also had to wait for the minister and others to gather on the sidewalk outside of the Prophet.

Lillian and Andrew wandered to the cement bench on the side of the church and sat down.

"Darn it, Lillian, I can't sit, don't want to stand! Mom's gone to the back of the church to the Pastor's office, so I'm going to walk over to King Center."

"Okay, Andrew. I'm edgy, too. Can't sit and don't want to walk, and I think I'm getting a headache. I have some aspirin in my purse. I'm going to look for some water."

"See you in a few," Andrew waved as he headed for King Park that was at the next corner down from the church. As he approached, he saw some wannabe jocks on the basketball court. Snake and Bucky were shooting hoops. Seated at a picnic table near the court were Ernie, Kelton and Fergie.

Reacie was just walking out of the recreation center's side door on his way to the funeral. He saw Andrew and veered over, saying, "Hi, Andrew! What ya doin' here?"

"I had to get away from the church and the old biddies, so I came over here to say hi to the homies. Lillian was getting a headache and those folks from the bakery wanted to talk about the murder. That's not what I wanted to talk about right now."

Reacie waved at the group of guys on the court, "See you guys later. We're going to the funeral."

Andrew turned around and Reacie joined him on the route back to the church.

"Man," Andrew said to Reacie, "Morris Brown University did you up brown! Who'd a thought a stint in Atlanta and a degree in Sports Education would have brought you back to good ole San Mateo."

Reacie was now a recreator at Martin Luther King Jr. Community Center in San Mateo, making a good salary and happy to see his old high school compadre Andrew. Reacie responded, "Man, I was coming to the funeral, specifically to see you. I've been at the Center for about eighteen months now, and I have good rapport with the folks here. I get to hear a lot of 'chit.' The word I hear on the street is that a couple of 'dung drops' who hang around here from time to time had something to do with your Mom's friend's death. They tell me they know who killed her."

Use specific color

Andrew said, "Man, why didn't you call me? Not now though. Hold it 'til after the funeral. I don't think I can take that type of information right now."

"Okay, Bro," Reacie countered. "But I can't talk to ya after the funeral. I have a meetin', but I'll call ya."

"Yeah, Dude, give me a call at the old house out on 37th." Andrew and Reacie separated. Reacie took an elaborate, colored program from the usher and was shown a seat.

Eva was standing at the door with Rev. Ellwood. "Mom, where's Lillian?" Andrew asked as he approached the front of the church.

"Someone told me they saw her in the social hall. She'll get here at the last minute," Eva answered.

The organ started and they lined up behind Rev. Ellwood with Tina, Ozzie, and the staff from the bakery.

◊

Lillian was this close to a headache. She wandered into the social hall and didn't see anyone she knew. Some of the church sisters were putting condiments and utensils into boxes to take over to King Center, where the after the funeral meal would be served.

Lillian walked up to a window from where food was served. Two young women working with the church sisters saw Lillian walk up, but ignored her. Most people who didn't know Lillian thought she was a white person and whites were in the minority of the congregation at Prophet. The conversation the two girls were having with each other was the most important thing they were doing. To hell with "Malibu Barbie," (Lillian) she could just stand there for all they cared.

The girls continued to disregard Lillian's presence, when Lillian interrupted, "Do you have a glass? I would like a drink of water."

Chapter 36
Sharing Information

about

"Now that I dun hert they kilt that woman whose funeral it is today, I'm staying away from um. Junebug and them needs to quit all that stuff they doin'. This is gone too fur."

The one talking looked up and finally acknowledged Lillian. They knew they weren't talking softly but what did this white woman know? She wouldn't know anything bout what goes on in the hood, and she hadn't been standing there that long, had she?

?

"Ma'am, kin I hep you?" One of the girls finally spoke.

"Yes," said Lillian, exasperated. "I need a glass. I would like to get some water."

"We ain't got no glasses in heyah." There were glasses. The young heifer just didn't want to get one. "Kin I gitcha a papah cup?"

usually refers to males

Lillian nodded, "That will do just fine."

The girl handed Lillian a Styrofoam cup. Lillian took it with plenty of attitude and walked away.

"Thank you, ladies," she clipped curtly over her shoulder while walking toward a water fountain near the door.

Whoa! They didn't care if I heard them or not. I guess I'm supposed to be invisible, Lillian thought to herself.

"Didn't make no difference. She don't know what we was talkin' about," one girl acknowledged to her buddy after Lillian left.

As Lillian stepped onto the sidewalk, exiting from the social hall, she heard the organ playing. Lillian popped the aspirin she had fished from her purse into her mouth. Slurping the water, Lillian ran to the front of the church just in time to catch Andrew and Eva heading down the aisle behind Rev. Ellwood, Tina, and Ozzie and the entourage of ministers and friends from the bakery.

The funeral was heart wrenching. The ushers provided fans, tissues, and water to Ozzie, Tina, and several of the bakery staff. They became so emotional that some of them had to leave the sanctuary. Although Rev. Ellwood preached one of his best services, he had to stop several times because the volume at intervals crescendoed through the church.

His most meaningful message to the congregation was, "Don't worry about today. Your name is in the guest book. You'll get a thank-you for your flowers and good wishes. You have hugged and kissed the family. It is not today that they'll need you most. It will be tomorrow and next week and next month. That's when they'll need you to stop by with that meal, that hug, and those consoling words.

"Your presence here today is wanted and needed, but there will be days in the future when this family, Tina, especially, will need to hear from you. Send her a card. Not today, but in the future.

"Now, all who want to go to the cemetery, please see the funeral director to get a placard for your car. Amen."

◊

On the way to St. John's Cemetery, near Hillside High School, the procession became one of the longest the city had ever seen. Due to the extra police that had to be put on, Eva vowed to herself that she would make a huge contribution to the Police Athletic League when things settled down.

Standing behind the family at the cemetery, Mr. Sullivan commented to Mr. Snieder, his partner, "Do you know what

Mrs. Garrett told me she is going to do the minute this funeral is over?"

"No, I don't. What did she say?".

"She said, 'When your city does wonderful things for you, you should give something back, if you're able.' That's what she said. She's one of the most generous women I've ever come across."

"You're right about that. I saw the bill for these white tuxedos. She's generous all right."

Mrs. Samms and Mrs. Johnson were also at the graveside service. They didn't want to miss a detail.

"Those girls sure are able to do the best of everything. White limos, white flowers, Tremaine Hawkins, Donnie McClurkin, an Lawd, Billy Preston I thought I had died and gone to heaven myself. She obviously didn't spare a dime," Mrs. Samms confided to Mrs. Johnson.

"You're right, Ms. Samms. Eva toe it up at this funeralizing. She just toe it up! Them gals was equal partners in everything they did. That business brings in plenty money. The gals were talented. One took up where the other one left off. What a business they have at that bakery," Sister Johnson said.

"Mrs. Johnson, both women used their talents and helped each other. 'Even-Steven' right down the line. None of this superiority stuff because one was white or one was in business. One didn't look up or down at the other. They believed in being equal. Their relationship was like a marriage. Together those talents melded. Now, one of them is gone. Killed by somebody or other. I wonder if the police will ever solve this thing?"

"I don't know, Mrs. Samms. I just don't know. But let me correct you. My marriage certainly wasn't like their partnership. My marriage was, 'Me Tarzan, you Jane!'"

◊

After the trip to the cemetery, Ozzie and Tina had the limo driver take them back to the house. They didn't feel up to being with a throng of people. In the limo going to 37th Avenue, Ozzie and Tina were talking at each other, each in their own world.

"Tina," sniffed Ozzie, "your mom and I were going to be married. I missed the biggest and best opportunity that ever came my way. We should have married."

"Ozzie, I should have come home. She wouldn't let me. She wanted me to stay in school, to keep my grades up. We were going to talk on the phone twice a day."

"Somebody said you need three hugs a day. I wanted all my hugs to be from your mother. I loved to hug her. She was my 'main squeeze.' I was helping your mom in the tutoring program one day and heard a kid use the term 'main squeeze.' It fit your mom. She was the main, major, number one woman in my life."

◊

"Andrew, will you please do the explaining. People are going to want to know why Tina and Ozzie aren't at the reception. I want to save my voice. I'm getting a sore throat, and I'm worn down. You be the family spokesman, okay?"

Eva, Lillian, and Andrew were in another limo by themselves on their way back to King Center.

"Sure, Mom, no problem. I'll explain it. People will understand that Tina's distraught because she was in New York when Kacy died. They'll understand."

"People saw how Tina performed at the funeral," Lillian added. "I told her where the sleeping pills are and told her to take a nap. Ozzie needs a nap, too. I hope they both take a pill. Reverend Ellwood had to stop the service four or five times so some of the people could compose themselves. Several of the stops were due to Ozzie or Tina."

Soon the only sound to be heard was the whip, whip, whip of the tires on the road and the hum of the engine. Eva, Lillian, and Andrew were deep in their own thoughts of beautiful Kacy and the impact she had had on their lives.

Lillian was also thinking about what she overheard in the social hall and Andrew's thoughts were intermingled with Kacy and the information Reacie started to share with him on their way to the funeral.

Back at the center for the meal and reception, Eva, Lillian and Andrew felt as though the afternoon would never be over. Finally, the crowd had dwindled. "Andrew and Lillian, thank those who are left, please. I'll be waiting for you in the limo."

Andrew and Lillian made their escape and almost ran to the long white car that was idling at the curb in front of King Center with their mother seated inside and not able to be seen through the tinted windows.

On the way to the homestead on 37th, "Why'd the driver take this route?" Lillian asked. "We're going by the bakery."

"I told him to come this way," Eva said, choking up.

On the front door hung a big black ribbon, a small sign stated, "Closed due to a death in the family."

"Mom," Andrew said, "Rei told me they all came in at four this morning to fill the orders. There were twelve cakes to be picked up. Did you know the staff paid for a temp to come in, in order to take care of the customers?"

"No", Eva sniffed, "The little stinkers didn't tell me a thing. I'll have to give them a big bonus for coming in so early and thinking to bring in a temp. Wait 'til I get them. They're all so sweet. Kacy would never have wanted customers to go without their cake."

◊

At the family house, as the three of them passed the living room, they noticed that Ozzie and Tina had been in there. Tina's jacket was on the piano bench and two programs from the funeral were on the coffee table. Eva, Andrew and Lillian continued to the kitchen, made a pot of coffee and sat around the table.

"Ozzie and Tina must be taking a nap," Andrew said in a low voice.

"They're allowed," Eva said.

The phone rang, Eva picked it up, "Hi Mrs. Garrett," came the cheerful voice of Reacie. "Andrew, it's Reacie."

"Reacie, how are you, Hon?" Eva asked. "When are you coming by? Just because you have that nice po-zi-tion," Eva teased, "doesn't mean you have to be a stranger."

"Okay Mrs. Garrett, I'll be by to see you before long. May I speak to Andrew, please?"

"Sure, sweetheart," Eva said.

Andrew headed out of the kitchen to pick up another phone. When she heard Andrew say "Hello," Eva hit the off button and laid her instrument on the table.

Lillian deep in thought, elbows on the table, chin in hand, was sitting quietly.

Eva placed her hand on her daughter's shoulder, "You okay, Hon?"

"Yeah, Mom," she sighed. "I'm okay. I'm just mulling over something I heard today in the social hall. I went to get some water - that's why I was almost late for the beginning of the service. Two young hoochies I'd call them, were talking to each other, and I don't believe they knew I was standing there as long as I had been. Or, if they did know I was standing there, it didn't seem to make any difference to them. It's more like they were trying to ignore me. Didn't know I was 'the Black thing', you know!" Lillian shrugged her shoulders and contorted her face, adding, "But they had the oddest conversation."

Lillian related the conversation to Eva. "Mom, you remember when Kacy was trying to help some boys and she mentioned two odd names? I believe the names were Skeet and June, or Junebug. Do you remember that?"

"Girl, you have got to be joking!" exclaimed Eva. "Are you sure you heard Junebug? Who can forget a name like June? I remember that name!"

"Mom, I'm positive and I can't get it out of my mind. This is one of those 'said what I meant' times."

"Lillian, you can't be serious."

"Mama, I know that's what I heard. I know it! I thought about it during and after the funeral. I thought I was going nuts, but I know that's what I heard those girls saying."

Andrew was walking back into the kitchen. He interrupted. "What did you hear the girls saying? And what girls are you talking about?"

Lillian explained to Andrew what she'd heard the hoochies talking about in the social hall before the funeral.

Andrew's eyebrows began to raise. "What, Sis? I can't believe what you're saying! Do you know I had a crazy conversation with Reacie before the funeral? He called to bring me up to date and to finish what he started to tell me this morning. Sis, did you say Junebug?"

Lillian nodded her head and repeated, "Yes, I said Junebug."

"Damn, Lillian," Andrew blurted. "There can't be too many people in San Mateo named Junebug! Reacie was telling me about two 'crud-buds' who hang out at the center and cause havoc. Also that the word on the street has the two characters involved in Kacy's killing."

"If the word on the street is that good," Lillian sputtered belligerently, "why aren't the cops able to infiltrate?"

"I don't know that answer, Sis," Andrew shrugged, "but Reacie said Skeet and Junebug are slicker than snot on a doorknob and have been getting away with stuff for years. They have a tight network, but this time many of the homies are scared. Reacie said most of the brothers can see through the undercover cops San Mateo puts on the street, but they still talk to each other. He also said this damn city needs more Black cops. More cops of color period. They want Black cops to have Ph.D. brains, when they hire dumb- ass white boys every time they do the hiring. But they seem to do all right when it comes to hiring women. They surprised everyone when they hired a woman Chief.

"I know some of the bloods aren't happy with this police force. A lot of them say they're still being harassed, profiled," Andrew confided.

"Yeah, Lillian remarked, "The new cops like to use the King neighborhood for 'Junior Nazi' practice. Two guys have hired lawyers about the profiling that's been going on. People thought it wasn't happening in San Mateo, but it is."

◊

The young men who were regulars at the center considered

Reacie to be cool. "I'm going to be with you knuckleheads on a daily basis, and I'll be bringing in a lot of new programs that I hope will suit your taste," he told them. "Also I want you to give me suggestions on what you think should be done around here." That's the speech he gave when he first got the job.

"Basketball!" was the chorus from the juvenile adults.

◊

"I'm going to invite medical people, some politicians and maybe even some celebrities to come and visit. Ya'll need to hear more about condoms, respecting women and turning down your sounds when you're in a residential zone. Especially here in the parking lot."

"You down wid it, man," one of the perennials shouted. "Ya sports da latest gear, drive a 'tallic blue Escalade an you bumps da sounds wid da best of 'um."

Reacie was top of the line: he gave, got, and earned their respect.

The young men under Reacie's sphere of influence still had a hard-on for Junebug and Skeet though, because of the way the dung-drop brothers had let those high school kids take the rap for them a few years back. The young male frequenters of King Center were willing to talk to Reacie about June and Skeet, but to no one else. And Reacie kept their confidence. He didn't even tell the cops.

sexual here?

◊

Eva sat listening to Lillian and Andrew, taking it all in. She picked the phone up from the table and called the San Mateo Police Department. Not getting her party, she left a message for a good friend, Detective Edwin McGinnes.

"Detective McGinnes? Edwin, dahling? This is Eva Garrett. Will you give me a call as soon as you can?" She left her phone number, clicked the off button and looked at her children, who were looking at her with startled expressions.

"Mom, why'd you call the police?" Lillian asked, in an unbelieving tone.

"Edwin is a great guy, and I want to know if he can find us a good – private detective."

Lillian and Andrew almost said in unison, on exhaled breath, "Mom, that's a great idea!"

Eva said, "I know it is. Your Mama can do something beside decorate cakes."

"How do you know Officer McGinnes, Mom?" Lillian asked.

"Do you remember the time we had a break-in at the bakery? The night the guy broke the glass door? When the police arrived, the poor boob was drunk and sitting in a refrigerator with the door standing open. He was lazily eating cold cake."

"Yes, Mom, I remember that," Lillian chuckled. "That's the guy who wanted to go back to Mexico and couldn't afford to buy a ticket."

"That's the one! That little break-in and a raise in my insurance rates were his ticket home. He wasn't dumb. He was just acting dumb with alcohol as his backbone that night.

"Eddie was one of the police officers who showed up. He started buying cakes for every occasion after that incident. We went to Jazz on the Hill and the Blues Festival down in Monterey together. Eddie's a big lover, but he loves all the ladies. Being part of a harem wasn't in my plans. We still go to lunch sometimes, and he stops by the bakery fairly often. He's nice, smart but not for me. And it doesn't hurt that he looks like Dennis Haysbert."

◊

Tina and Ozzie rose from their naps at about the same time. Ozzie came down the stairs and Tina came out of the bedroom that she and her mother used to share. They stepped into the kitchen at about the same time, too, joining the family.

Tina asked, "Were people able to understand why I wasn't there?"

Eva rose from the table, walked over to Tina and embraced her.

"Yes, Tina, they understood. How're you feeling? I hope you took some of those sleeping pills I left on the night stand."

"I'm fine, Eva. I'm going to be just fine. Sounds like my mom, doesn't it? She would always say she was going to be just fine." Tina began to well up. Tears streamed down her cheeks.

Ozzie crossed over to Tina, put his hand on her shoulder and squeezed. He looked funny with red spiky ends growing back on his head. Ozzie's uncombed red hair made him look a little like a "Chia Pet." Not in his face but definitely about the head. Although this was a somber moment, Eva, Lillian, and Andrew looked at Ozzie and they all thought, "Chia Pet" at the same time and started laughing.

Ozzie and Tina were startled as to why everyone was laughing. Tina looked up, with a hurt expression on her face, Lillian said, "Ozzie, man, you look like a Chia Pet."

Tina now looked at the tall redhead. Even she could see the resemblance and started laughing, too. Ozzie got the picture and they all went into convulsive, stomach-aching, laughter.

Eva grabbed her crotch and ran to the bathroom, exclaiming, "You people are going to make me pee my pants."

Eva flew to the small bathroom off the kitchen and barely made the toilet seat. When she came out of the bathroom, Lillian was on the floor with tears of laughter running down her cheeks. They were all still laughing and so was Eva.

"Lord have mercy, Ozzie! We'll be glad when you get that lovely red hair back. Everyone will be glad when you do." Eva continued to laugh, now holding her stomach!

As the laughter subsided, Ozzie said, "But I did it for my main squeeze."

Those words sobered up the group.

Eva and the staff shaved their heads to show support for Kacy while she was going through chemotherapy. But her tall redhead kept shaving his head. Everyone else had his or her hair back.

Lillian rose from the floor and sat back at the kitchen table. She looked at her mother and opened her mouth to say something. Eva shook her head no, very deliberately. Thankfully, the others didn't notice. Lillian lowered her chin and picked up her cup of now-cold coffee. Eva's daughter had been about to say something concerning the previous conversation relating to Junebug and Skeet, but Eva wisely didn't want to go there.

The family drifted into chitchat about the funeral. They brought out picture albums and reminisced about their lives with Kacy.

The doorbell began ringing and various friends and neighbors dropped in, bringing food and comfort.

Eva helped entertain the folks for as long she could. She finally gave all the kids a kiss, then gave them a slip of paper with Geraldine, the housekeeper's telephone number.

"Be sure to give Geraldine a call in the morning. This house is going to need a good straightening up. I have to get home to Clifford and see if he's had something to eat. He had to go teach right after the services. Gotta go take care 'uh mah main'," she said in mock ghettoese.

The next day, Eva received a call from Detective Eddie McGinnes.

"Eva, sweetie, how can I help you?"

Eva explained that she needed a private detective. "Someone at the bakery is putting their hand in the till and I need someone to look into it for me."

"Nothing to it, 'Hot Stuff'," Eddie cracked, "I've got a woman over in El Sobrante who I think can help you out. Great detective. She used to be with the Oakland PD. Sharp as a tack and a looker, too. I was going to marry her, but then. . ."

"Yeah, I know," interrupted Eva. "You were going to marry all of us. You're still a bachelor and will remain one until the day you die." They both laughed. Eva continued, "Thanks for the info, Eddie. You're an angel, as always. Thanks a million!"

"Okay, Eva. Let me know how it works out," Eddie ended his side of the conversation.

"I definitely will, Eddie. Thanks. Bye now." She clicked off the phone.

Chapter 37
Cheyenne

Detective Cheyenne Norman, Investigative Services,
Background Search Specialist
Professional, Ethical & Confidential.
Domestic - Corporate.
Will Find Information You Can't.
Call with your investigative needs - we can help!

Eva made an appointment to visit Cheyenne's El Sobrante office. Monday morning, while driving across the San Francisco/Oakland Bay Bridge to meet with Detective Cheyenne Norman, Eva remembered a conversation she'd had with the Dennis Haysbert mirror image, Ed McGinnes. Eva played her own brand of detective and took Eddie to lunch, so she could learn more about this Cheyenne person.

Eva invited Eddie for a quiet noon lunch at Cappellini's. Eddie swung by the bakery to pick her up. They drove to the underground parking garage at the railroad station and walked across B Street to the restaurant. Eddie ordered calamari steak and Eva order a crab salad. While waiting for the entrée to be served, they both enjoyed dipping crispy-crusted sourdough bread into saucers of oil and balsamic vinegar.

"Tell me more about this woman you recommended to me. I'm going to visit her next week," Eva said.

Eddie wiped his mouth with his napkin and began. "I remember Cheyenne telling me her family moved to Oakland when she was three. She attended the Oakland schools and knew she wasn't getting the best education because she heard about how bad Oakland schools were through the media. Cheyenne told me that due to the negative stuff she heard about the schools in Oakland, she became a library devotee. She spent as much time as she could at the Oakland Public Library, out at the Eastmont Town Center. That was just as the neighborhood was beginning to change," Eddie explained. "She was determined to get a good education. As she told me, 'Cheyenne Norman isn't going to be a statistic.'"

"Good for her. What made her so wise at such a young age?" Eva asked.

"During her growing years, Cheyenne told me, all she ever heard about was how downtrodden Native Americans were supposed to be, and she wasn't about to be what the dominant society chose for her to be. Cheyenne and her family weren't downtrodden. Her mother and father treasured education and they both had good jobs. Mom and Dad Norman always told her how great the Navajo were. They told her how education was passed on through word of mouth, much like among African people."

"Wow!" Eva said. "Everyone needs parents like that."

"Cheyenne would always brag to me that her people didn't need paper and pencil. They were able to use their memories and pass information on to the next generation. She'd say, 'I know paper and pencils are necessary tools and I need to use them, but I also know I come from greatness and that I have to develop my memory, just as my ancestors did. Why don't the media and the movies put more emphasis on that aspect of being Native in this damn country?'"

"This woman sounds like Lillian to me. Are you sure I should hire her?" Eva laughed.

"Eva, no one is as tough as your Lillian. Maybe Cheyenne is a mild version of Lillian. I've known your baby girl for almost her entire life, and Lillian will knock a person into next week and then give them a lecture. But, Cheyenne is a trained officer of the law.

She asks questions first and then lets that person run into her nightstick, accidentally on purpose. Nah, I'm just kidding. I don't think anyone in this world has a temper like Lillian."

"As her mother, Eddie, I have to agree with you about Lillian. Don't cross that girl."

Their entrées arrived. They thanked the waiter and dug into hot calamari and cold crab salad—as only Cappellini's could serve the two dishes. A glass of white wine for Eva and iced tea for Eddie rounded out the meal.

Eddie continued, "Cheyenne's grandfather had been in World War II and was a Code Talker. He knew the Navajo language and helped the US Forces defeat the Japanese because they couldn't break the Native American code. The code was concocted from the old Navajo, along with words and phrases that the Code Talkers made up."

Eva and Eddie finished lunch. She thanked Eddie for the information, and he drove himself back to the department office on Delaware Street. Eva chose to walk back to the bakery.

The memory of that conversation and the lunch spun through Eva's mind. She entered Cheyenne Norman's office and was pleased with the vision that rose from a desk and walked toward her with a hand extended and a warm smile.

Cheyenne was an impressive and stunning looking, thirty-something woman. She was about five feet two inches tall, with three-inch heels that brought her up to five-feet-five. Her skin was the color of a new penny. She wore her straight black hair parted in the middle and down to her tiny waist. She was wearing a light gray silk suit with a matching sweater.

After the warm greeting, Cheyenne inquired, "How can I help you, Mrs. Garrett? Ed McGinnes tells me there has been some theft at your store."

"That's the story I told Eddie because I don't want him or anyone else to know why I really need you. You may have to confide in a young gentleman named Reacie Florence, but he's the only one. Reacie has more information than my children and I do, and he works where some of the lowlife's involved in this puzzle hang out.

"Ed McGinnes said you would be able to do any type of investigation I would need. And the truth of the matter is, my dearest friend was murdered two months ago. My son and daughter and I have some suspicions and have heard rumors about people who might have done it or who might be involved."

Tears started forming in Eva's eyes. Cheyenne reached into a lower drawer of her desk, pulled out a box of tissue and pushed it over to Eva.

"Thanks, Ms. Norman." Eva dabbed at her eyes. "I'm still not over her death. Her name was Kacy Murphy. She was my friend and business partner." An hour and a half later, Eva completed the story.

"Thanks, Mrs. Garrett. That's bad business, but I think I can find something out for you. It's going to be a challenge, but I'll do my best."

"Ed gives you high marks. Now it's my turn to know more about you. What can you tell me about yourself?"

"Well, although I was born in Arizona, I'm an Oakland product: Franklin Middle School, McClymond's High School, the police academy, Oakland PD, Boalt Hall, assistant D.A. and now I'm a private investigator. In the Oakland PD, we had the opportunity to rotate. I served a year on patrol, a year in narcotics, a year as a detective, a year as a community officer and so on. I found my calling in the detective bureau. I juggled school and work. But after awhile, sending the same people to jail and hearing their sad stories over and over again made me feel I wanted to try something different - and *voilà*, here I am in this one-woman operation. I get many referrals from my old colleagues and sometimes I work with a friend in San Mateo, a guy named Rick Sanzeri. And, of course, you know my old sergeant, Ed McGinnes!"

"Yes, I do know Ed McGinnes. When did he say he wanted to marry you?"

"Mrs. Garrett, he didn't pull that stuff on you, too?

"Yes, Cheyenne. He pulls that stuff on all the ladies. He's so damned handsome, I wish I could have taken him up on it. But Eddie loves all females."

"You're right about that, Mrs. Garrett. But every time I see that Haysbert guy in those commercials, I think of Eddie."

"Me, you and a thousand other women, Cheyenne. You can call me Eva. And I hope we can be on a first name basis. What tribe are you?"

"I'm Navajo on my Dad's side and Pima-Maricopa on Mom's side."

"Aha, Salt River, about ten miles east of Phoenix."

"How'd you know that, Mrs. Garrett? I, I, mean Eva."

"A little bird who looks like Dennis Haysbert told me about your background, and I thought I'd do some research on my own."

"That's nice, Mrs. Garrett. I'm flattered."

"But one thing about you that I couldn't find through research. Why would a Navajo/Pima-Maricopa be named Cheyenne?"

"My mom and dad have a sense of humor. They knew people would ask, and they said they wanted me to have an important name. Cheyenne kind of sticks out, and I love it."

"I think it suits you to a tee. It's a lovely name! Just don't forget, I'm Eva."

◊

"Mrs. Garrett. . . Oh, it's going to take getting used to calling a client by her first name. I'll need a retainer. I charge two hundred and fifty an hour. I'll submit weekly bills in the mail."

Cheyenne rose, went to the file cabinet and pulled out a contract. "This is standard procedure, Eva. Umm," she chuckled, "I remembered. You can take it with you so you can read it carefully and send it back by mail."

Pulling out her Mount Blanc pen, Eva said, "No need. There's a song we sing at my church: *I've come this far by faith, leaning on the Lord.* I'm praying you'll be successful in finding something." Eva signed the bottom line on the contract.

"Please call me on my cell phone, if and when you have information," Eva said. "No need to bother calling my home phone. We wouldn't want to disturb the good Reverend." Eva winked at Cheyenne and rose to leave.

Walking to the door, Cheyenne said, "Thank you for the retainer and the name of Mr. Florence, I'll have to get inside and learn the lay of the land."

"No, Cheyenne, I thank you," Eva said. "I expect you to do a great job, and I expect you to do it quickly. I know this money will go fast, but keep the bills coming and send them to me at the bakery in a plain envelope, please. No need for too many people to know my business."

"Gotcha!" said Cheyenne.

Stepping out into the sunshine, Eva felt a sense of relief.

◊

Cheyenne Norman was able to come up with a good-looking fake ID. With her connections through San Mateo City government, she also landed a part-time job at Martin Luther King, Jr. Community Center. Cheyenne knew some people, who knew some people, who knew some people. And through the Mayor of San Mateo, a real nice Black woman, Cheyenne was a temporary hire with the City of San Mateo.

Cheyenne and Reacie Florence met in a private room at the San Mateo Police Station. Detective McGinnes provided the space. Detective Norman was waiting in the room when Reacie arrived.

With hand extended, "Reacie Florence, my name is Cheyenne Norman. I'm here to do some undercover work for Mrs. Garrett. No one is to know what I'm doing, but because some of the information the Garret family needs was provided by you, I'd like you to be a silent partner in this investigation. You will be sworn to secrecy."

"Ms. Norman, are you telling me that even Detective McGinnes doesn't know the true nature of your being here?" Reacie asked.

"That's right, sir. The fewer people who know what's going on, the better. Mrs. Garrett wants Ed McGinnes to think I'm working on some thefts at the bakery. Mrs. Garrett is my employer and, that's the way she wants it to be.

"Reacie, I'll be working with you at the Center. McGinnes thinks some of the dudes who hang out there may be friends with the dishwasher or the janitor at the bakery. That's the connection for him. I've already been to the Center and looked around. I've done my surveillance at night, so I know the layout of the area. From today on, I'll be known as Sally. The last name will remain Norman. I've filled out all the employment papers as Sally Norman."

"Sally it is," Reacie said. "I'll fill you in on what I know so far."

During the two hours Cheyenne and Reacie spent together at the Police Station. Reacie told her everything he knew about the word on the street and the turd brothers, Skeet and Junebug. And he told her how the Center was run and some of the local color. Cheyenne's assignment started Monday morning at 8 o'clock. Her job was as Reacie's assistant for after-school activities.

◊

That afternoon, in the Center lobby, one of the guys yelled. "Hey, Reacie! Introduce us to Ms. Fly."

"Guys, this is Sally Norman. She is going to be my assistant. Don't bug her!"

"How'd you find her, Reacie? She sure is fine."

"Woo, woo, woo!" One of the guys feigned a movie Indian war whoop.

"Hey, Pocahontas, ya need a date?" another jerk in the crowd asked.

"She's a little on da thin side, but I'd shake the sheets fuh 'er."

Sally was wearing her hair in two long braids with a beaded headband across her brow. She wore tight jeans and topped the jeans off with a basketball jersey and a Starter jacket.

"Now," said Cheyenne, "Whose Momma did I see out there on the corner sellin' somthin' stinky!"

"Ooooohhh, she sure capped on you!"

"Not on me. She talkin' bout yo Momma!"

"I'm talkin' bout all yall's mamas. My name is Sally Norman. I'm here to help Reacie keep your sorry butts doin' something positive. I'll be as nice to you as you let me be."

"Okay, Ms. Sally. I gotcha back!"

"Sistah Girl, sound like she's gon be okay."

"Welcome, Ms. Sally. Glad ya here."

After she weaned them from the Pocahontas and other stereotyped Indian/Native American bullshit, she was in.

"Anyone who doesn't understand how to give respect as well as demand it is going to be singing soprano. I'm a Viet Nam vet. When I was over there, I rearranged several male anatomies. I sliced and diced and now I have several pairs of cojones draped on my dresser mirror."

"Man, what's cojones?"

"Nuts, dummy. Nuts!"

"Dayum!" And several of the guys grabbed their crotches.

"Baby, you just think you bad. If you wuz mines, I'd put some meat on ya an whup ya inta shape," one of the guys proclaimed.

Sally countered. "Baby, if you wuz mine, I'd have you on a leash. Woof, woof!"

The guys roared, "Woof, woof, woof!" And did the howling that used to be done on the Arsenio Hall show. Cheyenne was in solid with this crowd.

These guys loved what was between their legs better than anything else and they got the not-so-subtle hint. But they were really dumb. If they had been able to do basic calculations, they would have realized Sally was too young to have been in Nam.

These boy-men were stuck in the famous old rut of "nothing but basketball."

More dudes came into the lobby to meet Sally. "Hey guys, I'm handing out a questionnaire. I want to know what types of activities you're interested in. Fill out this sheet. I'll compile the results and we'll see what new and innovative things we can do."

"Sally," Reacie said, standing by her side, "You're wasting your time. These dudes are interested in basketball. Plain and simple bas-ket-ball. They don't want to learn to play chess, and they don't want to play checkers. They don't want to play Scrabble! In fact, most of them can't play Scrabble—they can't spell. There are twelve computers to work on in the library, and they won't touch 'um. They're too afraid someone will find out they don't know how to read."

"Reacie, that's awful. I'm here to help. But if it's basketball and sports, we have to go for what we know."

The questionnaires came back with most of the boxes empty and with some of the poorest writing and printing Cheyenne had ever seen. Scribbled all over the questionnaires was pick up games, organized games, horse, new slam dunk methods, one on one, two on two - just basketball.

"Good googa mooga!" Sally exclaimed. "How many of you guys own your own portable baskets? Those contraptions are in every driveway and yard in the neighborhood." Almost every hand shot up.

"I'm going to introduce as many new activities as I can, but you guys are a tough crowd. I think I'm going to have to call in some backup." At home that evening, she went to the phone and called her old friend, Dr. Harry Edwards.

Cheyenne knew Harry well. He had been her brother's roommate when the two were freshmen at San Jose State University. Dr. Edwards was now the premier person in the field of Sports Sociology. This was a new academic discipline in the United States, One that he started back in 1968, after the Black Power Salute Olympics in Mexico.

"Hi, Mrs. Edwards. This is Cheyenne Norman. Is Dr. Edwards in?" Cheyenne always displayed a professional manner toward Mrs. Edwards. Although Cheyenne was many years younger than Harry Edwards was, she considered him one of the finest hunks on the planet. Detective Norman wanted to say to Mrs. Edwards, "Girl, your husband sure is fine!" But Cheyenne knew what Aretha was talking about: R-E-S-P-E-C-T! Single women don't hit on married men. Ah! At least Cheyenne didn't hit on married men.

"Hi, Cheyenne," Mrs. Edwards greeted her warmly. "Yes, he's in. I'll get him for you."

"Hello."

"Hi, Harry! It's me, Officer Norman, although I'm not Officer Norman anymore. I'm doing private investigation. I have a case over in San Mateo and I need your help. My cover is a job at a recreation center. I'm working with some hardheads and to impress them, I need to invite some Warriors, Kings, Giants, A's and Sharks to give me a hand. I have some contacts, but I need a steady stream of guys to help some wannabes with attitudes."

"Cheyenne, fax me a schedule and I'll get the office to set up some folks for you. I'd love to talk more, but I have a meeting downtown. You know I'm running Oakland Park and Rec these days."

"Yes, I do. And that's a deal, Harry. I still have your fax number, so the info will be there tomorrow morning. Thanks for your help. Good night."

Cheyenne had become friends with Harry and many other athletes when she was an Oakland police officer and headed the Oakland Police Athletic League for a year. All of the professional athletes she worked with respected her because she was all business and not a groupie.

Of course, the brothers in the Oakland Police Department thought Cheyenne Norman was the bomb personified. They didn't mind giving compliments to this police officer. Her fellow male officers were fond of her yet careful to not cross the sexual harassment line. They appreciated her as a team player and a good-looking female. "Fine as wine in the summertime," "Foxy Brown," and other such compliments always came her way at the Oakland PD, and they weren't all from the brothers. But wise Cheyenne took the compliments and made sure to do her dating outside of the force.

Back at King Center the next day, Cheyenne thought to herself, "Okay, okay. I'm not in here for the long haul. I'm going to get in, get the information and close the case."

Sitting at her desk, she stopped Reacie as he walked by. "Hey, Reacie, what are the best pizza places around here? I'm not above playing cheap tricks. Food always mellows people out. Plus bringing in professional sports friends, I'm going to take the guys out for pizza or bring it to the center. We're going to eat hot dogs, hamburgers, ice cream, doughnuts and as much food as I can ply them with. I have a supply of sports chatchkes and goodies to give the guys, too. I think filling bellies and 'a Greek bearing gifts' will help loosen some tongues. Also, Harry Edwards, one of my old friends, is going to help me bring in a few names from local teams. With the help of some local stars, I'll finish this case quicker than fast!"

◊

Cheyenne met Skeet and June on several occasions. They were usually hanging around the basketball courts or just hanging around the park looking ugly. They both did that well. She was trying to stay out of their way though, because one day, from both Skeet and June at different times, there came a glimmer of recognition. Skeet and June both asked similar questions on separate occasions.

"Don Ah know you fum some place? Yo face is sho familar?" asked Skeet.

"Dayum, Sistah, I knows I knows you fum some place," remarked Junebug.

"I seen you someplace befo an just cain't place it," commented Skeet.

"Yeah, Skeet," Cheyenne said, "you probably saw me in some Western or at the rodeo. I'm a rodeo rider. Didn't you know?"

When June asked his question, she told him, "June, you saw me at the Fourth of July Parade in Redwood City. I was riding a pinto. That's where you saw me 'cause I saw you on the sidewalk."

"No shit, baby!" June replied incredulously. He was dumb enough to believe that line.

That she talked to Junebug and Skeet at all threw them. Most people who worked at the Center tried to ignore the older fellows. Their jobs were to work with the youth. Cheyenne came off as nice and friendly. Her explanation, except for the movies, sounded plausible. They just thought she was a hot mama, flip, and one of the "guys."

Later in the week, during a telephone report to Eva, Cheyenne reported, "Mrs. Garrett, uh, Eva, I've been close to the 'subjects', and now I have to keep my distance. I don't look the way they remember me, but they've seen me someplace before.

"I've read their rap sheets. They both have been arrested in Alameda County, and I know they've probably seen me in court, the lineup or something over there. They could have seen me in uniform, with my hair up, with more make-up on. Who knows? I may have been on a backup at one of their arrests. I realize that my little girl look, with the braids, has them baffled.

"They've been racking what they call brains, trying to put it together. When I see them coming, I get out of the room or off the playground. I don't think I'm a priority for them, though. Skeet and June are too busy selling, trying to get new recruits and ducking an honest day's living. But I'm learning a lot."

"You certainly are," Eva agreed.

"Bucky, Snake and a homeless man named Shoji all sleep under the bleachers at King Park. They tell me they had an altercation with June and Skeet the night of the murder. The homeless man is mute, but he writes on a note pad. Most people don't know he can do that. He is very secretive. But that puts the turd brothers as Reacie calls them in the vicinity. And I've been able to charm Shoji with hot tea in a thermos."

"Hot tea is a nice touch, Cheyenne. Your patience is worth paying for. I sure couldn't do it!" Eva reflected.

"It's not patience, Eva. It's being thorough. That's what you're paying me for. I also hear that Junebug and Skeet have been talking to some mules that used to sell for them. The mules are scared. They've been dropping big hints about the fatal, the night Kacy was killed. They only hold these conversations among each another. They don't know I'm listening, but I'm listening hard."

"Thanks, so much, Cheyenne. I hope we'll talk again soon. It looks like you're getting to the bottom of this crazy thing. I look forward to your next report."

"De nada. Goodnight, Eva!"

They clicked off.

Chapter 38
Ray & Stevie

"Hey, Sally," Reacie said. "Come with me. We've got to go over to City Hall to pick up some stuff for the meeting the brass is having here tonight.

"Do I have to, Reacie? I have some work to do."

"Sorry to take you away from your work. You can finish it when you get back."

In the car on the ride over to City Hall, Reacie confided, "I'm just following instructions. We can't talk too much at the Center. I wanted you to know I woke Bucky up this morning to get him from under the bleachers before the Little Leaguers come to play. He told me he was there at the Railroad tracks when Shoji kicked Skeet's butt couple a months ago. He told me Skeet had a gun, but Shoji took it away from Skeet and, then, for some reason, Shoji threw it back at him and June."

"I guess Shoji was letting them know he wasn't afraid of them, even if they had a gun. Shoji was telling them, if he could take it away one time, he could do it again," Cheyenne surmised.

"A little while later," Reacie continued, "Bucky and them heard gun shots and took off runnin' scared across the tracks toward Claremont Street. Bucky though, claims they didn't see anything."

"Glad you took me away from the Center, Reacie. All the stories I'm hearing are beginning to jell. Stinky stuff is beginning to stick to the Halitosis Brothers. When you get a chance to talk to one of the big shots in the city, please tell them their undercover folks are whack. Even Ray Charles and Stevie Wonder could see what those two nut buckets are up to! Those two guys are as transparent as windows at Macy's. The dudes at the Center have diarrhea of the mouth, but they become shellfish when San Mateo's lame under-covers show up," Cheyenne fumed.

Reacie added, "I think our folks down at the PD are trying to find out some deeper information on Skeet and June. Most folks think they are just middlemen for someone higher up. I have connections, too, ya know. Cops have to get stuff off their chests, but it's all confidential."

Reacie knew Cheyenne needed a breather from the intensity of the work at the Center, so they rode up to the College of San Mateo before going back to King.

On the way up I-280, Cheyenne closed her eyes and leaned her head on the leather rest as they rode and listened to some cool jazz from a Quincy Jones CD.

Turning into the campus drive, Cheyenne said, "I'm not going to pump you for information, Reacie. But I'm still learning what I needed to know. The two at the bottom of the killing of Kacy Murphy and the two at the bottom of a lot of shit in the King Center neighborhood are Junebug and Skeet. From the information I've compiled it looks like Scott Gonzales, Jr. and Jerome Wainwright are guilty as hell."

"I agree, Cheyenne, but now for a diversion. Since you're from the East Bay, I want you to see some San Mateo sites."

"Beautiful place, Reacie. Where are we?"

"This is 'Harvard on the Hill,' better known as the College of San Mateo to the uninformed. It has a great view from the eastern parking lots. I'm taking you there and I can point out where you live in Oakland from that vantage point.

"But, back to the main subject. Do Junebug and Skeet talk much when you're around, Cheyenne?"

"Nah, they don't talk to me. And I don't want them to, anyway.

I try to stay out of their way. I think they might have seen me sometime over in Alameda County. But they don't need to talk. Others do.

"In my opinion, they shouldn't be at the basketball courts at all. They're too old and their attitudes exude the fact that they think their shit doesn't stink. The only thing they could play for me, Reacie, is dead."

"I know how you feel, Cheyenne. They think they're above everything because they've gotten away with so much. But believe me, the cops know. This isn't their first murder, according to what I've heard. They've made others come up missing and the buck never stops at their door. But big brother is watching."

"Reacie, I don't understand it. Their crimes have taken place over the years, and they manage to stay out of the line of fire. Skeet and June have been in and out of jail most of their lives, but going in and out has only made them think they were like tarps. They think they can cover everything. Going to jail has only been part of their higher education," Cheyenne sighed. "I hope when the information is compiled, it will help put a stop to their bovine excrement."

◊

One day at King Park, during a bull session of Crime 101, the guys exchanged war stories, with Skeet and June as the major instructors.

"Man, when I was in jail, Ah learned how ta beat a dude so the bruises dint show. The cops taught me good. Deyed put ah bar uh soap in ah sock, an beat the shit outchew," Skeet bragged.

"Sheeit, man, you don know the haf. Lemme tell ya wud Ah do," June chimed in. If you dint want da dope took out cha pocket right away - all you wud do is vomik in ya pocket. 'Notha way to keep the cops from finding shit on you when you sellin' is you tawk to da brotha. That is if he be uh regalah. You cain't do dis with peeps ya don't know. Stash yo shit in the bushes foe you make da sale. You extricates a nickel bag and sits on the curb with the potential, an yo puts the shit on the sidewalk 'tween ya. Put ya groceries ovah the shit, or yo cap. You sit there and tawk shit fuh ah minute uh two.

Den ya shows respeck, grasp, shake, grip an tap da brotha's hand, an pass da change. Moo da groceries. Put da cap back on. Dey got da shit, an you git ya geetahs."

"Off da hook, man!" One of the listeners exclaimed.

◊

After nine weeks, Cheyenne felt she'd learned enough pertinent information for Eva to give to the San Mateo Police Department. She typed her report in full, called Eva and set up a meeting. At the meeting she gave Eva two very large folders.

"Ms. Norman, I want to thank you for a job well done. I'll go over this information and give it to the proper authorities, after my kids and I have given it plenty of thought," Eva said.

"Yes, Mrs. Garrett, I mean Eva, it took nine weeks. Just about the same time that it takes to give birth to puppies dogs, if you get my drift. Those guys, Junebug and Skeet are dogs."

Eva pulled out her checkbook and her Mount Blanc pen.

"Mrs. Garrett, I mean Eva, I'll send you a bill."

"That won't be necessary, Ms. Norman. I want to thank you. I have confidence that you've done a good job. This check should cover everything."

Cheyenne looked at the check and gave a slow whistle at the six figures. She rose from her chair, came over and pecked Eva on the cheek.

"Thank you, Mrs. Garrett."

Cheyenne Norman handed in her resignation at the Martin Luther King, Jr. Community Center and was out of sight, literally and figuratively.

Chapter 39
The Meeting

"Professor Webb, this is Lillian Garrett."

"Lillian. How are you? I understand that you're in California due to a death in the family." Arnold Webb was Lillian's forensics professor at Yale. "I'm going to take a few more weeks off before coming back to school. The funeral was devastating and I want to re-gather myself before heading back to Connecticut. Are there any outstanding assignments I can do on line?" She wanted to spend more time with Eva. And this respite would give her some time to mull over the offer that had been made to her by the International Olympic Committee.

"Lillian, the group came up with several subjects: Brokers, Drexel Burnham Lamber Files for Bankruptcy, Mikel Milken Pleads Guilty to Securities Fraud, Noriega Arrested in Panama by US Agents for Drug Dealing and Nolan Ryan Pitches a Record Sixth No-Hitter.

"All of us felt you would like the Nolan Ryan story, but the majority chose the Mikel Milken story. I want you to state an affirmative case for Milken."

"Yuk, I hate Milken."

"Then pleading his case will give you a stretch. I'll send you an outline to help with your preparation. The debate is in three weeks at Harvard."

"Thanks for being understanding Professor Webb, but Nolan Ryan and a sixth no-hitter - I'm salivating. I would have given anything to tackle Ryan. But, I'll do you proud and see you in two and a half weeks. Please give my regards to the group."

"I will, Lillian, and you take care of yourself."

"I'll do the best I can, Professor."

She was staying by herself at the family digs on 37th Avenue, where she, Andrew and Tina had grown up.

Andrew had taken a position in Silicon Valley with a group of venture capitalists and remained close to home.

Tina was back at Columbia, trying to pick up where she left off and get her life back on track. Family and friends in San Mateo, including Ozzie, kept in touch with her. She was, as Kacy would have said, doing just fine.

Eva called Andrew and Lillian early Thursday morning, asking them to meet her at Bogie's Restaurant that night for dinner. Bogie's was a classy little restaurant tucked in the back of a complex of shops that used to be the San Mateo Theater.

Andrew arrived first but took his time before going downstairs to the small private room with shuttered doors. He'd been there before to have intimate dinners with his mom and friends.

He took his time because Bogie's was famous for the old movie posters and photos the owner, Humdi Ugar, had collected over the years and displayed on the walls of the restaurant. The posters were of various sizes. Some of them were huge. Andrew noted that the text on several of the posters was in Turkish, Hungarian or French. Humdi had been born in Turkey and had taken a circuitous route to the United States as a young chef. It was obvious that he was a fan of everything Humphrey Bogart had done in his film career and Humdi had amassed quite a collection, including photos of Lauren Bacall, Peter Lorre, Sidney Greenstreet and several others.

The Bogart estate once called on Humdi, asking him to pay royalties for using the Bogart image. Mr. Ugar told those upstarts to take a flying leap. "Humphrey Bogart is my idol," he exclaimed. "This restaurant is a tribute to him."

Eva asked Humdi, better known as "Bogie" to his friends and customers, to make sure that after the meal was served, she and her children would be left alone and uninterrupted. She asked for a pot of coffee on a burner, a bottle of rum, some coke and ordered dinner for the kids, knowing what they loved. Filet mignon and vegetables for Lillian, calamari steak, mashed potatoes and green salad for Andrew and a big crab salad for Eva with extra crab.

When Andrew finished his tour of the Bogie exhibit, he went down the stairs and opened the shutter doors to the tiny, well-appointed salon that was perfect for intimate parties.

"Hi, Mom," he greeted, giving Eva a kiss. He sat down, noticing the thick folder that was on top of the charger plate and asked, "What's this, Mom?"

"It's Cheyenne's report. Please start reading."

Lillian made her appearance about five minutes later. She, too, took a tour of the upper floor to see if there were any new additions to the Bogie gallery. After completing her walkabout, she descended the stairs and entered the cozy room, complaining about the lack of parking; she'd had to use the valet. Settling in at the table, she leaned over, kissed her mother, and blew a kiss to Andrew, who barely looked up from his reading material.

"Doggone!" he whispered, putting the folder down.

"What's this all about, Mom?" Lillian asked.

Andrew interrupted, "It's the private detective's report on Kacy and who killed her," he said soberly.

◊

Eva ate more of her meal than Lillian and Andrew did. They asked long questions. She gave short answers, punctuated with, "You're going to read that in the report." Finally, they finished what they could of their meal and started on the coffee and rum and coke.

Eva, still seated, placed her hand on her left hip and began to explain as much as she could, emphasizing that the report was explicit and thorough. "Cheyenne Norman was worth every penny I gave her, plus the big bonus.

"Lillian and Andrew, I've read this report twice – once in stunned silence and the second time with a box of tissue. I've gone to the park on several occasions. I've walked the field. I've sat in the bleachers. I have been in the playground when Slug, Snake, Bucky, and all the rest were out there.

"First, I think it's a crime that people like Junebug and Skeet can use public facilities. I cringe when I know my tax dollars are being used by those creeps and others like them. They all need jobs, but they use the park to drink, do drugs, and God knows what else.

"The park is well kept. The playground equipment is state-of-the-art. The swimming pool is used by most of the community. But the park is also a safe haven for people like those two murderers.

"I've sat in the car and watched them. I've eaten my lunch at the picnic tables and watched them. I know who they are, and I'm seething inside. My stomach is upset, and my head hurts when I think about what's in this report.

"I want you both to read the report several times. I want you to digest it and do it slowly."

"What are we going to do, Mom?" both Lillian and Andrew asked.

"I've just given you your instructions. Read the report. Digest it – both of you. Then, we'll have another discussion.

"After the next tête à tête, I can hand this over to the Police Department, or I can do something about it, myself."

"Mom, what do you mean do something about it, yourself? You're not a murderer!" Lillian exclaimed.

"And you don't have an Uncle Guido who can do a hit for you. You're Black, not Italian. That's 'Godfather' movie stuff," Andrew added. "The Italians don't like Blacks anyway. I'll always remember that line in 'The Godfather' when the character said, 'You can sell the dope to the coloreds, those people don't have souls.'" Andrew quoted dolefully.

"I want you kids to internalize this report from Detective Norman. Get it down pat and when we've given the material a lot of thought, we'll discuss if we should turn the folder over to the Police Department. There is no statute of limitations on murder, so we have time to think about our options. And from what is in this report, we'll have to stand in line. These two characters have many sins to atone for," Eva said.

They finished off the coffee and Eva had one more rum and coke. They gathered up their belongings and went upstairs to an empty restaurant. Mario, the Maitre 'D, was usually at home by this time on a Thursday night. It was past twelve.

Eva walked over to him and put a fifty-dollar bill in his hand. "Tell Bogie I'll be here tomorrow to settle the bill," Eva told the sleepy man. The fifty is for your personal use. Thanks for staying so late for us, Mario."

Eva and her children went out to the street to find their respective cars. The valet attendant was miffed because he usually didn't have to stay this long either. Lillian scruffed through her purse until she came up with twenty-five dollars. She handed it to the valet, who immediately became a little happier because the bill was only five dollars.

"Good night, Miss. Good night!" The valet brightened as he handed her the keys for the car he'd already parked at the curb.

Chapter 40
McNairy's

Lillian called King Center as soon as it opened the next day and asked for Reacie. Reacie hadn't yet arrived so she asked to be put into his voice mail. "Reacie, the minute you get in would you please call me? This is Lillian." She left her number and hung up.

When Reacie arrived and heard the message from Lillian, he thought he had died and gone to heaven. Reacie remembered a conversation he'd once had with Andrew many years back when the two were high school buddies. "Man, would I like to date Lillian, but she's got such a sharp tongue and she's such a brain, I'd be afraid to ask her out."

"That's not a bad decision, Reacie. Lillian is my little sister, and I love her to pieces, but she'd probably eat you alive after cussing you out." Andrew laughed.

"Well, anyway Andrew, I didn't feel it would be right to date my best friend's sister."

Standing at his desk and thinking about the telephone message, Reacie chuckled to himself. Ms. Unapproachable Lillian is calling me. She has grown into one 'brick house.' She's the spittin' image of her very good-looking mother, just a paler version. Dayum, to what do I owe this opportunity? A call from the prettiest jock in San Mateo! My, my!"

He returned the call and was shutting the door to his office as Lillian was saying hello. He wanted some privacy to get next to "Miss Fine."

"Hi, Reacie," Lillian opened.

With all the warmth in the world in his voice, Reacie returned the pleasant greeting, but Lillian immediately started a rapid-fire inquisition.

"Tell me, Reacie, do you know anybody named Jerome Wainwright or Scott Gonzales? Do they come to the Center? Do people call them by Jerome and Scott? Where do they hang out? How can I meet them? Are you free tonight? I'd like to go where they hang out, and I need someone to go with me."

That's not quite what Reacie had in mind, but if he could get close to Lillian, he'd try anything. "Don't ask so many questions. Let me check my calendar to see if I'm free tonight."

Of course he was free, but he didn't want Lillian to know that he was just going to rent a movie and sit home alone to watch it. "They usually hang out at a little spot on the tracks called McNairy's. Are you sure you want to go there?"

"Absolutely sure! I'll meet you there around eight, okay? What's the address?"

"It's in the Tens block on Railroad Avenue. Between Cypress and First Avenue, close to the creek. Okay, Lillian. I'll see you then." He hit the off button. I'd better let Andrew know what's going on, he mused.

"Andrew Garrett here." Came the voice from the driver's seat of the metallic-maroon Porsche – top down, headed north on 101. "May I help you?"

"Yeah, man, this is Reacie. Where are you?"

"On my way into San Francisco for a meeting with some people who need money."

"How you doin', Andrew?"

"Fine, fine, fine and fine!" Andrew answered.

After a few more pleasantries, Reacie said, "Man, I just talked to your sister. You know I always wanted to get next to her, but I didn't think I had a chance and didn't think you would like it. But now she's no longer 'San Quentin Quail,' I can go for what I know."

"Yep, you sure can Reacie," replied Andrew. "You don't need my permission. So why the call?"

"Man, Lillian called and asked about those knuckleheads whose names I shared with you at the funeral. Now that Cheyenne's gone, I surmise that she's filled you folks in on the information she gathered."

"Yeah, Reacie," Andrew said. "Cheyenne finished her report and Mom's read it. Now Lillian and I are in the process of reading it. With Lillian's speed, I wouldn't be surprised if she hasn't finished it."

"Ahh!" Reacie said, "now the light comes on? Most of the questions Lillian asked me she already knew the answers to. I found it a little curious and," Reacie lied, "she wants to go on a date with me down to McNairy's. So I thought you should know."

"Veddy in-ter-esting," Andrew dragged it out. "When's the date?"

"Tonight at eight," Reacie continued and gave more details.

"I don't think my sister's thinking straight. I'm going to show up," Andrew said. "When I walk in, please act surprised to see me. Lillian will kill both of us if she thinks I'm checking up on her."

"Okay, man," Reacie said. "I'll see you tonight!" They both clicked off.

That night, three late-model cars pull up at three different locations near McNairy's on Railroad Avenue, between First and Cypress, near the creek, in San Mateo's hood.

Andrew parked at the lot across the tracks and lingered there a while, checking the place out. He wanted to let Reacie and Lillian get settled before he went in.

Reacie and Lillian arrived in time to meet each other at the door. They entered and Reacie raised his hand to the bartender, "Two Buds, please."

They found their way to the back where a funky little band was playing some Lowell Folsom-style blues.

"This place is a time capsule out of the 1940s," Lillian commented. "It looks like something out of *Cabin in the Sky* or *The Color Purple*. Really retro."

McNairy's was a true throw back to another era. There were

men and women, mostly Black, of every size, shape and color. "Miss Thang" waitresses held forth; they were a cross between slut and siren. Short skirts, halter tops, fishnet hose and high heels. One of them wove her way though the room with a tray of drinks and bottles of beer.

"Thank you," Reacie nodded as he put some bills on the tray.

◊

"Sure thang," responded Miss Thang, clunking the two bottles on the table of the booth that Lillian and Reacie had placed themselves in.

"Where on earth do places like this come from?" Lillian asked Reacie.

"I actually visited a few places like this when I was in Georgia. I didn't know they existed in California."

Lillian had been to clubs in San Francisco, New Jersey and New York, but this seemed to be right out of the juke joint lore of Mississippi, Alabama and yes, Georgia.

Their eyes became accustomed to the haze in the room. The smoking section did not isolate the smoke. Reacie and Lillian, seated in the booth, moved close to one another, so they could hear themselves over the little band that was now swinging a bluesy version of the classic, *Night Train*.

Reacie had been to McNairy's several times, but he didn't want to let Lillian in on that tidbit. As he pointed out this one and that one, he was pleased to be cheek by jowl with her.

◊

McNairy's was a huge rectangle. The floor was covered in green and black linoleum tiles. Along the walls hung posters of coming events at the Fillmore Auditorium in San Francisco, the Patio in Redwood City and Slim Jenkins in Oakland. After customers passed the L-shaped bar and mismatched chrome stools with various colored Naugahyde seats, an unplugged jukebox stood beside the small bandstand. There were booths that could seat four to six people on two of the walls.

Reacie and Lillian were seated midway along the north wall and could see the people at the bar and almost everyone who walked in.

"That's Corabelle Jackson sitting in the motorized chair," Reacie nodded his head in her direction.

"Should she be drinking beer?" Lillian asked.

"She's only legless. Why not? Little Donny is the small white man with the scraggly beard over in the corner."

"Who's that huge brown sister draped all over him?"

"Her name is Delilah Spirit. The Spirit kids live at the Center. Delilah's never at home. That couple across from us is Tennessee and Grady Kimball. They live in the apartment below me. Nice people."

"I know that guy with the round, brown, bald head," Lillian said. "That's Cabbage and the man he's with Red used to clean the bakery for Mom. Mom said he had red hair in his youth."

"That tall, thin, real dark guy is Blackgold. He used to work at the race track."

"I can see why he was given his name. That single large gold tooth and his complexion are a dead giveaway. But I would call him Black Fang," Lillian commented.

The music stopped and Lillian moved away from Reacie. Reacie didn't mind at this point. He had been so close to Lillian that their knees, arms and cheeks touched. Reacie was happy; he had touched Ms. Fine. He could tell Lillian's head was swirling with the colorful monikers and even more colorful people. They silently sipped their beers.

When the music started again, a hard knot of a woman walked into McNairy's. "That's Little Blue," Reacie said. "They call her that because they say she's so black, she's blue."

"Ooo whee, Reacie! Little Blue looks like she's been in the ring with Muhammad Ali. She has scars, welts and keloids all over."

Little Blue and her partner, an ex-Marine named Pickens, headed for the middle of the floor. Some other couples followed, because the beat of Amos Millburn's *Bad, Bad Whiskey* was too good to sit through. But Little Blue and Pickens were the gold cup winners for dance that night. Not that the others were bad dancers. The other couples danced jitterbug, slow drag and bop, each in his or her own way, but Little Blue and Pickens were Lillian's favorites.

The front door of the establishment opened again and a familiar figure entered the room and looked around. It was Andrew. Reacie, Lillian and Andrew saw each other at about the same time. "Andrew, over here!" Reacie beckoned.

Lillian growled, "What's he doing here?"

Reacie explained, "I thought I'd better let your brother know what was going on. I owe him that respect, if I'm going to date his sister." He kept emphasizing and teasing about the dating aspect of their being together because he knew he was irritating Lillian. And like a naughty schoolboy, Reacie was enjoying Lillian's irritation.

"This isn't a date, Reacie. We're just having a few beers and soaking in some of the local color," Lillian snarled.

She kicked Reacie hard in the shin. Reacie grimaced as Andrew reached the table and sat down.

"What's wrong with you, man? And thanks so much for acting surprised," Andrew asked and commented as he saw the pain in Reacie's face.

"Man, your sister just kicked me! She wanted us to have this wonderful evening by ourselves," he teased again.

Lillian kicked him again.

"Girl, would you stop?" Reacie said through his pain, bending to rub his sore leg.

"Hi, Bro!" Lillian said, not looking too happy. "And what surprise are you two talking about? Glad to see you. NOT!" Lillian griped. "You know I love you, but some things I want to do on my own, Andrew."

"Never mind the surprise. Private joke between me and Reacie. I know, Sis, but you're home now and big brother has to keep an eye on you."

"Humph," Lillian pouted, drinking a sip of her beer.

Reacie caught the eye of one of the Miss Thangs . . . "Three beers, please."

After the third beer and a wonderful floorshow that wasn't

really a floorshow, Lillian had Reacie move, so she could go to the restroom. On her way across the floor, she looked down the bar and saw two of the most unappetizing men she had seen in a long time.

Rushing back from the restroom, Lillian asked, "Hey Reacie, how's about a dance?"

Pleased and surprised, Reacie grinned, "I've been dying to get you in my arms, Ms. Garrett. But only if you'll promise not to kick me again!"

"I promise, Reacie."

Reacie was surprised when he put his hand on her upper arm. The girl had more muscles than he had. She was well shaped, well proportioned, and hard as a rock. Lillian must spend hours in the gym, he thought to himself.

As they were doing a modified slow drag to a thumping, Duke Ellington, *Things Ain't What They Used to Be*, and making small talk, Reacie said, "Lillian, I know you ran a little track with Chrystie Gaines, Marion Jones, and Inger Miller. Do you still see those ladies?"

"No. I was nowhere as good as they were, but I still workout. Gotta take care of the body. Reacie, I asked for this dance because I want to know who those two uglies are, sitting at the bar. Could that be Junebug and Skeet?"

"In all their unsavory glory!"

"Just the people I want to meet."

"What? Are you nuts? You want to stay away from those two assholes!"

Like clockwork, Skeet and June showed up at one of the two Black establishments in San Mateo, and it was fate that Lillian didn't have to go to Sullivan's, the other bar, to look for the subjects of Cheyenne's report. Not only Lillian, but Andrew.

Lillian's brain was going like Michael Johnson running the 200 meters. "Reacie, I'm going to get next to one of them, and I'm going to do it tonight. Which one should it be?"

"That's up to you, Lillian. They both look like dammit to hell. How you gunna carry this one off?"

"I don't have a plan, but I'm going to do something with one of these guys before the night's over. And whichever one of them it is, he isn't going to like the outcome."

Lillian looked at Shit and Shittier, thinking, the bastards are responsible for killing Kacy. These are the anal sphincters from Cheyenne's report. I get to meet them up close and personal. Beautiful, loving Kacy, a woman who came into my life and the lives of my family. She brought nothing but joy and love. Agape love. That deep, grinding, down-in-your-soul type of love. Kacy was mine. And she was Andrew's and Mamma's. She was Ozzie's and mostly Tina's and those two drizzlin' shits, Junebug and Skeet, didn't have the right to take her away from us. No right at all!

Reacie and Lillian left the floor before the music stopped. When they reached their table, Lillian said to Andrew and Reacie, "I'm leaving you guys. You can keep an eye on me if you want to, but I have a date with one of the two scum buckets at the end of the bar. Maybe both of them, but I really think I can only handle one. We'll see."

Andrew protested, "Sis, are you crazy?"

Lillian retorted, "I meant what I said, and I said what I meant!"

"My sister is one of the most hard-headed people in creation. Reacie, she's going to drive me crazy."

Lillian bid good night to Reacie and Andrew, picked up her bag and her beer, put a wiggle in her walk and sauntered down the bar. She was looking for an empty stool near the two assholes who claimed to be humans - and who made her want to puke.

As she came closer, a guy left his stool and headed for the door. Lillian immediately hopped up on the seat and said "Hi," to Dam and Dammit, the ugly twins. These two men were definitely not her type or style. Not in this millennium nor in the next.

Lillian flirted. "Hey, Big Daddies, hope you have some time for me tonight?"

"Yeah, Snow. 'Pens on what ya got in mine."

"I need something big, black, and filling." Lillian demurred.

"Hah, Ah cun do dat," guffawed Skeet.

That mouth of gold on Junebug made Lillian want to ask one of the Miss Thang's for a barf bag.

With stony, emotionless faces, Andrew and Reacie kept their eyes on the image of Lillian reflected in the mirror behind the bar.

"Your sister's a magician, man. She's playing those two dog biscuits like a piano. I bet they think she's Madonna, and they're Taye Diggs and Denzel Washington. She's working it and them," Reacie spat, disgustedly, slightly in awe.

Andrew and Reacie rose from the booth, left a tip on the table, walked past the bar and out of the restaurant, giving Lillian a slight nod. Reacie went home. Andrew didn't.

"Wasn't ya with dem two guys and ain't dat Negro from the Center?" asked Skeet.

Skeet was the one with the ponytail and jogging suit made out of fabric from a used car or couch, or so it seemed to Lillian.

"I don't know nothin' about no Center. And yes, I was with them, but I'm free, white and twenty-one. When I see something I want, I go after it. Ya'll look like something I want, so here I am!"

With their tongues wagging like hounds at the Westminster, both Dumb and Dumber asked, "Which one uh us, baby?"

"Well, we're going to have to pull straws, cuz I just can't make up my mind," Lillian lied.

June and Skeet were falling under the "I want a piece of white ass, and I think I'm gonna get some tonight," spell! Lillian was doing just what Reacie said she was doing, playing those two jerks like Mrs. Wainwright, Skeet's mother, played her Steinway.

Lillian had asked the bartender for toothpicks. She broke one and held two of them in her hand for the two cow pies to pull. "Which one will it be?" Lillian giggled. Skeet pulled the long straw.

"Lawdy!" Skeet exclaimed. His eyes rolled all back in his head. He was going to be in hog heaven tonight in San Mateo, California, on the railroad tracks or close by.

"Sheeitt!" June exclaimed. "Me next time, baby?"

"Sure. You next time, big daddy."

"Waz yo name, boodiful?" Skeet asked.

"Ethel," Lillian said" My mama liked substantial, old-fashioned names. My name is Ethel Bailey."

"Well, Effel baby, lez shake dis joint."

"Not yet," Ethel said coyly. "We need another beer or two I'm enjoying the music. What's your name, Daddy?"

"Okay, baby! Ma name's Skeet. Juz call me Skeet."

"Skeet's such a sexy name."

"Yeah. He he he," Skeet tittered like a sick chicken.

Lillian hopped off the stool, saying, "I'll be right back. Gotta go to the john."

She left her empty bottle on the bar, wanting to be sure she'd get her place when she returned. But she needn't have worried. Skeet wasn't about to let anyone have this stool at this bar this night.

Lillian entered the little alcove that separated the restroom from the main room. She stood there until she could catch the eye of one of the Miss Thangs. Beckoning the girl to follow her into the area that had the vanity and mirror in it, Lillian whispered, "Here's fifty bucks. I want you to keep the beer coming to me and the dude with the ponytail. Make sure the beer is in dark bottles Bud, whatever. Even better, make it the strongest malt you have. Make sure mine has been diluted more than a third of the bottle. In fact, the more water you put in my bottle the better."

The two women walked out of the restroom. Lillian returned to the nightmares at the end of the bar, and Miss Thang went to the bartender.

The waitress knew the routine. "George, the ofay with Skeet and June wants you to keep 'um coming and she wants hers to be mostly water. She slipped me a fifty. Half of it is yours. This is a new day! None of these other cheap ass ho's who work this bar are that generous. Fives and tens are the best we get, but if Miss Whitey wants hers poured out, pour it anyway she wants it."

"Where in the hell did you come up with 'ofay?'" George laughed.

"Heard my daddy talking about ofays to some of his poker buddies. Says the word was popular during the '40s. I like it."

"It's Pig Latin for foe. Can it," George said. "I don't like nuthin' old but money." They both laughed.

Miss Thang took three dark bottles of Cooper & Son's naturally brewed beer down to the end of the bar. The alcohol content of Cooper & Son's is 7.10, whereas a bottle of Bud is 4.82. The conspiratorial waitress carefully and deliberately handed a bottle of beer to Lillian, while placing June and Skeet's bottles on the bar.

While Lillian had been away, Skeet had said, "Dawg, June! I love you like a brotha, but Ah'm gonna scowe tonight. Ya know what three is, so ga bye! See ya tamorrah."

"Man, you know I gotcha back. Have a good one. Lawd, how Ah wisht it was me, but she look like Ah might get a chance bye n' bye. See ya, blood." Junebug rose off his stool, leaving his half-drunk beer and diddy bopped out the door.

Now that Lillian was back on her stool, holding her personal delivery of brew, it was time to start the pick and shovel work. The hatred in her heart for this out- house deposit was gnawing at her core.

When Skeet started putting his hands on her, she could feel the bile from her gut rise to her throat. She had to choke it down.

"Sheeiit, baby, you as hard as a rock! ~~He he he.~~ Hee, hee, hee"

Allowing him to fondle her breasts and get as familiar as his increasingly drunken state permitted sickened her.

At 1:30 in the morning the band stopped playing and began packing their instruments. In half an hour, everyone would have to vacate the premises. Lillian slipped Miss Thang another twenty, winked, and put Skeet's arm over her shoulder and helped him wobble out of the bar and down the street to her car.

Across the tracks from McNairy's was a metallic maroon Porsche parked in the railroad station parking lot, the only car left. On a bench sat a man bundled in a navy pea coat and a black watch cap. The man looked homeless. The black watch cap was pulled down over his ears and in the dark, it was hard to tell where the watch cap began and the man's face ended. This man was so dark he was almost as dark as the cap. It was Andrew Garrett.

Lillian struggled to help Skeet into her car. "Man, you feel like cooked pasta!" He won't be able to get anything hard tonight, she said to herself.

She closed the passenger door and ran around to the driver's side. She put the keys in the ignition and started north on Railroad Avenue.

When she approached the Mt. Diablo intersection, Skeet asked, "Baby, kin you pull ovah? Gotta take a leak."

"Sure, boo. How's right here?" Lillian continued her coquette act.

Skeet struggled out of the car, fumbled with his fly, and peed for as long as it would take Lillian to walk 3,000 meters. He was emptying six bottles of strong ale in the gutter. It was now nearly two-thirty in the morning. There wasn't a soul around and not a light on in any of the apartments or houses close by.

write out?

Chapter 41
The Trestle

Lillian, in a loud whisper, said, "Skeet, let's do some gymnastics." At McNairy's, she had told him what a jock she had been in high school and in college and that explained why her arm was as hard as steel to the touch.

He slobbered, "Effel, that be cool, baby. Gynnastiks, cool, baby. He he he." *hee, hee, hee*

"Let's go up on the tracks. We're going to walk across the trestle, no hands." She scurried up the rocks to the trestle, leaving him staggering in the street. In seconds, Lillian appeared above, walking across the silver and black ledge with her arms outstretched.

"Whee," she exclaimed, "I'm free as a bird, I'm in the Olympics. How many points do I get, Skeet?"

"T-t-t-ten baby. You git uh t-ten. He he he."

"Shhh," she said with her fingers at her lips, attempting to keep him quiet.

After his small outburst, Skeet started climbing up the rocky slope to the tracks.

"Hold on buddy. I'm coming to get you," she said in a loud whisper.

As she was walking across the trestle, an idea popped into her head. Lillian agilely hopped down the embankment, watching her footing in the loose rocks. She hurried past Skeet. He drunkenly reached for her, but she was fast and kept just out of his way.

"You keep going up," she whispered. "I'll be right back."

Lillian popped the trunk of her car, pulled on a pair of leather driving gloves and lifted out a long length of orange nylon rope and an old towel.

Lillian used to help remove graffiti and political signs from the poles in San Mateo when she volunteered with the early morning sweeping crew. She remembered the rope and throwing it over the signs that were high on poles. Standing on a ladder or on a stool, she'd catch the other end of the rope and yank the sign from the pole.

Because of Lillian's years as a Girl Scout, she knew a lot about knot tying, and she had earned a badge for her skills. All the girls used to fool around making nooses. Lillian quickly tied a noose in the rope. She wound the rope around her waist and stuffed the towel into the back pocket of her jeans.

Scampering back up the embankment to the tracks, she reached the top just before Skeet shakily arrived. He was so unsteady and drunk, it had been slow going for him.

"Skeet, walk on the rail. You have to do that before you can walk on the beam. You have to keep your balance before you earn your ten."

Skeet placed an Air Jordan-clad foot on the rail. It slipped off. He wiggled his foot up from the railroad tie and tried again. He bent his body, taking a nasty handkerchief from his back pocket, bent again and wobbly wiped the sole of one shoe. His balance looked like that of a ten-month-old toddler learning to walk, but he kept slipping off the slick steel track.

"Let me put you in a harness. Let's see if I can keep you steady." She unwound the rope from her waist and threw the looped end at him. "Put it over your head. Let it rest on your shoulders. I'm going to lead you with the rope and keep you steady."

"Okay, okay, Effel baby . . ." He had trouble finishing the sentence. "I gone move the rope down . . ." He struggled but couldn't get the noose past his shoulders. It was around his neck but loose.

"That's okay, Skeet. Let's do it this way." Lillian came to him helped him onto the steel rail. "Now stretch your arms out, like you're going to fly."

It was difficult for Skeet to keep his arms up, but once they were up, Lillian walked away from him but gently led him with the rope. The rope was about fifteen feet long. She kept him steady enough to walk, very slowly, on the narrow, slick length of train track.

The rope was long and it was strong. Lillian played like a cat with a present for its owner. When they neared the trestle, "Come on, Skeet, come over here to the beam. I'm going to help you get up for the Olympics." She helped Skeet mount the trestle, and he was thrilled, wobbly but thrilled. He could put his hands on her. The smell of his beer-soaked breath and unbrushed teeth made bile rise again in Lillian's core to the gagging point. On his way up, he slobberishly tried to kiss her.

Lillian wanted to knee him in the groin and give him a karate chop. "Now Skeet, stand still and spread your arms again, like an eagle but don't move. You're on the Olympic beam. This ledge is wider and I'll lead you, but stay still 'til I tell you to move."

Skeet was having a wonderful time on the top of the trestle at Mt. Diablo and Railroad Avenue.

They were playing Olympics, something Skeet had never done before, drunk or sober. This took his mind away from the sex he thought he was going to have.

Boiled spaghetti again entered Lillian's mind. "You're doing fine," she encouraged Skeet. "You're looking good! Skeet at the Olympics! Go Skeet!" As she talked, she was looping seven feet of the other end of the rope to one of the metal buttresses with a spool-type shank at its edge.

Lillian moved back and forth, steadying Skeet and leaving plenty of looped rope on the gravel surface, next to the tracks, so she could walk beside him. She looked like a rodeo rider tying off a calf. When the rope was securely tied to the shank, she now concentrated solely on Skeet and held the rope gently in both gloved hands. She whispered, "You can walk now."

She took the towel from her back pocket, wiping away dew and previous fingerprints from the top of the eleven foot, one inch trestle. She moved with him, wiping, wiping, before each fall of an Air Jordan.

Because she had tied the other end of the rope to the spool-like buttress, the eight feet of remaining rope would only allow Skeet to walk a short way across the trestle. Lillian played the rope gently, like leading an ox.

As they headed back to the south side, where they had started, Lillian touched his arm to keep him steadied. She softly clapped her gloved hands. "You did it!"

Skeet had reached the portion of the trestle that was over the sidewalk.

"Congratulations, Skeet! Take a bow. Pose. You just won the gold medal! Turn to your audience!" As he bowed, Lillian bowed, too.

On Lillian's direction, Skeet had turned from south to east, facing Railroad Avenue. Lowering his arms, he put them at his sides, bowed, slipped off the trestle, and hanged himself. The loop of rope allowed his body to dangle about three feet above the sidewalk. His bent form, forward momentum and alcohol allowed the rule of gravity to tip the scales of justice. He moved so fast, he couldn't even let out a scream.

Head down, still holding the rope, Lillian felt it whiz through her gloved hands. She felt a jerk, looked up – Skeet had disappeared from view. She sprang forward, peered over the edge, and there he was, dangling like the Scarecrow from the Wizard of Oz. "I had intended to push him, but he slipped," Lillian murmured to herself.

She took the towel that had been draped over her shoulder and wiped where imprints of her gloves showed on the ledge of the trestle. Lillian stuffed the damp terry cloth back into her back pocket again and started down the embankment on her butt. She heard a car approaching and froze. Flipping herself over on her stomach she tried to melt her body into the rocky slope.

The car had no headlights; it edged forward slowly, coming to a stop behind her car.

Although it was a cool night Lillian was sweating, as though she has just finished the four hundred meter hurdles. She turned

Add earlier ←

her head just enough to see a metallic-maroon Porsche. Andrew! My brother!

Her muscles were as tight as spandex hugging Mo'Nique's thighs. Lillian exhaled when she realized the car belonged to Andrew, she flipped back to her behind and continued to scoot down to the street. Andrew jumped from his car, sprinted to the edge of the embankment, just in time for Lillian to fall into Andrew's arms. His brawny biceps were there to comfort her and to try to hold her still. Lillian's tremors were as though she was standing on top of the San Andreas Fault during a point 8.0 quake.

"You, okay?" Andrew whispered as he walked her to her car and opened the door. There was enough light from the street lamp for him to see that Lillian's complexion was the color of snow. "Drive slowly. I'll follow you home."

With teeth chattering, she nodded her head. "Y Yeah, I'll s s s see you at the house."

Before Andrew closed the car door, he said, "I saw what happened. Watched you put him in your car. I left the train station where I was parked and followed you up to the corner of Tilton where I watched the two of you on the trestle. I saw him slip. I couldn't get into my car and down here fast enough to do anything."

"Thanks, big brother. I didn't know I would need you tonight." She closed the car door, released the break, let the car coast down the incline to the stop sign, keeping her eyes forward. Trying to avoid the vision of a dangling Skeet. When she reached the intersection, she started the ignition with a shaking hand, turned left under the tracks, switched on her lights and drove to the house on the other side of town.

Lillian parked the car in the familiar driveway, flew in the house and ran straight to the bathroom. She vomited. It seemed as though she emptied everything in her guts that had been there for the last four days. She undressed, turned on the shower, stepped in and stood under the hot water until she heard footsteps in the house and Andrew calling her. She reluctantly stepped out of the shower wrapped herself in a big sheet towel and ran to her brother who held her and tried to stop her from shaking.

"Damn, Lillian! Is that what you had in mind?"

"Absolutely not! Not in the beginning. But when I got up there, it came to me. I didn't know I was going to do the noose and all, at McNairy's, but when I walked across the trestle, I knew what I was going to do. I was going to push him with his dumb-drunk ass. But I didn't have to. He slipped. He was so damned drunk that he slipped."

"Sis, I hope and pray that you will never, ever, be that upset with me."

Looking at her brother as though he was just a little loco, Lillian was calmer now and went back into her room to put on pajamas and a robe.

Lillian walked into the kitchen where Andrew had already pushed the button on the Hamilton Beach to warm up a pot of coffee from the morning.

"Whoa, Lillian! Grab hold of something. There you go again, doing a jitterbug all by yourself," Andrew said, trying to lighten the mood.

"Andrew, I wanted to push him, but I didn't get the chance. Whatever I did, I'd do it again and again . . . That bastard!" Tears rolled down Lillian's face.

Andrew reached into the cabinet for a cup and handed it to his sister. Her hands shook as he poured the coffee to the brim for her. "Are we going to tell Mom?"

"No way!" Lillian countered. "No way! She doesn't need to know."

Sipping and blowing the hot brew, she said, "Andrew, what am I going to do when the cops come? You know there's going to be an investigation. I was the last one seen with him. What am I going to say? What am I going to do?"

"Don't worry about all that stuff until tomorrow," Andrew comforted. "Let's sleep on it. We'll have some answers when the sun is shining."

"Yeah, but to get some sleep after seeing that hideous thing hanging from the trestle, I'll need a little help. Do you remember which bathroom those pills are in? Upstairs or downstairs?"

"I don't remember, but Tina was the last one to take one. They're probably in the bathroom in her room."

They went looking for the bottle of sleeping pills. Andrew yelled out, "I found them. They're in Tina's room."

Returning to the kitchen and after reading the directions, Lillian spilled part of the contents into Andrew's palm. He popped one into his mouth and chased it with a handful of water from the faucet. He returned the rest of the tablets to the bottle and handed it to his sister. Lillian took one and drank a sip of coffee to get it down. They went to their rooms and slept drug-induced sleep.

◊

Brother and sister woke around nine-thirty the next day. Andrew rose and went outside to pick up the paper. Lillian lingered, sitting on the edge of her bed.

Andrew opened the newspapers and yelled to his sister, "Hey, Lillian! Get down here! You have to see the Chronicle." The banner headline read 'Man Found Dead, Hanging from Railroad Trestle.' He showed the paper to Lillian who quickly moved to the small black and white television on the kitchen counter. The newsreader on Channel 7 was doing a special report.

"At the Mt. Diablo and Railroad Avenue overpass, an obvious suicide." Lillian blew air from her mouth in one forceful rush. She was seated at the kitchen table and Andrew was standing next to her with the Chronicle in his hand. Both were looking incredulously at the column heading, stating the same words they'd just heard on TV. "Suicide in San Mateo. Local Man Hangs Himself."

Andrew said, "Well, I'll be dad gummed!"

The telephone rang. It was Eva.

"Mom, is that you? I thought you'd be calling. Wait a minute Andrew's here. Let me get him on the phone, too."

"Andrew, Lillian, have you been listening to the news?"

"Yes, Mamma," they both answered.

"Can you believe what you're hearing?"

"No, Mom, I can't believe it," Lillian lied.

"Jerome Wainwright killed himself."

I can't believe it either." Andrew added. "Mom," he asked, "do you still have that report from the detective? Have you turned it in to the cops yet?"

"No, Andrew. I haven't turned it in to the cops. I still have it."

"Mom, why don't you keep the report awhile longer. This stuff is too weird. We need to sit on this. Don't do anything irrational," Andrew said.

Eva exhaled, "I agree." She folded the newspaper with a banner reading, "Neighbors Find Body Hanging from Trestle."

Chapter 42
A Pharmacy

Eva entered the bakery, "Hi, everybody. Any interesting orders today?"

Jason filled Eva in on the twelve orders that had been taken. "Eva, we need to tell the baker to make three, twenty-four-inch chocolates. And don't forget you have to clean out Anita's cubby. We need the room for storage."

Who?

Eva walked over to the computer and turned it on. She had been to lunch recently at the Mills/Peninsula Hospital Auditorium, on San Mateo Drive. The guest speaker was a well-known internist, Dr. Calbert Crane. His talk was about the tendency of American consumers to over-medicate with over-the-counter and prescription drugs.

"Prescription medicine shouldn't be consumed indiscriminately and the instructions given by the doctor or pharmacist should be strictly adhered to. Many people think that if they have been prescribed two pills a day, four will be better. Or, they take all of the pills at one time rather than taking them at the prescribed and timed intervals through the day," Dr. Crane said. Eva had been impressed by the talk.

"Jason, why don't you get started removing Anita's stuff? My heart just isn't in it."

"Should I put the stuff in a box?"

"Yeah, Jason. I'll sort through it later."

"Eva, when did Anita start working here?"

"Anita came here about a month after I opened. She was looking for a job. I trained her how to split and fill cakes, and she ended up being one of the best decorators I've ever had. She was seventy-two when she first walked through the door. Unfortunately, Anita started becoming confused. It was either dementia or Alzheimer's, but her son and daughter-in-law lovingly came and took her to live with them over in Oakland, near Lake Merritt. I haven't heard how she's doing."

"Dang! Eva, I wish I had had the opportunity to meet her. Was Anita ill? She had a whole pharmacy stored in this cubby," Jason complained. He handed a cardboard box that once contained cake rounds, to Eva.

Curious, Eva looked into the box and gave a verbal inventory of the contents, not waiting for the end of the day as she first stated.

"There's Coozar for high blood pressure, Premarin for menopause, Zocor for high blood pressure. Two different blood pressure medications?" Eva laughed. "Digitalis for her heart, Avlamil for her sex life. Sex life!" Eva laughed again! "The woman is in her eighties, but bless her. If she was still sexually active, there is hope for all of us."

Eva continued the inventory silently. Anita had analgesics, anti-inflammatories, anti-anxiety agents, anti-depressants, antihistamines, beta-blockers and stimulants - a pharmacy!

Digitalis: what had Dr. Crane said about digitalis? Eva couldn't remember but made a mental note that she'd look it up on the Internet whenever time permitted getting back to the computer.

At days end, and with research on her mind, Eva removed the bottle of digitalis from her apron pocket. In the search box on the computer, she typed in the word. She read page after page of information on the drug and learned that digitalis can poison a person if taken in the wrong quantity.

Symptoms: Pain in the stomach, nausea, violent vomiting, vertigo, muscular stiffness, fatigue, pain in the head, somnolence;

*pulse at first rapid and violent, but soon weak and irregular; dilated
pupils, dimness of vision, maybe delirium.*

"I don't want to kill anybody, Lord. I just want to make someone
extremely sick. I just want to make someone as sick as I can possibly
make him," Eva murmured. She went to her table and patted the
bottle of Anita's digitalis that was once again pocketed safely on
her thigh.

The day at the bakery went as usual. Happy customers, happy
children, people coming in to buy one of several books about cake
baking that Kacy had compiled before she was killed. Customers
purchased tapes of various cake decorating shows hosted by Eva,
candles, balloons and extra crunch for crunch cakes.

The world was not a bad place to be - except that someone had
taken the life of her beautiful friend Kacy. Eva was a church-going
woman. She was married to a devout man. She had given birth
to children who were steady churchgoers. But she didn't want to
involve the God she believed in, in what she was about to do. She
knew that to knowingly hurt or injure another person was against
everything she had been taught and believed in.

Eva took the Golden Rule seriously. "Do unto others as you would
have them do unto you." She practiced the Ten Commandments. In
the Protestant and Hebrew versions, "Thou shalt not kill" was the
sixth commandment. In the Catholic version, it was the fifth. Yes,
Eva knew better. She kept the digitalis in her pocket though, along
with information she had printed out. And anyway, I'm just going
to make someone extremely sick. I'm not going to kill anyone! She
rationalized.

When the last employee finally left for the day, Eva went to
the back and locked and padlocked the door. She walked through
the bakery to the front, locked the door and turned the sign from
OPEN ABRA to CLOSED – CERRADO.

She turned off the lights for the front of the store, leaving only
those in the cake decorating room. Reaching her table, she sat on
the stool and took Anita's prescription of digitalis out of her pocket.
Eva also pulled the sheets of paper about the pills out of her pocket
and began reading.

When she read the last word on the last sheet of paper, Eva lifted a plastic tray out of a box from under the table. These discarded meat or fish trays had been washed and cut into squares to be used as a base on which to make roses for cakes.

Into the tray, Eva dumped all the digitalis tablets. There were over twenty. With a large spoon, she crushed the tablets into a fine powder, just as she had done to the mints the first night she met and invited Kacy and Tina to be her houseguests. She picked up one of the pastry bags and squeezed a clump of white frosting all over the now powdered digitalis. She mixed the frosting and the pulverized pills thoroughly, until there was no evidence of the granulated tablets. The powdery substance mixed with the goopy white icing, as easily as confectioner's sugar.

Eva went to the sink, bent down to a low shelf and selected a pair of tight-fitting disposable plastic gloves. She walked over to the freezer and took out two large cupcakes. With a spatula, she scooped the white mixture from the tray and iced both cupcakes. In script, with black frosting, "In Memory of Skeet, R.I.P" was deftly inscribed on each cupcake. One plump, pale-pink rose and a small orange one, along with a border of green leaves finished off the perhaps deadly desserts. She placed the cupcakes in a brand-new pastry box that she had thoroughly wiped with a clean towel, before assembling.

Still wearing gloves, she went to the ribbon rack, and selected black and white ribbon. She tied the ribbon around the box and curled the ends with scissors. She laid a piece of newspaper on the counter, and set the box on top of the counter. Then she put the newspaper and the box into a shopping bag.

Eva went back to the table. She took everything she had used to make the digitalis-laced frosting to the sink and with detergent and bleach, plus the hottest water the heater could put out, she washed and scrubbed all of the items.

Eva tore up the plastic tray, placed it in a pie tin and burned it. She put the Clorox-washed spoon, the pastry bag and tips in separate Baggies, then went to the back door and unlocked it. She put the items in larger bags of various types and deposited each bag in a garbage can belonging to other merchants, knowing pick up would be at four o'clock in the morning.

After re-locking the back door, she put the ashes of the plastic tray in the toilet. Eva flushed the toilet several times and added Clorox to the water in the bowl and in the tank, letting it remain without flushing a final time.

She locked the safe and turned off the lights, put on her coat and a pair of mittens that were in the pocket of the coat. She had a delivery to make. There would be no problem finding Scott Gonzales, Jr., AKA Junebug. His address had been provided in the folder given to her by Cheyenne Norman, Private Detective. 101 North Claremont Street was just a few blocks away from the bakery.

"If he dies, God, please forgive me. But if he just becomes sick and retches his guts out, that will be okay, too. But he's not going to die."

It was about eight o'clock and dark enough for people walking on the street to not pay attention to her. Instead of the company van, she drove her blue Honda and parked it around the corner on Mt. Diablo between Delaware and Claremont. She walked around the corner to 101 North Claremont, put the box on the porch and rang the bell. After hearing the sound of the bell, she ran like hell. She felt like a ten-year old on Halloween, playing trick or treat. Reaching the corner, she hid behind a hedge. She could hear a front door open and in a few minutes, she heard it close.

Eva ran to her car, jumped in and made a uie in the middle of the street. When she turned the corner and looked out the window at June's house, she saw that the box was no longer on the porch. Eva pumped her fist and clamped her teeth on her lower lip. She felt triumphant, sad and regretful.

She scooted down Claremont, turned right on Tilton and headed home. "God, I'm sorry. Please forgive me." She muttered. Her heart was pounding. She was cold, sweaty, shaking – worried about being caught and asked God repeatedly, "Forgive me, Lord. Forgive me. Please!"

Eva was a nervous wreck. Opening her front door, she hollered to see if Clifford had made it in from teaching. Hearing no response, she went into the kitchen and made herself a big hot latte in a tall, thick mug. She wanted to sleep and forget the bad, awful, rotten, no good, sinful thing she had just done. All the while begging and pleading, "God, please forgive me!"

Eva made a promise to God. "If you take care of this sinful sister this time, Lord, I promise you I'll wear a white dress to church for Clifford, and I'll go and sin no more."

One day went by. Two days went by. Three days, then a week and two weeks.

Reading the newspaper exactly two weeks after her visit to 101 North Claremont, a small article in the back of the paper caught Eva's eye. "Man Found Dead at Home." Not much more than that, just a few sketchy details. It seemed neighbors saw flies swarming around the window of the house next door and called the police.

The police had knocked on the door to no response, but they knew there was someone dead inside. The smell was familiar and unmistakable. Inside, they found a man who evidently had had a heart attack. The police said they didn't find anything out of the ordinary. There were a few dishes in the sink, an empty pastry box, and the man was still clothed. He had been dead for about two weeks.

No relatives or friends had been by to see him, so he was like that television commercial for LifeAlert. He had fallen down, couldn't get up. His best buddy in the world had preceded him in death by committing suicide at the Mt. Diablo and Railroad Avenue train crossing.

You know you haven't lived as you should when your own mother and father won't come to claim your body. Eva felt like the girl in Chorus Line. She felt nothing!

The next day at work, Eva went into the back office and made a three-way telephone call to Lillian at the International Olympic Committee headquarters in New York and to Andrew at his posh office in Menlo Park. Eva reached Lillian first and made her hold until Andrew came on.

"Andrew, Lillian, this is a conference call. It's me, Mama."

"Hi, Mom. You don't sound so good," Andrew said.

"How are things, Mom?" Lillian asked.

Eva was extremely tired, it was in her voice.

Lillian and Andrew were talking over each other, but when they found that Eva was okay, they settled down to listen to what she had to say.

"I have a newspaper article to read to you." She read the small article about a man found dead in his home. After a short silence, she said, "Kids, it's over."

"Mama, what are you going to do with the folder from the detective?" Andrew asked.

"The next time I have the two of you together in San Mateo, we - just the three of us - are going to Coyote Point. We're going to go to the beach with a small barbecue grill. We're going to light a match and burn the folders."

"Mama," Lillian said, "I'll be home at the end of the month. I love you, Mama," Lillian said. "I love you, too, Andrew," Lillian repeated.

Eva and Andrew said the same things to each other and Lillian. They all clicked off.

Later that day, the phone rang and Eva looked at it quizzically. She wasn't in the mood to talk to anyone right now. The screen on the phone read, "Detective McGinnes, San Mateo, Police Dept." and gave the number.

Eva picked up the phone, "Hi, Eddie. How are you this fine day?"

"Eva, my love, I'm fine. I have something to discuss with you. Do you have a few minutes?"

"Sure, Eddie, anything for you."

"Have you read today's newspaper? There's an article in there about a guy, who was found dead in his house. His street name was Junebug, AKA, Scott Gonzales, Jr., He and his friend, Jerome 'Skeet' Wainwright, had been under surveillance by the department for quite some time. I learned from Cheyenne Norman, sometime back, that you had some interest in Gonzales."

Eva's heart rose to her throat. Her business with Cheyenne was confidential! If Cheyenne betrayed her, Eva thought, I'm going to kick her ass. And as quickly as her anger had risen, she told herself, calm down.

Eddie continued, "Cheyenne didn't give me any details. She told me it was confidential, and that you paid her dearly to keep the information under her hat. I honor that. I just wanted you to know that good old June seems to have died alone and of natural causes. His corpse was pretty well beyond help when it was discovered. Maggots, ants, rats. There were no guts left for the medical examiner."

"Yuk, Eddie! I don't need a description. TMI! TMI! Too much information!"

"They think he'd been dead a week and a half, two weeks. Usually there's an autopsy and a big investigation, but because he and that jerk he used to hang around with - a 'hanging' suicide by the way - were such bad actors, we did something that is also confidential."

"Who's we, Kimosabe?"

"Confidential, Eva. You can dig that?"

"I can dig it!"

"Nobody came to claim the body, so the attitude was good riddance to bad rubbish. Out of sight, out of mind. Gone and let's hope, forgotten. One of my Sergeants, Robert Ross, shared with me a sentiment that was shared with him by one of his old colleagues, 'You can't polish a terd.' Those two guys cost the City and the County of San Mateo far more than they were worth. The body was cremated and that's the end of that story. Those two dudes went through life throwing rocks and hiding their hands. I just wanted you to know that."

"Eddie, you have given me news that doesn't mean a thing to me," Eva lied. "But I'm glad you thought I should know. We must do lunch one afternoon."

"Yeah, sweet meat, I'll give you a call. Give my best to all your family."

"I will, Eddie. You know you still hold a warm place in my heart. I'll talk to you soon."

Eva clicked off the phone, pulled a paper napkin from the napkin holder on the desk, wiped her brow, which was beaded with sweat. She sat her behind on a chair to relieve her wobbly legs. A huge weight had just been lifted off her heavy-laden shoulders. A smile crept across her face. "Thank you, God!" she almost screamed, with hands raised into fists that she kept pumping and pumping in the air. Eva let out another burst. She squeezed her eyes tight, drew her lips back over clenched teeth and screeched, "Thank you, Jesus!"

Then she started to cry.

Chapter 43
The White Suit

The next Sunday was First Sunday. The women of the church wore their white hats, suits and dresses. The usher opened the door right after everyone had returned to his or her seat from the meet and greet session.

Down the main aisle of the church just as Corley, Hackett and the music department swung into *I Feel Like Praising Him* by Sandra Crouch in walked one of the most beautiful Black women the church had ever seen. She was wearing a white St. John knit trimmed in gold, with a white felt Sha-Ma-Ael hat tilted over her right eye. Mrs. Clifford Davidson, better known as Eva, strolled into Prophet Baptist Church. She came late on purpose and resisted placing her left hand on her hip as she strolled down the center aisle to one of the front pews.

As she proceeded forward Eva looked straight into Clifford's face. He was seated on the left side of Rev. Ellwood and looked straight back at Eva. Clifford displayed the oddest expression on his face as he watched his wife saunter down the aisle in her white outfit.

The End